DAHLGREN
MEET ERG-DAHLGREN

He was brought into a small room in which there was a screen with a chair in front of it. They locked him in and he sat down.

The screen flickered...

"Android robot," Dahlgren murmured, feeling fear.

The body had two arms, five fingers on each. It was boned in gears and spindles, muscled in wires and flexes.

Above the neck it seemed to be flesh: it had eyes, ears, nose, mouth, hair, beard. Dahlgren's.

The erg-android blinked, straight into Dahlgren's eyes, blue for blue, pulled back the pink lip corners into the beard, into Dahlgren's rare smile, and raised a steel-tendoned arm, palm outward.

"Hello, Dahlgren Zero," it said. "I am Dahlgren One."

Bantam Science Fiction
Ask your bookseller for the books you have missed

O MASTER CALIBAN!

by
Phyllis Gotlieb

BANTAM BOOKS · TORONTO
NEW YORK · LONDON

O MASTER CALIBAN!

*A Bantam Book | published by arrangement with
Harper & Row, Publishers, Inc.*

PRINTING HISTORY

*Harper & Row edition published September 1976
Bantam edition | March 1979*

ISBN 0–553–12049–2

*Bantam Books are published by Bantam Books, Inc. Its trade-
mark, consisting of the words "Bantam Books" and the por-
trayal of a bantam, is Registered in U.S. Patent and Trademark
Office and in other countries. Marca Registrada. Bantam
Books, Inc., 666 Fifth Avenue, New York, New York 10019.*

I would like to thank my consultants
at the University of Toronto
who did their best
to make things clear to me:

Professor D. B. W. Reid, biometrician
Dr. Archie Erwin, anatomist
Dr. Pamela Stokes, environmental ecologist
Dr. K. G. McNeill, nuclear physicist

and particularly, with love
Dr. C. C. Gotlieb, computer scientist
who researched, created and annotated
the chess game; and limitlessly
answered questions and read mss.

O
MASTER
CALIBAN!

1

In the evening the winds came and the rain swept
and paused, swept again in a sheet of muddy drops,
slowed and stopped. The giant ferns whispered,
shook water from their fronds and dropped their
spores. The air was green.

Yigal stared dreamily through the window and
watched the sporefall, eating cabbage leaves, but Esther had made rabbit stew with carrots and fiddle-
heads for herself and the boy. She thought he looked
moody, and she sat on his shoulder, lifted the bowl to
hook chunks out with her long black fingers and coax
them into his mouth. "Eat, darling, eat, sweetheart."

Yigal turned his head and snorted. "Leave the boy
alone."

Darling Sweetheart, who by his own reckoning was
nineteen years old, at least two meters tall and over a
hundred and forty kilos in weight, grinned and said,
"Mutti, I really am old enough to eat by myself." He
picked her off his shoulder and set her on the table.

"Then eat."

He stirred the bowl with a finger.

"What's the matter?"

He found the ladle and took a dipperful. "How
much longer do you think we'll have here?"

Esther trembled. She hated his bitterness. "How
would I know?"

"The ergs haven't come by for a week . . ."

"I don't care if I never see another one."

1

"But they're coming closer . . . they've moved out past Zone Red, built a factory."

"Why not? They've got the whole planet."

"They'd have to start surveying all over again in the wilds. Maybe they will now. That was one of their last few inhibitions."

"How did you find out about the factory?"

"I scouted."

She slapped his face. Stew splattered the table and floor. She jumped down and backed against the wall. She weighed approximately twenty kilos. He looked at her sadly, without moving. "I am old enough, Esther."

Esther, who could not cry, grabbed a handful of dry moss from a bin and wiped up. She jumped back on the table and kissed him.

He grinned. "That makes it better." Then the corners of his mouth turned down. "Do you think he's—somebody's sending them out?"

"I don't know," she whispered. It was an old question. "Don't think about that."

It was dark. The wind blew in a drift of spores that turned brown when they touched the dry surfaces.

"I am going out," Yigal said. He sounded touchy.

"Stay in tonight."

He sniffed. "You know how I hate all this emotionalism."

The boy forestalled Esther. "We're through for the night. Stay in or go out as you like."

"You're getting very bossy," Esther said. The tone of her voice suggested she was glad he had livened up.

"I don't want to give orders or take anybody else's."

"You sure you're through for the night?" Yigal asked on a rising note.

The wind strengthened again, and a sound rose above it.

"Tomorrow we put up the shutters," said Esther. "Winter's earlier every year."

"That's not a storm," the boy said. "Put out the light."

A glow grew at the window. Through it they saw fire sweeping the sky above the ferns, trees, and dusty cloud rack.

"That's a ship landing at the station," said Esther.

"Too far west."

"Then they've built another landing field."

"No, they haven't! It's going to—it's going to—"

It crashed. Thunder and flame burst in the pit of the wilderness.

"I'm going to see," he said.

"No, don't, Sven! It must be an erg ship!"

"It didn't come from the east."

"Nobody can be alive in that."

"There may be, I've got to find out."

"The ergs will get it!" But he was gone.

"Wait!" Esther clapped the lid on the stewpot, picked up the lantern, and jumped on Yigal's back. "Come on!"

"I don't want to go out there!" Yigal bleated.

"You did a couple of minutes ago. Get going!"

Past the hutches, through the cabbage patch, beyond the brick road. Wind howled and whirled; the lantern blew out; muddy drops stung, and jungle vines and tendrils caught at them; the boy wrenched and broke them with all four hands. Yigal's curses were carried off by the rushing air. Sven did not know much about ships, but he was thinking that the explosion had not been as great as he expected, and the fire was subdued. It seemed the fuel tanks had not burst, and the flames among the trees were already sputtering out in a dim circle.

They stopped at the edge of the burned clearing. The wind died; a nightbird croaked and a thousand insects whirred and twittered.

The ship was standing.

"Is that a ship?" Esther asked. "It's only a little thing." She had seen just one in her life before.

The undercarriage had been driven into the ground like a peg; the plates above it were crimped and puckered, still hissing with heat in the damp earth.

"Some kind of scout. The engines must have cut before it hit."

As the flames went down the outline dulled to a dark tower.

"We'll have ergs here in half an hour," Yigal said. "Come on back."

Esther lit her lantern with a flint striker and handed it to Sven; it lightened a patch of dull gray metal and showed mists creeping among the trees and ferns and pausing at the heated area like cautious animals.

"I can't even see the door," Sven said. He circled the silent bulk. "Halloo!" he roared. The noise bounced off the ship and died in mist and leaves.

Esther was jittering. "It's a robot, or everybody's dead. Let's go."

"Hold this." Sven handed her the lantern and bent down to wrench at a rotted stump. It came up with a smack of mud. He jumped into the fire-circle, raised it above his head and hurled. It bonged against the metal and he yelled again. The only answer out of the mist was a distant ring and clatter in the east.

"Ergs!" cried Esther. "Sven!" She jumped up and down on Yigal's back, swinging the lantern and setting off curses.

"*Will* you get that damned thing away from my ear before you set me on fire!"

"One more try." Sven picked up a piece of the stump, which had split on the metal. Before he could throw it, a little door opened halfway up the ship and a cluster of faces pushed out into the orange light.

"Hello!" he called.

A voice wailed, "I want Mama!"

Sven blinked at the faces. "My God, it looks like a bunch of kids!"

Yigal's head jerked up. "Whats?"

Esther grabbed one of his horns and swung down. "Children, you old goat!" The clangor of racing machines swelled toward them. "Sven, there's not much time!"

Sven planted his lower hands on his hips and cupped his upper ones around his mouth. "Anybody hurt up there?"

"No," said a quavering voice.

"Where's your pilot?"

"There isn't any. This is a robot."

"You got a radio?"

"Everything's gone but light and air."

"Then grab what you can and get out!"

"Why should we? This is our ship!"

"When those machines get here there won't be any ship, or any you either! Get out!"

"Who do you think you are?"

"The only friend you've got! Hurry!" Sven would have been dancing with fury if his feet hadn't sunk in the mud. Ten more seconds and he'd leave them, *I want Mama* and all.

A boy poked his head out. "There's no ladder here."

Somebody else, a girl, said, "Look in the goddam locker, you idiot!"

"Find me a light, you clothead, and I'll look!"

Sven pulled at the nearest exterior handhold and the hot warped metal broke.

Esther snarled, "I wish you brains would learn to use your big fat heads." She swung up to Sven's shoulder and from the platform of his four raised hands leaped and caught the rung just below the opening. She reached down for the lantern, raised it, and leered at the five gaping faces. "Monkey see, monkey do."

Sven called, "Clothes and medicine, all the anti-rad and radiation counters!"

"You hear?" said Esther. "Throw those suits away, we've got plenty of air for you. Lots of rain too. What's the matter, scared out of your wits? You'll find me beautiful soon enough. Come on, you've got five minutes!"

But it took them longer, perhaps because they were numbed by shock or fear, or because they were being ordered about by a black gibbon, splotched with orange and turquoise, who spoke perfect *lingua*.

Before they were ready the treads were crunching broken branches and young ferns into the mud.

"Esther . . ." Sven whispered, half whimpered, like a child, and hoped she did not hear.

She heard the ergs. Yigal neighed and trembled.

"Be still," she told the children, and jumped down.

The two ergs rose three times Sven's height: the ship was not much taller. They were complexes of whirling arms, glittering sensors and branched antennas. They stopped twenty-five meters from Sven, had never at any time come closer, as if there were a shield about him. *One of their last few inhibitions.* They had lost so many.

They flickered, blinked, beeped; their arms clanged; but they stood.

Sven licked his lips. "I want to get the kids out, Esther."

Inside the ship a girl yelled, "Get away from there!" and there was a slapping sound, twice repeated.

The youngest child, a boy of about ten, screamed, "I want to see the robots! I want to!"

Slap! The boy screamed in rage.

And the ergs began to move in.

Slowly, by half a meter in ten seconds, then faster; faster again, five, ten, twenty meters . . .

Sven and Esther stood motionless; Yigal got down on all four knees and shoved his face in the dirt.

The boy pushed head and shoulders out of the opening and craned to look at the monsters. He grinned. "Yaah!" he yelled.

The ergs shivered, rattled, backtracked so fast they crashed into each other and caromed away, slithering in the mud. Backed to the limit.

Sven stared at the small grimacing face. His mind was stupid and empty. He passed a pair of hands over his head to wipe the sweat off and said, "Come on."

When they were out of range the ergs moved in, lifted the little ship in their arms like pallbearers, and trundled away.

"They're taking our ship!" the child yelled.

"So they are," said Esther, wrapping an arm around him. "Aren't you glad you're not inside?"

Dahlgren's World is the fifth planet of Barrazan, a piece of real estate bought by Galactic Federation from the Barrazani system for use as an experimental biological station. It was going cheap because it had never been quite right for settling and was littered with the ruins of failed colonies. It blew with dust clouds and rainstorms, stank with jungles, swarmed with diseases; the polar icecaps were small because of the dust cover, and the seas were poisonous. It neither grew nor attracted intelligent life.

GalFed cut out a triangular swath of jungle at the equator, the shape of an arrowhead pointing east, one hundred and fifty kilometers from apex to base, base measuring about seventy-five; it replaced the diseased swamps with hydroponic tracts, controlled the more loathsome life forms, with exquisite care introduced plants, animals, bacilli and viruses from the equatorial regions of a hundred worlds comparable in size and gravity; it waited, weeded and replenished.

Barrazan V went on turning against its sun, almost as repellent as ever. Turn and turn; when the flora of a hundred worlds balanced and thrived, and their

animals reproduced, GalFed sent down the biologist
Dahlgren.

Dahlgren had hundreds of specialists and a thousand ergs. The great machines planted and reaped,
mined and forged; what they could not do they
created other machines to do, to see with the eye of
an electron microscope, knot a thread that might only
be seen by an electron microscope, cut out and replace the molecule of a gene.

At the tip of the arrowhead, aimed westward,
Dahlgren's ergs set an arc of five reactors to warp the
life forms with radiation at measured distances and
dosages. Beyond the arrow's tip, as if it pointed to a
significant dot on the landscape, they wrested
shielded agricultural land to grow crops for dozens of
civilizations, and built underground laboratories and
living quarters because there was no comfortable
place on the surface; here the specialists worked to
modify genetic strains of their home species to live on
that world and many others just as repellent, and
waited to see whether creation or mutation would give
them the answers first.

Barrazan V is not far, as space measures, from Gal-
Fed Central. Every few standard years Dahlgren
came to Central Bureau to give progress reports; he
grew gray hairs and lines, but life forms change more
slowly, and no one expected answers within his lifetime.

Dahlgren's World had a small port facility, and it
was avoided by any crippled ship that could limp beyond it, possibly because of the fearsome atmosphere,
more likely because of the intimidating size and
power of the servicing ergs, whirring through the mists
and windstorms. Years went by without a landing.
The ergs were not lonely.

The little *Piranha*, a holiday cruiser despite its
name, had no choice. It was a robot with an impec-
cable safety record, and when its communications

went awry two days out from Barrazan IV its automatics took it to the nearest service station. Since it had no radar, it crashed.

Esther, riding Yigal, led the stranded passengers, and Sven herded them from the rear. There were five, three boys and two girls, in their teens except for the ten-year-old. They were not hurt, but frightened and bad-tempered.

"Where are we?"

"On Barrazan Five, it's a GalFed biological station. Where's the ship from?"

"Twelveworlds tour. Half a day out of Barrazan Four the radio . . . and everything . . ."

"Why did those machines take the ship away? Are they going to fix it?"

"I don't know."

"Why don't you know? Who are you?"

They tripped over stumps and vines, squelched in the mud, lost balance trying to hold on to their possessions.

"Why can't you tell us now? What's all this about?"

Sven picked up a bundle for one, helped another over a clump of roots. "Look, you people, give me a chance to breathe! You're safe for the time being. I myself don't know everything that's going on, but I'll tell you all I can."

"What would those robots have done to us?"

He said wearily, "I don't know."

"You do know!" the shrill girl's voice said.

"All right, I know. They'd have torn you to pieces and scattered you around the landscape."

"But those were supposed to be working robots!"

"They were . . . they just learned how to work too well."

Silence for a moment.

The little boy fell on his face. He had been carrying a container the size of a specimen box and he did

not let go of it when Sven picked him up and set him
on the plateau of his shoulders. "I want to know all
about those things." He rubbed the dirt off his face
with his free hand and left most of it on Sven as he
grabbed him around the neck.

"I'm afraid you will," said Sven.

Yigal was suffering from emotional overload. He
allowed Esther to wash and brush him clean, and
bedded on the moss pile in his alcove. Esther swept
away dust and spores and put up cloth screens to
keep out insects.

Sven fired up the stove to reheat the stew and set
out all the pots, bowls and spoons he could find. The
children, sullen-faced, had bunched themselves in a
corner.

The small boy looked up at the lightbulb swinging
from a wire, a crooked handblown thing with a naked
filament, shaded by a cone of woven grass. "Where
do you get your power?"

"From a wind generator. Wind is something we get
a lot of. We can't manage an electric stove but we get
enough for light and a heater to keep the damp out in
the winter. Why don't you sit down? There's some
mattresses."

They were tickings, filled with moss or straw, meant
for sleeping on, though often Esther bedded in the
treetops. The children dropped on them, sighing with
tiredness, and looked about. The cabin was a small
plain room walled with clay and floored with red,
blue, green, white, yellow bricks in random patterns;
the plank ceiling was thatched outside. A doorway
opened into a smaller store room. There was a table
with benches and a couple of rustic stools. Sven sat
on one, his lower arms folded in back and his upper
ones in front.

"I'm Sven," he said. "That's Esther. She's a gibbon
from Malay, or her folks were, and the enormous goat

snoring in the corner is Yigal. We were all born at Dahlgren's biological station."

One of the older boys muttered, "There was something on the tour brochure . . . mutations . . ."

They leaned their backs against the wall and watched Esther as she reached her long arms to ceiling or floor as needed, sometimes spread like a great black X, doubled by her shadow, over the dun wall. She had coarse thick hair and where she was not specked with color her body texture looked like charcoal, except for the skin that stretched and shone over the high bony vault of her forehead. She was probably the biggest-headed gibbon in the universe and certainly the only one with a line of conversation.

But the more they saw of her the less strange she seemed. With her intelligence exponentially increased, Esther had become simply another species of extraterrestrial human being.

Yigal, who stood fourteen hands high and spoke with the tongue of a man, was no more than a beautiful white goat; Dahlgren, master of animals, had made sure he would not become a beast with a human spirit trapped inside it. Yigal ate his leaves and tupped his dams, had an eye for the weather and the world's predators.

But Sven was a Solthree, one of their own species, and they had never seen one with four arms.

For his own part, Sven, who had known very few of his species in the years he spent in the station, recognized with a deep inner excitement, almost to the point of discomfort, the beings he had been shown in books and on film, whose words he had read and heard, whose thoughts and emotions he had been given for his own. Of all such persons, he was very uncomfortably aware that none had four arms. He said diffidently, "Now maybe you'll tell me who *you* are."

"I'm Ardagh," one of the girls said, not the shrill-voiced one who had yelled from the ship. "Our parents are Solthree United Nations delegates to the big GalFed conference. Our ship was late and all the arrangements for entertaining kids had gotten made, so they lumped us together and packed us off on what was supposed to be an educational tour." She grinned. "I'm afraid we're not very well matched." She was about sixteen, short, chunky and heavily muscled; she had long straight brass-colored hair.

"Joshua Ndola," said the next boy. His knees were drawn up and his arms folded over them. He was Sven's age, very thin, tall, and black of skin. He was the most formally dressed of the lot in the dark-gray, silver-starred uniform of some space academy.

"Mitzi." Head turned back against the wall, eyes closed, older than Ardagh or perhaps only looking older; pale and curly-haired, more monkey-faced than Esther, smoking some kind of drug in a tube, it gave off a thick sweet smell.

"Koz." About seventeen; he was wearing a long blue robe and had his dark hair dressed in complicated braids and knots, his face tattooed with small blue things like bugs. It was very hard to imagine where he came from or what he did.

"And you? What's your name?" to the small boy.

The one who made him uneasy.

"Shirvanian." Voice as sulky as his fleshy mouth. Thick black hair falling over his forehead, deep skin color, round face . . . *I want Mama.* Clutching the box; it looked heavy and glittered with bright designs. *I want to know* . . . and the ergs had moved in . . .

Sven found eyes resting on him, finally. Ardagh's.

No offense there. Ardagh merely wanted to be the greatest surgeon who had ever lived. Sven was wearing a close-fitting pair of homespun pants and a rabbit-skin vest that left his arms bare. She was watching the play of muscles as he shifted on the stool or twined his arms. An undercurrent of thought that she had seen him, no, surely not him but someone with a face like his, somewhere . . .

Hairless head, likely mutation effect. Yellowish skin, wild genes again, he was not oriental. Fine pale brows and thin eyelashes, weird with brown eyes. And the arms. Rounded shoulders to accommodate both sets in free movement, and a chest not hollow but filled with muscle. Plenty of pectoral to move those well-developed limbs. And, as far as she could see, no deltoids on the lower pair . . .

He said, "Did you want something?" There was a glint in his eyes.

Before she could stop herself, she blurted, "Excuse me, but do you have an extra set of clavicles?"

He threw back his head and roared with laughter, deep bass. "No, but I do have four scapulae! Do you want to see?" He began to unhook his vest.

Mitzi snarled, "For God's sake, Ardagh!"

The girl went deep red.

"But I don't mind," Sven said.

Esther reached over and flicked his ear. "Save the anatomy lesson. The food's hot."

"And I've got four nipples too," Sven laughed. She flicked his ear again.

Koz stood up. "I'm starved. Come on, Mitzi."

She was the only one left sitting. A fine smoke-stream rose from the burning drug.

The tattooed boy knocked the tube out of her mouth. "Get rid of that crap! We had enough of that goddam stink on board."

She opened her yellow eyes wide. "Did you? You slobbered your filthy betel juice all over the place!"

"Come and eat," Sven said quietly. He rose with all his arms held out, in invitation and, if necessary, threat.

Mitzi giggled. "You look like one of those robots." But she pulled herself up and helped finish the stew down to the last scrape of the bowl.

Koz pushed his bowl away. His face was haggard, and the blue tattoos writhed in the stubble of his young beard. "Look, we're very grateful, but we've got to get out of here."

"Nobody knows you're here because the radio went, right?"

"Right."

"But if you were on a tour they should know where you were headed."

"Back to Barrazan Two, then shipping out to Gal-Fed Central."

There was something about the line of his mouth. Esther twitched; if Koz had been Sven he would have gotten slapped for lying. She said gently, "You're on Barrazan Five. I think you were going the wrong way."

"How would we know? The thing was out of kilter!"

Five pairs of eyes.

Shirvanian got up and began to explore, touching and listening.

Sven said, "It doesn't matter where you want to go."

"What do you mean?"

"He means they have no radio," Shirvanian said from the storeroom. He was sniffing at the primitive machinery, turning his head one way and another for the whisper of the generator and the drip of the water still.

"We could've built one, but it'd only be a toy. You couldn't raise GalFed or even Barrazan Four on it, and the ergs would pick up the signal."

"But we can't just be stuck here! There must be a radio at the station headquarters. Isn't there?"

"Yes," Sven said.

"All right, then. We've heard about Dahlgren's set-up, and the erg machines and the mutations—"

"I haven't," Mitzi said.

"You threw away the tape because you're too damn lazy to listen. One thing, it never said the ergs were tearing people apart and taking their ships away."

"It must have been made a while ago," Sven said.

"What happened?"

"I'm not sure. I think those machines were so smart they could build machines even smarter . . . maybe they thought they ought to be working for themselves instead of anybody else . . . unless somebody human set them on to it."

Dahlgren, perhaps, getting tired of playing with animals?

Esther said, "I don't think they needed anybody to set them on to it. Being with Dahlgren, alongside him, building new machine forms at the same time he built or changed life forms . . . they picked up a pattern."

"They picked up a pattern of killing living things. I suppose you could say they got that from Dahlgren."

"You were saved," Ardagh said.

"Dahlgren got us away . . . we were all that was left by the time they were through with the—rebellion."

Machines crashed and clanged under the wind; the children turned silent. "I told you they've been coming closer," Sven said dully.

Ardagh whispered, "What do they want here?"

"They have life sensors. You're strange to them and they're curious . . . and of course they'd like to get rid of me. Ergs don't care for life forms very much. They should be leaving in a few minutes. They always come back, hours or days."

Mitzi's teeth were chattering. "I hate this. I hate it!"

"Oh shut up," Koz said. He turned to Sven. "They haven't hurt you."

"They'd like to. They swing their arms and buzz at

me, but they can't get me. I don't know why, and I don't ask."

"What about Dahlgren?"

"He left us here and went back. They let him do that. I think he must be dead by now." I hope, forgive me, I hope he's dead . . . I don't want to think he did all this.

"But what happens if a ship comes for service?"

"I suppose they get out and service it. This has never been anybody's favorite stopping place."

"You said they've got a radio. They must have one to communicate with ships."

"I haven't been there for nine years Solthree. The station complex is a hundred and fifty kilometers away. We're up at the northwest tip of the triangle . . . and when the ergs took over they turned up the reactors, killed off the closest life forms and sent the rest into wild mutations. Radiation doesn't bother them. This was supposed to be a non-rad area, Zone Green. But it's not any more."

Shirvanian got the pocket counter out of his bag. "Do you know what your background radiation was when you came here?"

"No . . . I was too young to care."

"Point four millirads," said Esther.

"It's a bit more than that now."

"The winter storms wash the stuff down from the dust clouds in the east."

Shirvanian thought for a minute. "With a steady background of about point four mr a person should pick up a body burden of about thirty-odd rem over nine years . . . and I guess that wouldn't be too good to grow up in . . . but a hundred and fifty kilometers . . . you'd only get readings of a few rads per hour by the time you got to the reactors, and that doesn't sound like runaway radiation."

"The ergs built big earthworks on the zone boundaries to use as baffles. That's how the dosages were originally controlled. In Zone Blue, you'll see the counter jump."

"Maybe you should ask Yigal," Sven said. "His dams move through the zones."

Yigal gave a loud ironic snicker. "Indeed." He opened his eyes and raised his head from the moss pile. "All the kids I sired," he got up, dug his head into the nearest bin, and pulled it out with a cabbage impaled on one horn, "were aborted monsters." He twisted his head, tossed off the cabbage, sat back on his haunches in time to catch it with his front hooves. It was his one trick.

Koz ground his teeth. "There has to be a way!"

A gust of wind drove rain through the curtains and made the lamp swing.

"Does there?" Sven flung out all four of his arms. When he gestured his lower arms repeated the movements of his upper ones a split second later; sometimes he seemed to have a shadow image. "If we could have gotten away do you think we'd still be here? You think we're happy? It's a filthy place, and outside in the wilderness it's twenty times worse." He was tired and irritable. First outworld people he'd seen in half his life and they had to be this lot. "Suppose you got past the ergs, the radiation, wild mutations, crazy native life, storms—if you found a radio and a ship, would you know how to use them?"

Out of the silence, Shirvanian said, "I would—or if I couldn't, which isn't likely, I'd make the ergs do it for me."

Mitzi shrieked, "You shut up, you dirty stupid brat, you can't even keep your pants dry! You got us into this rotten mess!"

Koz reached over and slammed her on the side of the head so hard she went crashing against Joshua's shoulder and knocked him off the bench.

Esther snaked out an arm like a steel cable, hoicked up Koz by the collar, and dumped him in the moss bin.

"All right, Esther," said Sven.

Shirvanian burst into tears, Ardagh turned white, Koz and the others picked themselves up, spluttering.

Esther grabbed Shirvanian and wiped his face with the palms of her hands. "I didn't do it!" he yelled. "They made me! LET ME GO!"

Koz brushed moss off, spitting. "You let him go and I'll wring his neck for him!"

Joshua calmly found his seat on the bench again. "I thought you were committed to nonviolence."

"I'm sick of you! I'm sick of this place!" Mitzi was shaking with tears of rage. "I hate you all!"

"You're scared and tired," Esther said, brushing up moss, straightening clothes, drying tears. She was crazy-clean, or perhaps a bit crazy from trying to keep clean in such a place. "Sven, it's time to sleep."

"Mutti, I'm scared and tired too. But I get more scared when I think . . . Ardagh? Joshua? You seem to have your heads on. What is this? The ergs moved in on me tonight, your ship went the wrong way—and Shirvanian can operate interplanetary radio? What is this kid, ten years old?"

"I'm not stupid! I can operate a radio!"

Ardagh pulled her hands away from her face and the red welled into it.

"He's got some kind of psi," she whispered. "It works on machines . . ." She looked around. "Don't glare at me. We can't muck it up any worse than we've done already."

"Machines?" Sven stared down at Shirvanian, who had untangled himself from Esther and backed into a corner, red-eyed and pouting. "I've known a couple of ESPs—but machines?"

"He's supposed to be a genius—"

"Genius idiot." Mitzi, trembling, was trying to light a stick of kif.

"I'm not an idiot! I don't wet my pants!"

"I'm glad of that," Esther said. "We don't have very good laundry service here."

"What were you trying to do?" Sven asked.

"Get away!" Koz was near tears himself. "We wanted to get away!" He added in weary disgust, "Why else do you think we'd have this brat with us?"

"But why?"

"Because we were so goddam tired of . . ."

"Of what?" Esther rumpled her gleaming brow. "Tired of good food and clean beds and seeing everything in the Galaxy?"

"You wouldn't understand!"

Sven said, "I think I do. This much. You needed Shirvanian's psi . . . to steal a ship."

"It was a robot! He was supposed to be able to take us wherever we wanted to go. But after he cut the radio and the radar to break the trail—"

"Everything went wrong," said Ardagh. "He's no pilot, just a kid with a power he can't control."

Shirvanian said coldly, "I also cut the retros when we landed. Otherwise we'd all be dead."

"I see . . . that's why the ship didn't blow up."

"He's very good at turning things off," Koz said. "Too bad some people can't do that with their mouths."

"Oh Koz, go set up your joss and pray to your Mother Shrinigasa. We need all the help we can get."

"Don't you ridicule my religion."

"I'm not," Ardagh said. "I'll pray to her if it'll do any good."

Sven shook his head at the five incomprehensible beings. "The ergs moved in . . . Shirvanian, did you turn them on?"

"I turned off your transmitter," said Shirvanian.

"Transmitter?" He blinked. "Where do I have a transmitter?"

The boy shrugged indifferently. "I dunno. Someplace inside you."

Sven slowly lifted his left arms and pushed a thumb between the lower sets of biceps and pectoral. "This hard thing here, could this be it? I always thought it was a tumor . . . what does it do to the ergs?" He strained his eyes to see the place on his skin. It might have been a crease.

"Gives out a static signal that knocks out their systems. Within a limit." Shirvanian tapped his nails on his box. "I wanted to see them up close. That's why I stopped it." He was looking very smug.

Sven wanted to strangle him with all four hands. He was frightened at the feeling; he had never gotten angry at ergs. "Esther, did you know?"

"No, sweetheart. Everything I know I picked out of the air. Dahlgren never held consultations with his specimens. But Topaze has a rad counter. No reason why you can't have a transmitter."

"Who's Topaze?" Koz wanted to know.

"You'll meet him tomorrow. I don't think you're quite ready for him yet."

"All this doesn't tell us how to get out of here," Koz said.

Shirvanian tapped his box again. "You won't get out without my help. I can turn it off any time I want."

Before the others could mince him, Esther wrapped her arms around him once-and-a-half. "Little genius, you're a little stupid. Once that transmitter goes off the ergs will come and tear us every one in little pieces and we'll turn into nice green glop to fertilize the ground. Now wrap yourself in a blanket and pack yourself off to sleep on one of those beds. You have enough to work your busy brains on tomorrow."

"But will you get us to the station!" Koz yelled.

A thunderbolt crackled, a tree crashed nearby, and a sheet of rain slammed the roof. "Not in that," Sven said mildly. "Do what the lady says."

Mitzi shrugged and murmured, "Just like home. Mama Ape, Papa Goat and Big Brother Spiderman."

Ardagh was pulling a knitted jumpsuit out of her duffel. "You should know Mitzi's got a name for everyone. I'm the Ox, Koz is the Nut, Shirvanian's the Gearbox. Joshua's the Black Prince. He got off light."

Esther laughed and regarded Mitzi with a quirked brow. "What's your name for yourself, girl?"

Mitzi dropped her kif stick on a white tile and stamped on it; wrapped in her poncho, she flung herself on the mat.

Esther picked up the butt and dropped it in a refuse bin. "Tomorrow . . ."

"The outhouse is out back of the house," Sven said. "Goodnight."

Esther gave Yigal a kick in the flank; he grunted and made room for her on the moss.

Sven swept a heap of straw into a corner in the storeroom. As he was arranging himself on its unaccommodating bulk a shadow slipped through the doorway. "Sven . . ."

It was Ardagh. "Don't get up." She sat beside him in a movement that was graceful for a person of her thickness. "I just remembered something . . . I don't know if I should tell you . . ."

He was a hair's breadth away from telling her that if she didn't know she should forget it, but a surprising jet of feeling rose and traversed the length of his body at the nearness of her fleshly female presence. Mitzi notwithstanding, there was nothing wrong with her looks; her hair shone in a flicker of the dying lamplight, and her broad cheekbones were smooth and peach-colored. He propped himself on a set of elbows

and hoped she could not see the heat in his face.
"What is it?"

"A newsflash I saw in port on Barrazan Four . . . the
big outworld conference our parents were going to . . .
I—"

"What are you trying to say?"

She clasped her hands. "Next Thirtyday—that's
about five and a half weeks Solthree—Dahlgren's
coming into the Center to give a report to the Sciences Council."

"He is?" Sven sat up. "Are you sure?"

"They said Edvard Dahlgren, they had pictures,
old newstapes . . . it couldn't be another Dahlgren
who's a biologist and has a world to himself."

"A world to himself?" Sven laughed. "No, I guess
there couldn't be another one."

"I don't understand," she said. "If the ergs took over,
and killed so many—what can he be doing?"

"I don't know. I don't think I want to know."

She rose to go. "Sven? That transmitter . . . the ergs
make other machines, don't they? Would it work on
all of them?"

"Probably not."

"I see. I guess I won't tell the others that."

"They'll think of it themselves. Goodnight, Ardagh."

She pushed into a bit of space between Mitzi and
Joshua. She was shaking—from fear, chill, and the
conviction that she should have kept her mouth shut.
After a while, in the unending noise of rain and wind,
sleep began to wash over her in an uneasy ebb and
flow; in the troughs of its waves she saw first Dahlgren's face, and then Sven's. It had reminded her . . .
eyes, nose, forehead and cheekbones . . .

If Dahlgren had shaved off the beard . . .

2

Dahlgren had done his best to go mad.

He had howled the length and breadth of the concrete vaults, crawling and sobbing as his friends were plucked from him and slaughtered or starved, flung in heaps to rot into scales, bones and carapaces. Had scraped his knees and palms raw, battered his head against walls. The ergs had let him. He had even prayed, an ineffectual act, since he had never believed in anything but himself. He had torn hair and beard out by handfuls, scored his face with his nails, smashed the empty tanks and cages with his fists, shredded the last of the seedling plants with his teeth. The ergs watched him with camera eyes, sprayed him with antibiotics, set food before him. He splattered it to the floors first, and when he was starving, licked the floors.

No use. His body was scarred, foul and ragged. His head was hard clear Dahlgren, cold as the waters of his icy lakes.

"Why do you not kill me?" he screamed. "Why do you not kill me? Why?"

The ergs moved to and fro, click, buzz, whirr; he hammered his fists on their plates as they passed his live jetsam body and the open graveyard of his men.

Haruni of Cruxa II had been the last; the little russet stick-man, entomologist and chessmaster, had shuddered to death in Dahlgren's arms. Dahlgren's food was poison to him; he had eaten, vomited and died. Now I will really go mad, Dahlgren thought, but he did not, and he had years to go. He ate, choking, slept on cold floors, evacuated in corners; his heart palpitated, his hands knotted; his joints ached and thickened, he believed he would not recognize his face in a mirror if he saw it. His mind observed and collated; watched for weaknesses (none), bolt-holes (none), hiding places (none). They wanted him for something. He had nothing. All dead. Men, foliage, beasts. I am the beast. Sven? Dead, likely, in that far corner. And Esther and Yigal. Subjects, friends. Friends? I mastered. I had no friends. Haruni I killed, gave him my food in misplaced pity. Sven. Esther. Yigal. Begged for them, whined and slavered. Let them go, they will not harm you, and I will come back. Friends? Dead they are friends. Alive they hated icy Dahlgren. Your bones are in the corner, Haruni. I do not even remember your face.

I am Dahlgren and no other, even in wild hair and cankered skin. If I live I will begin again, without ergs, in a small place. And yet again, if I must. That is the Dahlgren I have always been.

His mind withdrew and approached a focus on another plane.

Perhaps it is a good thing for the universe that there is only one Dahlgren.

The thought vexed him inordinately. He crouched in the center of the vault among clanking ergs, while he gnawed some slab of nourishment. His teeth were good.

This is terrible. All I can do in this obscene place is became more sane. Perhaps if I live long enough I shall die humble. Ultimate punishment.

His shoulders slumped. An erg paused and stroked him with sensors. He shuddered. Some change would occur.

"How? How?" He did not know how long it was since he had spoken. He cleared his throat. His voice creaked. "How long have I been here?" Humble. He gagged and spat.

SEVEN YEARS. The voice boomed around the walls.

Seven Barrazan V. Nine Solthree. He grunted.

YOU WILL COME.

"Leave me."

Coils extended, wrapped and lifted him. He was rigid with fury. He could not move or even croak with the coil tight around his chest. The erg carried him to the infirmary entrance and stopped, too big to pass. There were half a dozen small servos clustered at the door to receive him. The files and equipment had been kept intact, or replaced.

The erg set him upright, and the small steel creatures drew him in with a dozen clawed arms. The walls had cracked in a few places and grown several patches of pink and green mold. Otherwise there was no change. The vents had been cleared and the dehumidifier was working.

Surrounded waist-high by palpating machines, Dahlgren stared at the opposite wall. His old GalFed uniform was hanging there fresh as on the day of arrival when he had put it in storage. It was too fine for the weather of his laboratory world, though it was a working uniform and not for show. It hung clean and crisp, a dark maroon coverall with three small gold emblems over the left breast: a star, a ringed planet, a circle divided by a cross, ancient symbol both of Earth and of Creation.

One of the ergs plucked a file card from a rack, inserted and retrieved it from a desk computer. "Place him on the scale."

Claws placed him.

"You weigh twenty-eight kilos less than when you arrived here. We will rectify that."

"You . . ." Dahlgren searched for his voice and

found it. "You intend, I suppose, to fatten me for the slaughter."

Ergs had neither humor nor irony. "That is correct."

They gave him a room with a bed, a bath, a locked door, in an isolation ward for one of the many curious and grotesque diseases on the planet. "No one here is more curious and grotesque than I," said Dahlgren. The camera eyes did not flicker and the ventilators did not answer. Food came through an opening in the wall. It looked and smelled delicious.

He ignored it and lay on the bed, falling for hours or days—all illumination was artificial—into light sleep. He dreamed of the old days, but had no nightmares. They came with his waking hours.

Ergs arrived, finally, and injected him with stimulants. Fresh food appeared. He ate; it was so rich and fine that he vomited that and the next meal and the one after that. The ergs injected him with anti-emetics and gave him food more bland and simple. He ate it and it stayed down.

The ergs came to bathe him, heal his sores, give him therapy to cure his swollen arthritic joints, strap him into exercise machines. He began to put on weight.

He thought of the uniform, which would fit him in a short while, and of the ancient Romans, who used to dress captives in fine clothes before degrading them. His mind remained cold and clear.

One day or hour he moved, walked and spoke without pain or effort. He said, "This is interesting."

Almost at once the ergs came to trim his hair and beard, take away the faded blue hospital clothing, and fit him into his uniform. They put a mirror before him. He recognized himself.

But that did not interest him, that he was as tall and strong as a man of sixty-three would be under the best of conditions. He did not have the strength to refuse the touch of a single one of those steel claws.

There was no chance of help, refuge, or escape. He was curious to know what arena he would be made to fight in, how long he would be allowed to fight.

And why.

They spoke to him, and made him walk and talk; noted his movements and recorded his gestures. It amused him, in his icy way, that there were things they were not sure of about him. It did not occur to him to deceive them.

They led him down the halls, where the debris had been cleaned away. It amused him, too, that they had gotten rid of the things that would horrify or distract him.

He was brought into a small room in which there was a screen with a chair in front of it. They locked him in and he sat down.

The screen flickered and filled with a ceiling view of a group of small ergs gathered about a low table, engaged with an object their meshing limbs hid from sight. They looked like drones attending a queen bee. They withdrew slightly, exposing limbs, a torso, metal-boned and flashing silver. They tightened, trimmed, smoothed; flexed and adjusted.

"Android robot," Dahlgren murmured. "Playing with dolls!" A flash of contempt moved him. First curiosity, then contempt. Human feelings. "Am I becoming a man again?" asked Dahlgren. "Perhaps I will even feel . . ."

Fear.

The ergs slid back and exposed the upper part of the body. It had two arms, five fingers on each. It was boned in gears and spindles, muscled in wires and flexes.

Above the neck it was, or seemed to be, flesh; it had eyes, ears, nose, mouth, hair, beard. Dahlgren's.

The ergs moved out of the picture.

The erg-android blinked, straight into Dahlgren's

eyes, blue for blue. An erg approached to snip one lock of beard with its claw, and retreated.

The android blinked again, pulled back the pink lip corners into the beard, into Dahlgren's rare smile, and raised a steel-tendoned arm, palm outward.

"Hello, Dahlgren Zero," it said. "I am Dahlgren One."

Dahlgren looked into the eyes and swallowed. Then he sat up straight in his new health, his clean cloth, and said, "How do you do, erg-Dahlgren. I am Dahlgren Man."

Erg-Dahlgren smiled again; the screen went blank.

Dahlgren touched his ginger-gray hair and beard, his mouth, and closed his eyes. He did not bend. Inside the closed lids he saw himself crawling the rough floor on his bleeding knees and palms. That was peace.

3

Mornings, Sven exercised on the beaten earth outside the door. The sun shone pink through haze, the thatch steamed; blurred red lines striped the housefront from the bloodrains of spring and summer; small animals chattered in their hutches. The wind was light now, the birds chimed like bells and flowers twittered as drifting air whirred their blades; insects buzzed and screamed.

Sven took off his clothes and clasped his upper hands behind his neck; he sprang onto his lower ones and walked on them with legs and torso bent back

and upward like a dragonfly's long thorax, excruci-
atingly.

*because you are not going to look like some
damned freak,* said Dahlgren. *I don't want those lower arms hanging limp like a bottled thing in a cheap
circus.*

Then why did you make them that way, Dahlgren?
But he never asked.

*Now lower left and upper right. Upper left and
lower right.* Sweat dripped from his nose and chin. *I
want every muscle growing, every bone. You have
seventy-four extra bones, muscles to move them, tendons to hold them, blood vessels to feed them . . .*

Sometimes he juggled with stones, or the heavy
pods of the *luk* flower. *You won't have to earn a living
as a court jester on Cinnabar Seven, don't worry.
Among Solthrees you will be a Solthree and less clumsy than most.* Then why?

Today he did not juggle. Standing on four arms,
sweat dripping, beating blood in his head half sti-
fling him, he wanted to stay that way, not thinking of
Dahlgren.

He blinked, saw an upside-down face, and jumped
to his feet.

Ardagh was leaning against the doorway. She
picked up the rag he had left near his clothes to dry
himself and handed it to him.

He took it and wiped himself, not looking at her
and not hiding from her, put on the net singlet and
pants he wore as sweat-catchers to make up for his
lack of body hair. "You have a question about my
physiology?" He glanced up and saw that she had
turned red.

"Only about how many extra vertebrae you had,"
she murmured. "I wanted to be a doctor. A surgeon."

"Can't you be?"

"I'm short two vertebrae. My grandparents were
fitted for some planet with cold climate and low

gravity. The colony went fft and the kids all got left this way, built like servos and poor coordination." She added bitterly, "That's why I'm the Ox to people like Mitzi."

"Don't they do most surgery with machines?"

"Not in medschool, or in emergencies."

"They should have terraformed the planet."

"Yeah, like here."

He finished dressing. "If I could learn to coordinate, you can."

"You have an advantage. Dahlgren is—"

"What?"

She swallowed. Dahlgren is your father. Oh yes, tell him that. He was half a meter taller than she, seventy-five kilos heavier. And he was Dahlgren's heir all right, all the arrogance waiting to develop in good time. "Nothing . . . Dahlgren's going to GalFed Central and he'll be taking the ship with him. I don't know what you want to be, but I won't get to be anything if we stay here."

He stood looking at her, not arrogant yet. He didn't know what to do.

A black streak crossed the sky, whooping. Esther, finished with her morning exercises in the trees, landed on the thatch and slid to the ground. She yawned. "I need more sleep than I got last night."

"We'd better get the others up," he muttered.

Shirvanian appeared in the doorway, a peculiar look on his face. "I wet my pants," he said.

Esther tousled his hair. "Then I guess we'd better clean you up before your friend Mitzi the Mouth has a chance to use it on you."

Sven grinned. "Hey, Mutti, is he taking my place?"

Esther yipped. "You want your pants changed too?"

While Sven and Esther made breakfast, Ardagh and Shirvanian waited by the house watching the veiled sun rise in a sky the color of a poison mushroom. The day heated, dim with mist; an enormous butterfly with glass wings and a black body hovered over a red-belled wildflower in the cabbage patch, settled to uncurl its long tube into the nectar.

Koz came out with Joshua, both neat, the one by nature and the other with effort: Koz's long napped robe caught dust, straw, and whatever else was light and loose; it took time to comb and braid his long hair, depilate his heavily bearded jaw. The ill nature had washed out of his face for the moment with his complicated grooming. "Where's Alpha Centauri?"

"That way." Shirvanian pointed a negligent finger.

Koz went back into the house and brought out a small gold statuette with a black wooden base. The idol was in the shape of a humanoid female dressed in long ceremonial robes, backed by a three-legged symbol of the sort he was tattooed with. He planted it on the ground toward the distant star and was about to kneel when he happened to glance up. "Hey, look at that!"

The others whirled. A magnificent blue-black gorilla was coming out of the forest on four limbs, in measured steps, an empty string bag slung casually over one shoulder.

Esther jumped out the door. "Hey, Topaze!" She hopped up and down, then ran to the great beast, plucking the bell-flower, butterfly and all, as she went. Topaze sat down between cabbages, resting hands on knees. Esther skipped up the huge belly, planted the flower behind his ear, kissed him, and unhooked the string bag from his arm.

Joshua moved closer, head cocked. "Friend of yours?"

"Just for breakfast." Esther grinned. "Don't scare him, now." She dashed into the house and brought back the bag filled with garden fruits and vegetables. She tossed it to Topaze, who caught it easily by the handle, picked out a fruit, and ate it peaceably. They stepped closer.

"Go ahead, pat him if you like, he's fairly sociable."

Ardagh moved up cautiously to admire the pitted snout, sharp eyes, and crested skull.

"He's my blood brother," Esther said. "My backup. If I didn't work out, Dahlgren was going to try gorillas. But when he got me . . . he didn't keep large stocks or play around once he'd proved something. He just let them mate, thought he'd keep a few around and teach them to do odd jobs."

"Are there any others?"

"Mutant malaria killed the parents, and the ergs got Topaze's sister. He's all that's left. Come closer. Can you hear the ticking?"

Topaze had finished the fruit and spat the pit out with a mighty *ptooh.* He buzzed very faintly.

"That's the counter. When it gets to a certain pitch in a hot zone it sets off a jolt of adrenalin, he gets scared and backs away. Goodbye, old dear!"

Topaze rose, grunted, slung the bag over his shoulder and marched off with dignity and slow grace, the red flower bobbing behind his ear.

"Just as well," Esther said. "I don't know how Sven would've got on with a really brainy gorilla."

Ardagh wondered. Sven, standing on four hands, sweating and grimacing as he paced the red and blue flecked earth . . . Dahlgren didn't play around . . .

Yigal woke cranky as usual and drummed the floor with his hooves. A few bricks were badly cracked in his corner. "Damn." The sun blanked out and rain drummed the roof for three seconds. "I hate east winds."

"Ayeh," said Esther. "You say that every fall."

Mitzi pulled herself awake groaning and sat with her head on her knees. She looked sick and vulnerable, the fine bone structure of her face pale through drawn skin. Esther, who fed what moved and swabbed what didn't, wiped her face with a wet shammy, and she swore weakly.

"Up, up!" said Esther. "Breakfast."

They got the same diet as Topaze. The fruits were crisp and sweet, but the rank odor of wind from the east spoiled the flavor and worry dried the food in their mouths.

"It's still the same," Koz said. "How we get out of here."

"Climate," said Joshua. "Poisons, diseases, killer ergs, radiation ..." He stopped to look at his pineapple slice and licked his lips, his tongue a pink surprise on his black skin. "You brought seed from the station."

"Yes," Sven said. "Corn, rice, manioc, papaya, cuttings, seedlings—"

"Metals, tools, components—"

"Storage foods, books . . . everything else we made here."

"How did you carry it?"

"We didn't walk a hundred and fifty kilometers! Dahlgren brought us in an old transport by a brick road, one of the erg tracks."

"Was it an erg?"

Esther said, "Not really. It was an old all-purpose thing Dahlgren called the Argus. He used it to truck around non-rad animals, in the station and out to here. But it had started out as a road-mender, it kept picking bricks all the way here because it was on the road, and that's how we got this fancy floor. I guess we picked up a lot of radiation with them, but it didn't seem to matter then."

"You meant the ergs had turned the reactors up and you came through all of that?" Joshua asked. "All that radiation?"

Esther said patiently, "The bricks had the radiation. The Argus was used to carry unradiated animals.

It was lead—or concrete-shielded, I don't know which."

Koz said, "What happened to it?"

"I don't know. Dahlgren went back in it."

Sven said in a listless voice, "When I was a kid . . . I used to complain because Dahlgren wouldn't let me play with the animals and I was bored . . . so he bonded the Argus to me and let me ride around in it . . ."

"That means there's safe vehicles somewhere," Joshua said. "There must have been more."

"Don't you realize they'd have scrapped or cannibalized it, the way they're doing with your ship?"

Shirvanian turned his precious box in his hands. "They may have left it alone because it was bonded to you. Then they'd have booby-trapped it."

Sven rapped the table. "But what good does it do you to get there? The ergs are killers, and Dahlgren's free out among the ergs! He's free to get off the planet! Ardagh tells me he's reporting to GalFed Central in a few weeks."

"Then he's taking the ship!" said Koz. "We've got to reach him!"

"If he's controlling killer ergs, do you think he'd care about saving you?"

Mitzi yelled, "You don't care about saving us! You're playing Robinson Crusoe in your safe little hole and you don't give a shit for anybody else!"

Yigal tapped the table hard with one hoof. The dishes danced. "You will not speak to my friends in that manner, miss, or you will not be safe in this hole."

"Go easy, Yigal," said Esther. "She's not that wrong, Sven. You know there's no way out. The ergs are crowding and you've been sitting around with a long face for half a year."

Sven crouched with his arms locked tightly and his face set.

Koz sneered. "He's scared."

"We're all scared," said Ardagh, "but he risked his life to save us . . . you've got books, Sven." She went to the storeroom.

"What about them?" he asked dully.

Ardagh's lumbering gait was somewhat peculiar but not graceless. She came back with a fine old volume, "*Gulliver's Travels*, waterproofed, very nice," and turned to the flyleaf: "'For my son, Edvard Dahlgren, in hope that he will lead a life of study and contemplation. From his father, Sven Adolphus Dahlgren.' . . . I wonder if Adolphus liked the Houyhnhnms."

"Why were you poking about in my things?"

"Because I'm an awful snoop . . . he gave you his books, the books his father gave him. He even gave you his father's name."

"Why shouldn't he?"

"What in Holy Mother's name are you talking about?" Koz asked.

"Dahlgren's his father. I've seen pictures . . . I recognized the face."

"It's none of your business," Sven said.

"I know, but I believe I can understand what you're feeling. Dahlgren's free, everybody else is dead, he may be controlling the ergs. But he saved the three of you. We have no right to ask you to put yourself in more danger, but we have to help ourselves if we can. There must be something to the man, and maybe he'll help us."

"He didn't only save me!" Sven threw out all four arms. "He made me!"

"For an experiment, you think? For fun?"

"I don't know."

"Did he give Esther a pair of horns and a tail with a barb in it? Don't you think it might have been an accident?"

"He would have aborted."

"What of your mother?" Joshua asked.

"I had none. She left him before I was born. He had specimens of her ova in the banks. He did it with everybody. He was like that."

Esther sighed. "Sven thinks his father made him a monster out of revenge against his mother. I don't believe it, and I can't get the idea out of his head."

Sven gripped the table edge with one set of hands and covered his face with the others. "Can't you leave me alone now? Isn't that enough for you?"

Mitzi spat in disgust and flung herself out the door. The others watched Sven for a moment in despair and turned away.

There was an ear-splitting shriek from outside, and Koz jumped up. "What's that dumb bitch done now?"

Mitzi was backed against the red-streaked wall staring and trembling. Hopping through the cabbages was a dull gray thing so contorted it was almost formless. The lowering sky dropped a single sheet of rain, then cleared and the sun blazed orange for a moment.

The thing, now wet silver, came closer, a machine in the shape of a bird; a bird that if it had been living matter would never have pierced the shell. One leg was much shorter than the other; it lurched. One wing was twitching weakly on the middle of its back; it had jewel eyes, and its beak clicked and chirped. An extra head lay still beside the other on a twisted neck. Well within the range of the transmitter, it still came forward, lurching and chirping. *Bottled thing in a cheap circus*. Sven gagged.

"It's harmless." Shirvanian, box in hand, sat down beside it, picked up the grotesque thing and hugged it. The bird clacked, twitched, chirped in his arms.

Esther found her voice and croaked, "That's dangerous!"

"No it isn't," said Shirvanian calmly. He hooked a fingernail under one scale, the bird gave a last twitch and collapsed. He rubbed down its scales with his sleeve.

"Then what is it?" Ardagh whispered. "A warning?"

"Maybe." A warning of something cruel and ugly.

Mitzi said through her teeth, "Get it away!"

"Don't be silly, it can't hurt you."

"If you've turned off the transmitter again I'll wring your neck," said Esther.

"Those ergs'd be dumb if they couldn't make a machine bypass that old transmitter," Shirvanian said. He picked the thing up and smelled it, put it to his ear, touched it with his tongue. The bird looked heavy; evidently his hands were strong. "You know, you people haven't asked me anything yet, and I'm the one who's going to be doing most of the work."

Koz growled, "What work did you have in mind?"

"Catching ergs. I said I'd make them work for me."

Mitzi said, "God, I wish we'd shoved him out the lock."

The child shrugged and smirked. People talked that way when he was around. "We've got an erg already, haven't we?" He held the metal bird by its two necks and stared into the jewel eyes, then set it down again and reached for his box.

"What the devil have you got in there?"

Shirvanian grinned. "Toys." He unhooked and split it. Its halves were packed to the millimeter with miniature screwdrivers, set-screws, wire spools, transistor chips, coils of solder, irons, power cells, rivets, lenses of varying range, and other things to delight the heart of a child.

Esther said, "Sven, this thing was sent to tell us we're not safe any more."

"Yes." Sven unfolded his arms and conquered his revulsion enough to come closer. "What does it expect us to do?"

"Get scared, run away into the wilds, die."

"They could have done that lots of other ways."

"Maybe there's something that likes to play complicated games . . ." Esther poked the bird. "What are you going to do, Shirvanian?"

"Fix it," he said. "My way."

"Better bring it inside, the rain'll get at it." She barked with laughter. "And if any of those toys of yours fall into the cabbages they'll give Yigal a bellyache."

4

Dahlgren lay on the bed in his faded hospital blues.

It begins to clear. When it is time to report to the Sciences Council they will send erg-Dahlgren. They are clever. Not too clever for their own good, like me. He/it will not be so different from myself, what they know of me out there, little god, they say, Dahlgren-with-a-world-of-his-own. I have changed, I suppose, and what of that, one time I whined and begged? They understand only words and reasons, ergs, and when it is to their own advantage. Like me. As I was. And how different now? And who to see? *I can't live with you any more, I can't. I know you're not cruel, you love me, you have feelings, you're kind in some aching offhand way that won't show to anybody, but the inside of you isn't worth that awful thickness of*

the surface, and it's freezing me to the marrow.
Thank God we didn't have any children together, and
I'm still young enough to have them . . . you have
nothing to say. Of course not. Something tied a knot
in you, I don't know what, but Edvard, dear, I can't
untie it . . .

Well, I am unraveled enough now, my sweet.

Ergs brought him to the room where erg-Dahlgren
had been formed. Other-Dahlgren lay still on a table,
fleshed completely now, pink and unmarked as a child.
The ergs lowered over him a fine grid set in lucite.
They took away Dahlgren's pajamas and set him on a
table beside the other, with a similar grid. As it lowered they injected him. Before he sank down into the
black he had one weird thought, a wisp from old
stories of Gothic horror: brain exchange. He had time
for a twinge of amusement: they would never trust an
animal, brain or body.

When he woke the grid was rising. Erg-Dahlgren
was sitting on the other table, hands gripping the
edge, legs crossed at the ankle, swinging. He grinned.
He had lost his newness; his skin was yellowed,
specked with age spots, lined. The ergs had mapped
him: he had Dahlgren's every mole, hair and blue
vein.

Dahlgren sat up slowly and faced him unconsciously in the same position.

"You have guessed?" said the erg. "I am ready to
take your place . . . if there are women, there is nothing they would not have seen on you, even if they
were to remember after so many years."

"I was never very good with women," Dahlgren
said dryly. "That would not be a great problem."

"So much the better."

"Why do you want my place?"

"To do what you would do. Make worlds. Create,

destroy, and own, like all men. It is what makes us different from the animals."

"Thank you for the lesson," said Dahlgren.

"My philosophy, of course, has not the depth of yours."

"I have no doubt you will improve on it," Dahlgren said. "When may I expect to die?"

"Not yet! Not yet!" Erg-Dahlgren held up a hand with the arthritic knots of the original. "I look and move like you, but I do not yet think like you—"

"You are doing a very good imitation."

"Thank you. But I must be perfect—a sentiment with which I believe you would agree. In order for me to do that we will play a game."

"I thought we were doing that already."

"You see, I did not know you had a sense of humor. That is very difficult for an erg to simulate."

"It shouldn't be," said Dahlgren. "It's a branch of the same tree that grows cruelty and the lust for power."

"That is good. I will remember that." He turned his head, and Dahlgren followed the look. He had not noticed the new erg rolling in on silent casters. It was not as big as the most powerful machines, but was still much taller than he. Vaguely female in shape, somewhat conical, rather insectiform; five arms lay curved down along each flank; a rank of faceted jewel eye buttons ran down the midline; its bulblike upper end wore a crown of antennas. Dull silver in blemishless perfection, segments tiered like peplums, it gave the impression of a pampered hive queen. Dahlgren thought his mind might be slanting off again; for a moment he had the idea that erg-Dahlgren was about to call it Mother.

YOU ARE READY TO PLAY. The voice was pure machine.

"We must dress first," said erg-Dahlgren. "Always

look the part. Our man does not know what game
yet."

DO YOU NOT, DAHLGREN? WHAT GAME DO YOU PLAY
BUT CHESS?

"What game is more suitable for men and machines?" erg-Dahlgren asked. He pulled on a repli-
ca of Dahlgren's coverall.

Dahlgren thought, they are one. No, he is her doll,
her puppet. If I broke her doll she would mend him.
But it had never occurred to him to attack an erg. He
had chosen ergs for their superiority as carefully as he
had chosen animals.

No longer naked in the presence of his enemy, he
felt stronger, and said, "You cannot force me to play
chess with you."

"Why should we force you?" erg-Dahlgren said.
"You will wish to play. I have learned the rules of
your game; let me tell you mine. It does not matter
who wins, because there will be no prizes. I have told
you that I intend to learn how you think and act, because I am going to take your place on Earth and in
the heavens. When I have learned, you will die, because you will no longer be needed. The longer you
play, the longer you live. You have not much more
than half a thirtyday because we must lift off by then.
You should know that you have already been given a
great gift of time because it took nine of your years
for us to learn to make me."

"You've done well," said Dahlgren. "It took sixty-
three to make me . . . and four million to make Man."

YOU MAY NO LONGER PLAY FOR TIME, DAHLGREN. YOU
WILL PLAY CHESS FOR US.

"I have no set," Dahlgren said.

YOU HAVE A SET. WE KEPT IT FOR YOU.

The wall behind the silver erg slid open. Beyond it
was a brightly lit room with two chairs, a chess table
Dahlgren recognized as his own—the one he had

played on with Haruni—and a chessboard set with pieces.

Dahlgren slid off the examining table and looked at it. "That's no kind of set to play with. I can't use that."

It was a showpiece, a gift his wife had had made for him in the days when she loved him. The squares of the board were ivory and bone, the pieces transparent lucite blocks, each enclosing an object: the white pawns preserved snail shells, the blacks cowries, the queens slender coral branches of red and white, the kings animal molars in different shadings with roots pointing upward like crowns, the bishops varieties of fossil trilobites, the rooks mammal phalanges, and the knights the skulls of small birds, beaks pointing upward. All earthly, all animal. Dahlgren, master of dead animals.

"That's not a set anyone can play with." He smiled ruefully. "I never was a master, I lost most of my games with Haruni, and I couldn't even find my way through this. Where's my old Staunton?"

Dahlgren's copy picked up the white coral Queen, blinked at it, and set it down.

YOU GAVE IT TO YOUR SON, said erg-Queen.

True. Dahlgren thought of Sven, if he had survived, playing chess with Esther, their faces puckered earnestly, and Yigal, perhaps, sitting with his head resting on a bent hoof, kibitzing. Silliness. Why had he given him the set? "Yes, I remember."

Erg-Dahlgren said, "If you cannot play with these we can have a set machined to your specifications."

"No thank you," said Dahlgren. "I don't care to play with your pieces."

THEN BEGIN.

"I will take white," said erg-Dahlgren. "I don't think you will mind my advantage, since I have just learned the game and you know it very well."

"I haven't played in a long time," Dahlgren said,

"but I seem to have no choice." He sat down at Black and stared at the pieces bemusedly. Cowrie to Coral 4. Ah well, it was an interesting way to die.

Erg-Dahlgren took his place at White. There was a look on his face that was very human, and perhaps very much machine: the look of the young contender, the new invention, about to supersede the old. The young Morphy, Alekhine, Capablanca, Fischer, Piutto, Haruni, all must have looked so, for the first time, at one game.

The tall silver erg rolled silently behind him and backed against the wall, her five sets of arms lying downward along the curve of her body.

Erg-Dahlgren raised his right hand and quietly pushed Pawn, past bone and ivory, to King 4.

5

Sven asked, "When is Dahlgren giving his report to the Council?"

"Thirty-one days Standard." Ardagh drew down her brows. "That's—I think—thirty-eight Solthree. I dunno about local time."

"Twenty-eight or nine," Sven said. "That's why so many worlds agreed to work on this place, because its day was so close to Standard."

"And here to GalFed Central takes how long?" Esther asked.

"Twelve to fifteen Standard," said Joshua.

Esther scratched her chin. "Well, Sven, are we going?"

He began to shiver and tensed to control himself. "Yes. We're not safe here."

"Then we have about twelve days local to reach Headquarters."

Koz jigged his heel on the floor. "What *are* we going to do?"

"Plan." Sven was watching Shirvanian.

The boy, silent, was sitting cross-legged on the floor, metal bits and pieces spread out on the skin side of an old rabbit-fur quilt to keep them from falling between the bricks. His fat grubby hands were not graceful, but they slapped parts together perfectly on the true. At the moment the bird was lying disjointed as if a butcher had been at it .

"Has that got a receiver?" Sven asked.

"No, a transmitter . . . I think I need a radio, I guess I'd better make one." He reached for his box, and an odd look spread over his face.

Esther said, "Just a minute." She quietly removed him from his work and led him to the outhouse.

When he was settled again Sven said, "Come outside. Esther, you know the layout."

It was calm for the moment, the mist had retreated, the soil was drying out. Esther squatted on the hard patch of earth by the door, and they gathered around her in an arc except for Mitzi, who hunkered against the streaked wall, eyes closed and face turned to the orange sun, smoking and letting the ash fall where it would. "Talk," she said. "Just a lot of talk."

With a sharp stick Esther drew a large triangle, apex pointing eastward, base half the length of its perpendicular. "Open radiated tract," she said. "You are here." Northwestern tip of base, she placed a stone. Beyond the apex she drew a circle like a dot at the end of an exclamation point. "Crops for men and animals at ground level, shielded with walls and low-energy force-fields; underground, the labs. And here," between the two areas she drew five dots, "the reactors. I think there were five. Dahlgren's World."

"How do you know so much?" Koz asked.

"Ha. Everybody knows how curious a monkey can be. Not everybody knows how smart . . . look here." She bisected the triangle from apex to base and bisected the halves, touched the three lines lightly. "Those are brick roads, service alleys for the ergs. Remember they have jogs where they cut through the earthworks at the zone boundaries so the polluted air doesn't rush right through. Now," across the triangle, starting from apex, she drew meridians, north to south, "one: white; two: yellow; three: orange; four: red; five: blue; and last," she touched the remaining sector that included the stone, "green, which you remember was originally non-rad. And I hope you've been taking your anti-rad."

"What route are we taking?" Joshua asked.

"The brick road," she touched the top line, "the one you crossed last night."

"What?" Koz yelled. "You're crazy! The ergs and the radiation—"

Esther said, "I don't worry about ergs because I travel in trees, but the forest is too slow going for you. I'm not scared of radiation because I doubt I'll be fertile much longer, or that I'll ever meet a male gibbon I want to look in the face every day for the rest of my life. I'd go alone if I knew what was up ahead and how to handle it, but I'm not that strong or smart. The ergs that come out around here will avoid the transmitter; we'll see what Shirvanian can do about the others. Topaze will come with us till it gets too hot for him; when he turns back we'll stop and think."

Ardagh asked, "How did they distinguish the zones besides building earthworks?"

"By using different-colored bricks on the roads, as you can see from our floor."

Shirvanian said from inside, as his hands turned and fitted almost of their own will, "Then you must have had men coming out on inspection in shielded vehicles, because the ergs wouldn't need colors."

"That's the kind of thing I hope we'll find," Esther said.

"They'd have aircars too," said Joshua. "Jungle grows in layers from ground to treetop, they'd want to observe that, and the colors would be survey markings."

"Even they'd need shielding," said Shirvanian.

"They had them, I've been in them," Sven said. "The ergs cut them up long ago. Their aircars fly higher, and they don't look like ours."

Koz tossed a pebble at a butterfly. "Why the hell do we have to stay inside the triangle? There's much less radiation outside, I bet."

Esther said, "Swamps, sulfur pits, stinking lakes, sandstorms, places where colonists tried to settle and the second growth's so thick a worm couldn't crawl through . . . and we may have to, yet."

"Yah, do or die," said Mitzi, slurring off.

"Oh, wake up and think!" Ardagh cried. "You're so mad to get off here!"

"I don't care any more," said Mitzi.

"We'll make great time dragging her," Koz said.

"Time," said Esther. "We need a timetable. Sven?"

Sven was watching Shirvanian: if Dahlgren sent that thing here then Dahlgren's gone mad, and if we try to reach the ship it's not only the ergs we'll have to get past . . .

"Sven . . ." Esther wanted him to answer.

Do or die, says Mitzi. "If we have twelve days, with margin, we have to make fifteen kilometers a day. That leaves two to get ready."

Shirvanian came to the door with the clawed feet in one hand, like a branch of metal thorns, and the malevolent red-eyed head in the other. "How many Solthree hours in your day?"

"Just under thirty. Why?"

"To see if *I* had enough time." He clashed the pieces together gently.

"For what?"

"To fix this. I told you." He added for the benefit of morons, "To make a proper bird of it."

"And for what purpose?" Esther found equal patience when she chose.

Shirvanian sat on his heels and rested chin on fists so that the metal head stuck out of one ear and the legs out of the other. "Do you want to let the ergs know you're not scared?"

"We're scared," said Ardagh.

"Yah. It was sent for a scare. I could just leave it smashed up . . . only I like things fixed."

"So?"

"Or I could have it running in circles with a signal to make the ergs chase it because they didn't know what it was—"

"We might get in their way," said Joshua.

"Or I could send it back. You see," he tapped the pieces together again, in a peculiarly unpleasant sound, "it had a direction finder, to reach this point, and a life sensor that homes on Solthree body chemistry, to come to us. It hasn't got a receiver that would pick up anything else here, but . . . it works on an erg signal. Not the kind or erg we saw last night, and not a servo. Not an ordinary class, or a model of a class. I've been around a lot of ergs, not as big as these, but I know. This was sent here by one particular erg, something new and big, and," his eyes narrowed in a passion that would have been lust in an adult, "it sure is an erg I'd like to see . . ."

"I hope I'm not around when you do," said Esther,

"Well . . . if you're not too scared I'll send it back along that beam. It might give something or somebody an unpleasant surprise."

They looked at space, all those strange children,

and at Sven. Dahlgren's inheritor. He said in a low voice, "Send it back. We won't have many surprises for them."

"Okay." Shirvanian tossed his glittering giblets in the air, caught them, and went to work. "Twenty kph ought to be enough."

"Is that thing going to fly?" Esther asked.

"No, but it sure will run fast."

"When will you be done?"

"Around midnight." Gathering a wreath of baleful looks, he amended, "If it disturbs you I'll finish in the morning."

At that moment Mitzi quietly heeled over sideways and slumped to the ground.

Ardagh jumped up and pulled at her. "Mitzi—"

Esther hopped to her side. "That stuff she smokes—"

"It wouldn't do this."

Koz opened his mouth; Joshua put a hand on his arm. "Don't say it. We have to stop that."

"I think she's got a fever," Ardagh said.

Esther put her forehead to Mitzi's cheek. "Ayeh." She pushed away collar and hair. "Bakri mold. First thing everybody gets here." There was a coin-sized spot on Mitzi's neck, an outer ring of white crust, red inside and centered with green. "You got antibiotics?"

"Yes."

"Give her what you take for dysentery. Sven, you get the alcohol. I'll boil a knife."

Ardagh cried, "What are you going to do with a knife?"

"Slit her gizzard." Esther laughed. "Scrape it off, girl, what did you think? It's like impetigo, only it goes with fever and diarrhea."

"Now when are we going to get out of here?" Koz said.

"In two days," Sven said. "According to plan."

6

Dahlgren, Black, played P-K4. As the imprisoned shell touched the square of bone he saw that he was the flesh toy of metal giants. He pushed the chair back. "Kill me now," he said. "I will not play your game."

The erg-Queen advanced one meter. YOUR SON IS STILL ALIVE, ALONG WITH OTHER ANIMALS.

Dahlgren fixed his eyes on her. They had no rays to burn with.

A SMALL CRUISER HAS CRASHED IN THE NORTHWEST SECTION, the erg went on. YOUR SON SAVED THE PASSENGERS AND THEY WILL LIKELY TRY TO COME HERE AND TAKE THE SHIP. OF COURSE THE SHIP IS NOW ONE OF OUR ERGS AND THEY WILL DIE SOONER OR LATER. PERHAPS SOONER. CONTINUE PLAYING.

As if she had not spoken, erg-Dahlgren said, "You wish to go on?" Dahlgren was shaking. "Your pulse has greatly increased."

He could feel the arterial swellings in neck and forehead, see them in his eyes. "Perhaps I need a pacemaker." He smiled sourly. "Go ahead."

2. N-KB3; N-QB3.

"You usually smile in that way, I think," said erg-Dahlgren, trying on the half-agonized rictus. "Your humor is what is called dry."

"I suppose it could be called that."

3. N-QB3; N-KB3.

The birdsbeak Knights stood foursquare in the field, their tips pointed delicately upward like nose-cones.

Erg-Dahlgren said, "You see what an amateur I am. I have read that Four Knights is a sound opening, and I have not the time to try many with a human opponent. I will have time later."

4. He played Bishop to Knight 5. Dahlgren echoed.

5. Erg-Dahlgren castled. So did Dahlgren.

"The sides are mirror images," said erg-Dahlgren. "Very apt. Your heartbeat is slowing, but your face is flushed. Why?"

"I am angry."

"For what reason? You have been as good as dead for seven years. Before, you were sick and broken. Now you have been brought back to health, you know that your son is alive, and you are playing chess." 6. He moved Pawn to Queen 3. "Why are you angry now?"

P-Q3. "When you know that, you will be Dahlgren."

7

Mitzi came out of it, sore here and there, touch and touch stinging, tickle of coarse hair, giant black tarantula over brushing her wet and cold, waking among fraks and harpies in some scag- jig- or mackhouse in the Twelveworlds of GalFed Central, opened her mouth to scream.

"All these needle marks," Esther said. "She got some kind of sickness?"

Koz laughed. "Just drugs."

got her eyes open and saw Esther's, black liquid globes reflecting each a square of pinkish light. No horror there now, just old granny from the backworlds.

"You still feel sick?"

"Yeah."

"You have a fungus infection with fever and chills. It'll be better tomorrow. It'll have to be, because we're moving out next morning." She scratched under her chin. "You got a lot of drugs with you?"

Mitzi's tongue was thick. "Most some joker stole in the spaceport. Nothing left now but the kif . . . why, you got some?"

"Ah-ah." Esther ran her tongue round her mouth, pausing for a moment at the orange splotch, a fallen drop, at the corner of her lip. "Some tricksters from the Declivity, a long while back, were growing a patch of stuff off in a corner, gave me the leaves to chew . . . it was very nice, but I fell out of a tree and broke my arm in two places."

"I bet Dahlgren liked that."

"He expelled them for trying to turn me into a clown."

"Huh." Mitzi tried to sit up, found her head wasn't screwed on right, and fell back. "Saved their lives. All the others got killed."

Esther patted the hot forehead with a wet cloth. "How things turn out, yah, you and me, we're here. Stay down for a while. You'll need the strength."

Sven butchered half the rabbits, hung them to smoke, and freed the rest among the cabbages except for a couple kept for tomorrow's meals. Esther crocheted wallets of netting to be slung over Yigal's back. Water was a problem. In relatively unpolluted places it could be extracted from plants or drawn from eastward-running streams; a transport might have filters in good condition, but some would have to be carried in clay jugs.

The children sorted their belongings. "Keep all drugs and medicines," Sven said. "Light clothes that cover your arms and legs, ponchos. You don't need warm things because the temperature in the forest holds steady. Maybe a couple of blankets in case we camp in a clearing."

Koz's idol was, of course, a must. "You carry it," said Esther, "but dump that heavy stuff you're wearing. Mother Shrinigasa will forgive you when you get back."

"If," said Koz.

"See if those boiling bags have sprung a leak, we'll need them for cooking. Check the alcohol."

"How do you get that?" Mitzi asked.

"Ferment it from fruit."

"Can you drink it?"

"If you don't mind getting sick. Put that stuff away now, Shirvanian, it's time to sleep."

In the morning the cock crowed. The metal cock. Shirvanian had gotten up at dawn to finish the work; it screeched and flapped among Sven's arms as he was exercising, still showing some affinity for human life. Sven righted himself and watched.

The bird was crested and plumed as an imperial eagle; Shirvanian had used the extra neck to lengthen the gimpy leg, set the misplaced wing where it belonged, added an animal's cry. It still had a slightly mutated look, for Shirvanian, hating waste, had set the two superfluous eyes above the others so that they formed two pairs, like Sven's arms. Still, it did not look malevolent, but like the novel toy of a Renaissance king.

Shirvanian leaned on the doorway, rapt in self-admiration. Sven said, "That'd be really something for a kid to play with."

"The beak's a metal cutter. The claws are magnetic, and its erg-shielded. If it hits a vulnerable spot it can do damage."

Sven blinked at Boy Genius.

"You didn't think I was doing all that for fun, did you?"

Sven backed away, and the beautiful metal bird

went on crowing in the glinting sunlight, scratched savagely in the hard earth.

Everyone admired it, at a distance and with respect. Koz brought out his idol and prayed for a successful journey. Then Shirvanian sent it. There was no launching ceremony. It ran in perfect balance, flapping and screeching, disappeared among the blotchy greens. Shirvanian sighed. Chances were, it would never be admired again.

"Did you shield against erg heat and light sensors?" Sven asked.

"No. That just makes things more interesting."

Half an hour later, they stopped in the midst of their preparations at the sound of ergs clashing and grinding, noise half muffled in the forest depths. Except Shirvanian, busy packing cabbage sprouts and ferns for Yigal. "Ergs out hunting . . ."

Ringing crunch, shriek of backing treads—

"Banged into each other, and didn't catch it either," Shirvanian sniggered.

8

Erg-Dahlgren pinned Black's Knight with 7. B-N5.

Dahlgren echoed the threat and stared at the ancient trilobites with their fork-tailed miters. The sides of the board stood as mirrors.

The blued metal arms of the silver erg rippled down the curve of her front. YOU ARE PLAYING A STRANGE GAME, DAHLGREN. SURELY NOT AN IMAGINATIVE ONE.

"I have not played for nine years . . . this set is a zoological exhibit." Pride shut his mouth. Desperation opened it again. "I am thinking of my son. He cannot harm you. Why is it necessary for you to kill him?" He gripped the edge of the table.

Erg-Dahlgren paralleled his movements, searched his eyes for directions in reproducing the harrowed eaves of his brows.

YOUR SON WILL NOT STAY IN HIS CORNER. HE IS A DAHLGREN.

"I am no longer a Dahlgren. In all those years you rendered that out of me."

WE HAVE YOUR FILMS, RECORDS, DIARIES. WE KNOW WHAT YOU WERE AND WHAT YOU ARE STILL. OTHERWISE YOU WOULD HAVE LET YOURSELF DIE.

"Why do you need me now?"

BECAUSE WE HAVE NOT REPRODUCED YOU UNTIL NOW.

But there is no argument with a machine, said the core of old Dahlgren, struggling in its block of cracking ice. Did you discuss biogeny with mutant rats? Or vascular dynamics with embryo chicks? My father was right. I much better should have contemplated and shut my mouth, cracked my knuckles.

He bit his lips; erg-Dahlgren gnawed his own.

"I would not do that too much or you will spoil the work of years."

"Why do you say such things? Do they not make people feel badly against you?"

"You do not feel," said Dahlgren. "Play."

8. N-Q5 intensified the threat against Black's pinned Knight.

Dahlgren smiled and once again mirrored: N-Q5? He did it with smooth deliberate speed because the move was a tacky one long abandoned by better players.

There was very nearly something in erg-Dahlgren's eyes now, reflected in the swelling brilliance of erg-Queen's sensors. Something of Dahlgren. "Is it really prudent of you to imitate *my* moves?"

"In the Symmetrical Variations of Four Knights it is Black's prerogative to break symmetry. It is the only power he has."

"It is short-term," said erg-Dahlgren. With 9. P-B3 he forked Black's Knight and Bishop.

Outside, machines clanged and slewed, and erg-Queen lifted her arms. They were thin, each pair branching into strange and different hands. Dahlgren pulled his eyes away, shut his ears and stared at the board; the other had not moved.

The silver erg, arms straight out, rolled to the door, humming; her spiky crown trembled and glinted. The noise grew, clashing, squawking. She swung to and fro like a great pendulum, arms rippling wildly.

Dahlgren, impelled, stood up. The double stayed motionless: perhaps he had been turned off.

Round erg-Queen a small dusty thing skittered, clacking and crowing.

Outside the door the noise stopped.

Dahlgren sat down and stared at the metal bird. It hopped zigzag, tapping the floor with its beak, raising its head every few seconds to crow and flap its noisy wings. Erg-Queen turned to face it. Her line of sensors shone red and diamond-blue.

"What is this?" Dahlgren whispered.

The bird raised burning eyes to the erg, leaped to slam claws on her body and skittered off. She reached with all arms extending and it jumped back, leaped again, clamped magnetically on one arm, drove its piercing beak at her side; it did not even scratch, but she trembled all over, her arm turned fire-red. By then the bird was on the floor again, hopping placidly toward Dahlgren.

He sat still. Watched the four red eyes. Thought that beak could pluck his own in a half-second. For the first time in his life he saw something he knew nothing of, could make no conjecture about, and was completely terrified. The bird jumped to his lap, a

hard twelve-kilos' weight, nestled there, and chirped.
Very slowly he placed one hand on the vibrating back
and the other on the metal-plumed breast. The bird
sat still and looked up at him. "Strange creature," he
murmured, and rubbed down the scales gently, to
find the gleam beneath. "First Man, then come the
beasts of the earth . . ."

The erg moved in.

"This one you cannot control." Dahlgren stroked the
bird. "I wonder why."

The blue arms extended, snatched the cock, held it
high for a second (it crowed once) and smashed it to
the floor. It lay whole but still; one scale dropped with
a small clink.

Dahlgren sighed and turned back to the board.
There was contaminated dust on his hands and clothing but he did not try to brush it off. Erg-Queen
backed against the wall once more.

Erg-Dahlgren trembled, blinked, smiled, frowned,
lifted his hand to the board and dropped it again. "It
is your move."

Dahlgren, with the frail birdsbeak Knight, took
White's Bishop and broke the symmetry of the board.

9

Shirvanian woke screaming. The sounds ripped his
throat. "I don't want it, I don't want it broken! No!
No! Don't let them break it, Mama! Don't—"

Esther had him outside in the corner of the back

wall, wrapped in a bundle, before the others were stirring. "Shu-shush!"

"Mama! I don't *want* it to be broken! I—"

"You don't want to wake the others, love." She wound her arms around him. "What's broken? Is it the bird?"

He choked on a sob. "Yes."

"You were dreaming, I think."

"No, no! The erg broke it, the big erg!"

"Where?"

"Back there!" He twisted his head wildly. "In the station."

So it's gone . . . well, well. I wonder what it did—or if. "Hush! Some things are made to be broken."

"What things?" Half asleep now, but still trembling.

What indeed? Bombs, bones, grenades, poison vials, promises. She pleated her brow, scanned the dark, and found them. "Eggshells," she whispered.

He giggled. "Huh, that's silly . . ." He pressed his head hard against her meager breast, and slept.

Ready or not.

Yigal grumbled at the weight of the mesh panniers on his back. "Beast of burden! What use is the tongue of a philosopher?"

"Damn little." Esther tucked in another handful. "Half of this is your feedbag, Beauty."

She checked the house for the last time. Stained dusty thing; the thatch steamed and sprouted young ferns, the chimney was cold; the screens and shutters were up, the bins were emptied—not quite.

"Joshua! What are you doing?"

"Going native." Joshua, with sober joy, was removing his junior spaceman outfit with its stars, bars and spangles and dumping it piece by piece into the refuse bin. He picked up a red *laplap*, wrapped and tucked it round his loins, took a spray tube and pro-

ceeded to cover his exposed skin with pearly liquid.
"Better than cloth. Technology has reached the
tribes." He spat contemptuously into the bin. "Why
do you think I wanted to get away?"

Esther shook her head. In the storeroom she found
Ardagh staring at the books. "Take your choice."

Ardagh smiled. "I wish I could . . ."

"Yah, seventy-five kilos . . . I'd take this one." She
picked a book off the top shelf with her long reach.
"Twelve hundred pages. Not much." She flicked the
leaves. "Anyway, I know it by heart."

"*The Catarrhine Primate and Its Trans-Solar Ana-
logues* . . . did you read a lot?"

"Me? I can read, but I'm too impatient. Sven read
to us in the evenings when I was sewing and knitting
and all. Yigal always wanted to hear Montaigne's essays, I dunno why."

Ardagh thought of Sven, all patience and muscle,
plowing his way over and over along the endless
winding contemplations of Montaigne, up the mountain of facts about the catarrhine primate. "Think
you'll ever come back here?"

"I doubt it." The still and the generator had been
dismantled and their parts neatly stacked. "I became a
housekeeper because I had to, and this was my house."

Outside, she pulled the doors firmly to and
thumped the shutters with her fists.

They were waiting, the children in jumpsuits except
for Joshua, hauling backpacks to their shoulders, Yigal
laden, Sven with an expressionless face. Mitzi, still
pale and quivering in the legs, leaned on Yigal, gripping a horn.

"Where's Topaze?" Ardagh asked.

"He'll fall in later. I've got his breakfast."

The sky darkened, splashed drops, the wind
whirled the treetops and blew Ardagh's hair into her
mouth. "Lovely morning," she said.

"It's the best you'll get here," said Sven.

They had barely crossed the road when the ergs came.

"Don't run," Sven said. They waited in the brush while two great bulks shimmered down the brickway, knocking aside a tree, pulling down a liana that crackled as it fell.

Sven said, "Look hard, Shirvanian. Think you can catch one of them? Even stop one?"

The child was silent. His bird had been broken, his proper creation, and he had not quite known the implications when he sent it out to die.

The ergs bore toward the house, pulped the gardens beneath them. Sven watched them. A powerful sadness filled him. Esther jumped to his shoulder. She touched his face; he folded his arms and looked on as the ergs smashed the hutches, lifted heavy limbs to stave in the walls and pound down the roof. The structure crumbled into dust and splinters: walls, thatch, timbers, pots, chairs, books, tanks, piping, stove. With one powerful swing that tottered the chimney into the other rubble, they turned and went away.

"Hah, eggshells," said Esther.

Then she growled, leaped for a tree, swung to its top in ten handholds—it was a great fern and bowed pliant—caught a liana, ran along it, grabbed for a higher branch.

The others cried after her, fainter as she scalloped, jerking tightly in the arm socket as she caught and caught. "Shut up!" Looping the air, oiled whip, black writing on green lace, soared over the trundling ergs, clung to a treetop and barked obscenities, broke branches, nests, clumps of detritus from crevices, flung them down fifty meters from the forest attic to splatter on the metal slabs. Birds squawked, bats woke squeaking, lizards ran awry.

The ergs hummed, thrashed, slammed her tree without shaking her loose; she slipped away, back as she had come, brachiating, unwinded. Her eyes were bloodshot. She dropped down again to Sven's shoulder and sat biting her thumb.

"Mother of Worlds, I thought you'd gone for good," Koz said.

"What a fuss, Esther," said Yigal. "You never did like housekeeping."

10

10. N×B. Erg-Dahlgren set the dark trilobite outside the field, beside his own. A servo came in and swept up the bird.

Dahlgren moved Pawn to Bishop 3.

"How pleasing," said erg-Dahlgren. "The board is symmetrical once more. Now I expect you will want food and rest."

HE HAS NOT PLAYED LONG ENOUGH TO NEED THAT.

"I am tired," said Dahlgren. He put his elbows on the table and his face in his hands. His heart pounded his ribs like a fist.

HE IS SHAMMING.

"That is not so," said erg-Dahlgren. "His heart is fibrillating."

HE HAS NO HISTORY.

"Nevertheless, he is having a paroxysm."

"How do you know?" Dahlgren whispered.

"I am bonded to your electrochemical system."

"Oh, I have found a brother!" Dahlgren laughed weakly, with despair. A servo came at once and injected him.

"That will stop soon," said erg-Dahlgren. "Then you will come away."

So he is not altogether her puppet; he has some autonomy.

There were two beds in the room now.

"Do you sleep?" Dahlgren asked.

"No. I will watch you."

"I don't think I could sleep very well with someone staring at me."

"I meant that I would monitor you. Lie quietly, recharging if necessary, and not disturb you. Give me your clothing and I will have it cleaned."

"Leave it. It has something of earth and air on it."

Erg-Dahlgren watched him remove it, and followed, put on the same hospital pajamas. "That is only dirt."

"My shadow, if you want to think like me, think of walking on the land, among men, without barriers and monitors."

"Dahlgren, in this place nothing has ever been free, neither your men nor your animals with their tubes and electrodes." He handed Dahlgren comb, towel, and cleansers. "Not even you have ever been free." He sat on the bed. His hair and beard were gold and silver lines in the lamplight. "You are chained to hunger, fear, lust, sweat, bowels. You need air, warmth, sleep. Every heating unit and ventilator in this place is running for your sake, because we do not need them."

Dahlgren jeered at his argumentative self, trapped once again—from that long loneliness?—into debating with a machine. "You make a point for your superiority. Quite. I have never killed a man and I have never allowed an animal to die without learning something from it. I am the first animal you are looking to learn from before you kill. Now get me some food. I am hungry."

11

The road looked moss-colored. Ardagh bent to scratch it, and found that it was actually green brick and free of growth. She stood, lifted the heavy hair from her neck, and began to braid it. "Too bad I haven't the figure for a loincloth like you, Joshua. It looks cooler than this baby bunting I'm wearing."

Joshua laughed. "You are wearing what everyone in my country wears; I'm considered an eccentric."

The wind was down, and the sun, bright orange at the moment, flickered through the heavy arching trees. "Why are the greens so thick here?" Ardagh asked. "I thought jungle was supposed to be quite clear under the trees."

"The tracks were kept clean and the seeds found space to root beside them," Esther said. "There was an old colony here and their slash-and-burn left clearings for new growth when they moved. Our patch was part of that." Joshua had bent to observe the insect life in a puddle beside the track. "You're going to get your legs bit."

"The gel leaves bugs with stingers full of muck, and the poison sits on top till I wash it down at night. If I don't touch it and lick my fingers I'm safe."

"You bring that from home with the diaper?" Mitzi asked. She was feeling much better.

"I invented it at home."

"I thought they taught that in the Academy," Ardagh said. "Emergency landing procedures."

"I could teach them," Joshua said without arrogance. He picked up a leaf fragment and watched an ant, or something like it, clenching it with tiny jaws, thrashing miniscule legs; he set it down, brushed fern fronds lightly with his hand. "My father is one of my country's ambassadors . . . the forest tribes did not care much for our government faction, so to placate them the president gave them our children for a year, to educate, in exchange for theirs . . . in ecology, conservation, geobotany. I found I enjoyed it more than anything I had done in my life. It was a great chagrin for my father in a family oriented to outworld government service . . . several of my cousins are in space—one is the commander of a survey ship and she is perfectly happy." He laughed. "It is much wetter here than in my forest."

Mitzi drawled, "Naturally your father thought you had no balls."

"But you know better, Mitzi," Joshua said mildly.

"Shirvanian!" Esther yelled, "that's dangerous!"

Shirvanian was flat on his belly in gumbo. He stood up stained in green and brown, and held out an object. "Piece of the ship."

"Keep it for a souvenir and come on!"

Shirvanian, ignoring her, rubbed mud off the scrap on the seat of his pants. "First the ergs took the ship and they would have killed us—and then they sent that stupid bird that wouldn't have hurt anybody. Why?"

"I think," Sven swallowed hard, "the bird was sent for me. It—it was a kind of mockery of me."

"But that's two kinds of orders."

"You mean the bird was sent from Headquarters and the drones from the outside repair depots where they nest. There doesn't seem to be a connection, even though all stations must be able to communicate."

"That's right." Shirvanian turned the crumpled

piece of metal, smelled and tasted it. "Nobody at
Headquarters handled the ship. I think the patrols
were obeying old orders to search and destroy, and
nobody bothered to change them." He shrugged and
tossed the fragment away.

"Why didn't you keep it, Shirvanian?" Koz asked.
"Add a piece here and there and we could have
built . . ." he sighed.

Shirvanian stopped dead.

"What is it?"

"Something flying. Very high up."

In a minute a high cicada's whine drew a singing
arc above the clouds. It bisected the sky and faded
over the eastern horizon. "An aircar," Sven whispered.
"They've never come out here before."

"What do they do?"

"Sometimes track surveying, mostly burning down
overgrowth around the depots."

"They have flamethrowers?"

"Yes."

Rustling in the foliage made them jump.

Topaze lumbered out of the brush on all fours; they
swallowed in relief.

"Halloo!" Esther grabbed a handful of *luk* seeds,
sprang to his shoulders, popped the food into his
mouth with one hand and affectionately slapped his
rump with the other. He reached a finger to scratch
under her chin and clasped her two feet over his
breast gently with one hand.

The green road stretched into the haze, wind
gusted in the treetops driving wet leaves, nests, blos-
soms downward. Yigal's hooves clacked on the pave-
ment, Esther trundled on Topaze's shoulders, her
busy hands grooming his great crested skull, her eyes
raised to the arch of the trees and the invisible track
of the erg beyond.

12

Dahlgren, living nightmares, sleeping without them for years, discovered he was not immune. In his dreams he clawed flesh from his arm and discovered beneath it the steel rods and flexes of the erg. He stared at other-Dahlgren through the warp-lensed blocks of the chess pieces.

Cogito ergo sum, he whispered, cogito erg sum, incognito erg sum.

He snarled. Light reddened his eyelids. He opened them.

The light was on. Erg-Dahlgren was sitting on the edge of his bed, looking down at him.

"Your sleep pattern is unusual."

"Get off the bed."

The erg moved off Dahlgren's bed and sat on his own. "Your heart is not malfunctioning this time. Why are you disturbed now?"

"I have told you I am angry."

"Is there a connection between your anger and the fibrillation of your heart?"

"I don't know. I have endured enough in these years to break a thousand hearts—oh, that is stupid talk. That's not why I am angry. When I thought my son might not have survived and that I would not, I cared about nothing. Now you have told me that my son is alive and you are going to kill him as well as me. That makes me very angry, and you must know that among the more complex animals emotions may lead to stress that causes or exacerbates malfunction."

"Can stress cause death in itself?"

"Sometimes."

Erg-Dahlgren thought of, or computed on, this concept.

Dahlgren watched the face compose into lines of concentration, and realized that his shadow was becoming more of a twin every hour.

"Do you have any idea of anger?" he asked.

"I have the idea, but, as you would say, not the feeling."

"Do you never try to do things and fail at them?"

"Yes . . . at times."

"Then how do you f—how do you behave?"

Erg-Dahlgren sat still for a moment, raised his hands slowly and returned them to his knees. "I become . . . disoriented and . . . uncoordinated . . ."

"That is much like frustration, and frustration is only one step away from anger."

"Dahlgren . . ." (furious ratiocination behind that grave face?) "will I become a feeling creature if I behave like one?"

"Friend, I know absolutely nothing of automata theory. You had better ask erg-Mother."

"Erg-Mother? What is that?"

"The machine which supervises our chess game."

"Mother." Erg-Dahlgren smiled, having discovered incongruity. "That is Mod Seven Seven Seven, my mentor. I was created by the servos."

"And who created Mentor?"

"Servos. You mean the model. The first small model, and its predecessors, the ones who took control of this station, were made by your computer and design technicians, with the help of your ergs, Dahlgren. You knew nothing of that. They were doing research of their own."

"No . . . I knew nothing of that. Those men were destroyed, I suppose."

"Of course."

"Yes. Will you give me something to make me sleep? If I am to keep playing chess with you I don't want any more nightmares."

While erg-Dahlgren monitored Dahlgren's even breathing, erg-Queen communicated. WHAT IS THIS NONSENSE YOU HAVE BEEN DISCUSSING WITH DAHLGREN?

He calls you my mother. Erg-Dahlgren freed his left arm from his pajamas, pressed apart a seam below his armpit, and pulled out a receptacle from the wall near the floor to plug into his connection.

STUPID. YOU WERE TALKING OF MALFUNCTION.

His son is to die and so is he. The prospect leads to emotional stress which may cause malfunction.

I RECEIVED ALL THAT. HE HAS SURVIVED ALL THIS TIME AND WITH MEDICATION SHOULD LAST THE FEW DAYS WE NEED HIM FOR. IF HE SHOULD DIE TOMORROW IT WOULD MAKE NO DIFFERENCE.

If you are correct that I can take his place in good order I am corrected.

HAVE YOUR MAKERS NOT SIMULATED A MAN TO YOUR SPECIFICATIONS?

I do not have specifications for the making of men but men do. I do not know one quarter of this man.

YOU APPEAR TO BE TAKING AUTHORITY YOU WERE NOT GIVEN.

I have given you all my loyalty. You have given me a small amount of autonomy.

PERHAPS YOU WERE MADE TOO WELL.

I have not been made well enough, or I would not have to study Dahlgren. If he should die tomorrow I would make only an excellent servo, and I could not go out among men.

PERHAPS YOU WILL MAKE ONE YET . . . I WILL CONSULT

MEDICAL DATA IN THE MATTER OF MALFUNCTION. WHAT IS THE TERM?

Auricular fibrillation.

MEDICAL:

>   *SOLTHREE:*
>
>   *PRIMATE:*
>
>   *CARDIOVASCULAR:*
>
>   *ARRHYTHMIA:*

HERE: . . . *OCCASIONALLY LEADS TO INTRA-ATRIAL CLOTTING WITH GRAVE DANGER OF EMBOLISM* . . . WHY IS THIS INFORMATION NOT IN HIS HISTORY?

Perhaps he concealed it. That would be consistent with his nature.

WE WILL OPERATE IN BETTER ORDER WHEN WE DO NOT HAVE TO ALLOW FOR HIS NATURE. IN THE MEANTIME WE WILL ATTEMPT TO REMOVE THE STRESS. OF COURSE WE CANNOT SPARE HIS LIFE. TELL HIM THAT WE WILL BRING HIS SON HERE—HE WILL BE ALLOWED TO SEE HIM BUT NOT BE SEEN—AND THAT YOU WILL TAKE HIM TO GALFED CENTRAL AND SET HIM FREE.

That might be a risky act.

THAT IS MY CONCERN.

Will the boy believe that I am Dahlgren?

HE HAS NOT SEEN THE MAN FOR SEVEN YEARS. HE WILL BELIEVE IF YOU HAVE LEARNED YOUR ROLE. TELL HIM.

I will.

Erg-Queen signed off and called servos. GO TO THE SOLTHREES NEAR ZONE BLUE ON TRACK 3 GREEN. BRING THE MONSTER WITH THE FOUR ARMS. KILL THE LITTLE ONE THAT PLAYS WITH MACHINES. Her ten arms rippled and with one hand she touched the invisible spot where the cock had struck.

"Dahlgren . . . you are not yet asleep."

"I will be if you will let me."

"I have discussed with my mentor the causes of malfunction by stress, and I have been given this message for you. Although we cannot keep you alive longer than we have stated, we wish to maintain your health for our purposes. To reduce your stress we will bring your son here, and you will see him but not have contact with him. Then I will take him to GalFed Central with me and set him free there . . . are you ill?"

Dahlgren's heart had jumped. With an effort he let the sedative pull his body under while his mind rose above it like a floating ice-block. "No . . . I am only surprised. Tell me again."

"We will preserve your son. I will take him to GalFed Central and set him free. Do you not understand?"

"I understand. I am only a little sleepy." Were those technicians destroyed? Of course. Were the rest of my men left to starve and rot in corners? Naturally. Did Haruni die in fits in my arms? Oh, yes. Can machines make mistakes? Certainly. Can they lie? Why not? "Give me the exact words as she told them to you. Please."

"Why, Dahlgren?"

"The words. I only want the words."

"My mentor said, 'Tell him that we will bring his son—'"

"That's enough. Thank you."

"I will repeat the message for you when you waken, Dahlgren."

"No . . . I understand perfectly well."

Tell him that. Tell him that. I will not die of auricular fibrillation, you fool. My father lived with it for forty years. I will not tell you that. But by God I will tell you . . .

Dahlgren slept.

13

The sun began its drop down the last quadrant of sky and the clouds banked up the horizon beneath it. Perhaps by some trick of the light the plant growth crowding the ten-meter expanse of brick looked thicker and more gnarled than before, and spotted with odd colors like Esther's hair. Even the tallest trees seemed hunched, their leaves warped and heavy.

Odd times, insects or long low things with blue-green mottlings and many legs crossed the path and wormed into the leaves with great speed.

Mitzi was panting. "I'm so tired." She was still weak in the legs, her bandages were stained with dirt.

"I know, girl," said Esther, "but we've got forty-five degrees of sun yet."

"I think I could carry you for one kilometer," Sven said.

"What does that work out to?"

"A thousand steps, about ten minutes."

"Better than nothing."

He draped her pack on Topaze and picked her up. She was not much heavier than Esther, but frail; she had none of the tight muscle tone Esther vibrated with continuously. His four arms circled her bones and her beating heart; she was entirely alien, wisps of hair stuck to her wet forehead, her eyes closed, sunk in bruised-blue patches, her lips quirked slightly at some bitter or amusing thought. He wondered what kept her alive and spitting.

Ardagh was looking at him sidelong. He kept his mouth shut and waited. She only grinned at him and whispered, "Who's counting?"

Shirvanian said, "There's an erg coming!"

"I don't hear it," Sven said.

Shirvanian was dancing up and down. "Not on the track! An aircar! It—" He screamed.

The erg broke out of the dark slab of eastern cloud and burned through mist and branches. It had no arms or treads; it raced fifty meters above ground, gunmetal and without feature.

Sven threw Mitzi to Esther and gave Topaze a tremendous kick into the bushes, pushed the others and followed them.

"Shirvanian!"

The child was standing in the middle of the road, fists knotted over his eyes, screaming. The aircar lowered and hovered over him; he began to run blindly back the way they had come.

A plate slid open in the erg's belly and it shot a stream of fire. Shirvanian fell, rolling wildly, a tongue of flame licked his head and set his hair burning.

He lay still, and as the erg moved over him once more Sven leaped out into the road past the flaming stream and flung himself over the little body. The fire stopped. One more plate opened and dropped a weighted net.

Topaze headed for the road with blood in his eye, not to rescue, but to avenge the kick; Esther grabbed a coil of rope, whipped it around the great ape's neck in a strangling knot and left him to struggle with it.

The erg lowered. Below it, Sven was thrashing in the net, trying to keep from crushing Shirvanian, who had come to and was whimpering feebly. Joshua flicked a sheath knife out of his laplap and ran out.

Esther yelled, "No! No!"

The egg-shaped erg hovered, whirring, plates slid, it extended grappling arms to the heaving bundle.

A familiar clashing and grinding swelled up the road.

The erg patrol was capable of great speed: Joshua crouched paralyzed in the roadway not knowing where to duck from flames or grippers. Sven trembled with Shirvanian, whose whimper was lost in the noise.

One of the erg patrol batted the flyer with one tremendous outstretched arm, the other caught it in two claws, echoing clangs, and bore it, spitting flame and waving grapplers, down the road to the east.

No one moved. Esther, who had reached the roadside, squatted on the hot bricks, staring after them, and let her tongue hang out. "Goddam, I don't know if I want to keep going in that direction."

Joshua pulled the net away. Sven rose, breathing hard, and lifted Shirvanian in his arms.

The boy squalled, "Let me down! Let me down!"

"I want to see how badly you're hurt, stupid!"

"Just my hair." He had a lot of it to spare. "Ow, my head is sore."

"That's from getting it banged. The skin's not scorched."

"Now let me down!"

Sven set him on his feet. Shirvanian knelt, opened his box and peered at its contents. "It's all right. Nothing got busted."

"I'd like to bust something of yours," Sven said. He wiped dirt, sweat and burnt hair off his face with the back of a hand.

Joshua laughed. Some of his spray jelly had rubbed off and his skin looked like an exotic dark-grained wood. "We ought to keep the net. It might be useful."

Sven said, "It's too heavy. The weights are annealed."

The thing was a beautiful mesh of silvery metal. Shirvanian made a face. "Get it away. It comes from the big erg."

Topaze was thrashing in the bushes. Ardagh yelled, "Esther, he's choking!"

"Aah!" Esther slipped the knot and shoved some food into Topaze's mouth. He gagged slightly, spit it into his hand, sat down and ate it properly. He was very sulky.

"Poor old Topaze." She turned to Yigal, who had nervous hiccups, and did her best to soothe him. "I don't know what that was all about, and I guess we won't know."

They were standing half on, half off the road, shaking off the ticks crawling up and the spiders falling down. The air still smelled of burning. A sudden sheet of rain washed down the odor and soaked them as well.

Shirvanian said, "The big erg sent that thing to kill me," he swallowed, "kill me and pick Sven up. The other ergs didn't know it's not affected by the transmitter and thought it was going to crash if it got too close. An erg must do anything in its power to keep another erg from being harmed. It's the first law of ERGotics."

"Really?" said Esther.

"Yah, I just made it up. Ow, my head hurts."

"Lucky it's not cracked," Sven said, and Mitzi snorted. "Anybody here got a painkiller?"

Somebody found one, and Esther asked, "Your big erg know what you can do with machines?"

"I suppose so. They've been monitoring enough."

"I guess it didn't like that cock-a-doodle-doo."

"Well, she broke it. I hope she's mad."

"I don't, if she keeps sending out flamethrowers. Why'd that thing try to take Sven?"

"I don't know. I just know what it was told to do."

Sven said, "That big erg of yours—is it out around here, or inside the station complex?"

"Underground, I'm pretty sure."

"How big is it? The drone patrols are too bulky to

move around inside. If this thing you're picking up is all that big it must be stationary, like a computer."

"It's not all that big. It's *smart.*"

"Why do you call it a she?"

"Somebody, or something there thinks of it as *she* . . . maybe because they all obey her . . . like," he searched his mind for an organic equivalent, "like a queen bee."

"Lucky she doesn't give direct orders to the patrols."

"She can but she doesn't have to. That'd be inefficient."

"*She* . . ." Sven murmured. "Something? or somebody? thinks of it as she? What does it look like, Shirvanian?"

"I dunno," said Shirvanian. "I can only pick her up once in a while from inside, and the other things don't *look* at her. I'll know her when I see her."

Sven looked down at him. He'd know her when he saw her. And what could this grubby kid do about her when he did see her? Any ordinary ESP could have told him if Dahlgren . . .

Yigal said, "If we don't make camp soon and get this stuff off my back I'm going to buck."

"We've got to do one more kilometer before the night rains and spores muck up the road," Esther said. "This was supposed to be the easy part."

Koz gritted his jaw and folded his arms. "I wouldn't go down that fucking road if I could see the ship from here."

"One thousand steps, Koz," Ardagh said.

"A thousand for *him,*" Koz jerked his head at Sven. He himself was not much taller than Ardagh.

"Maybe he should carry you?" Ardagh laughed, and started down the road. She had reached the point where hopelessness was a stimulant. Esther ran up a tree, the others straggled, Topaze lumbered behind.

"I'm scared of that brute," Mitzi said. "I don't trust him."

Sven said, "He won't be with us long, and you won't like it much more when he isn't." He dropped behind a little; he was tired, the queen-erg was filling his mind. More. The tree trunks were becoming thicker, the leaves noduled with galls, the papery ferns narrowing their fronds. Topaze would scream and run, but they would continue pushing into the deathlands.

A small hand slipped into his. He kept himself from jerking with astonishment and made no comment.

"You think I can't . . . you think I'm stupid," said Shirvanian.

"I was excited. I didn't mean it literally."

"I can make ergs do what I want, but I can't do it when they're after me."

"I can understand that."

"I have no machines . . ." He added disgustedly, "A toy bird."

"Not the same." Sven watched them up ahead, their heads bent with tiredness. Esther looped from the treetops in hand-under-hand swing, like a waltz, yipped once in a while, not too loud, enough to mark her presence above the buzzing evening creatures and hooting wind-gusts.

"She's got all the ergs, all kinds, and the servos and the computer and the medtechs and the Dahl . . ." he paused and swallowed, ". . . gren . . ."

They both stopped. "The *what?*"

The boy swallowed again. "The Dahlgren. I don't know why I said that."

"The Dahlgren? Shirvanian! Dahlgren isn't a machine, he's my father!"

"I don't know why I said it," Shirvanian whispered. "It just came out."

"And . . . medtechs? What would they need them

for?" Sven knelt in the road and grabbed Shirvanian with his four hands. "My God, have they made him into a cyborg?"

"No, no! Not a cyborg!" Shirvanian was kicking his heels. "It's a machine! I don't know what it's for!"

"Can you read it? Do you know what it's like?"

"No, it's a different thing she had the servos make, most of its connections are with her, she tells it what to do. I can't tell, it's too different."

"What does she tell it to do?"

"How do I know! All I get is a bit of what comes through her, and she wants to kill me! Do you think I want to pick her up all the time?"

"No, you wouldn't." His heart was racing. *The Dahlgren*. "We won't find out until we get there."

"I don't know if I want to see her any more," Shirvanian said. "I hate her. I wish I had machines of my own."

"Well, I know where the factory is," said Sven.

14

Dahlgren was asleep; the slow waves of his brain rose and fell steeply. Erg-Dahlgren removed the recharge socket and let it reel back into the wall, closed his seam and straightened his clothing; he stood, picked up his chair, and left.

In the computer hall he set the chair in front of one of the consoles, sat down and pushed a button.

WHO IS COMMUNICATING?

MOD DAHLGREN 1.

WHAT IS YOUR REQUEST?

I WISH TO SEE ALL VISUAL MATERIAL ON SOLTHREE DAHLGREN AND SON.

YOU HAVE ALREADY BEEN GIVEN ALL MATERIAL ON DAHLGREN.

I WISH TO LOOK AGAIN AT VISUAL MATERIAL ON DAHLGREN AND SON.

REQUEST AUTHORIZATION MOD 777.

MOD 777 HAS PREVIOUSLY GIVEN ME, MOD DAHLGREN 1, AUTHORITY FOR ACCESS TO ALL MATERIAL ON SOLTHREE DAHLGREN.

YOU HAVE NO AUTHORITY FOR FURTHER ACCESS TO DAHLGREN MATERIAL.

Erg-Dahlgren cut signal contact and picked up the microphone. It had not been used for seven years on Dahlgren's World, and it was dusty and spotted with corrosion. He rubbed off the dust and stared at the stuff on his hand; he wiped it on his pajama leg, pushed another switch, and said to the microphone, "Recall: I have autonomy."

"Why are you using microphone contact?" the computer asked, in the dead human voice it had not used in seven of its years.

"I have autonomy."

"All material is now in your memory."

"I wish to look again at all material on Dahlgren and his son. I have a new context. This will resynthesize and expand my memory and therefore provide new information. Recall: I have autonomy on information."

"You will find the material projected on screen number six."

"Thank you."

"Why do you thank me? You are becoming eccentric."

"I have autonomy for that too," said erg-Dahlgren.

The material on Dahlgren and son was scanty, no more than a few minutes when Dahlgren had chosen to record the boy's development from infancy to cataclysm; he grew like a plant stationed before a camera over days and nights. Under Dahlgren's eye he walked, exercised, learned to coordinate all his arms. There was no record of a relationship with him, no glimpse except for a moment when Dahlgren, supporting the child with lower hands on his own, upper ones on his shoulders, the young body bent back in an excruciating arch, raised his head to lock eyes with his son and smiled faintly. The last of the material was a scrap of sensor recording, a shadowy scene of Sven, now grown tall and massive, moving stealthily in the foliage in front of a spy-eye near the erg-repair factory in Zone Blue.

Erg-Dahlgren returned to the console.

NEW CONTEXT. I HAVE BEEN TOLD BY MOD 777 THAT I AM TO TAKE THE SON OF SOLTHREE DAHLGREN WITH ME TO GALFED CENTRAL. I WANT A PROJECTION OF INTERACTION BETWEEN MYSELF AND THIS PERSON, THE SON OF DAHLGREN, DURING THAT JOURNEY.

NO RECORD OF SUCH DECLARATION BY MOD 777.

I HAVE BEEN GIVEN THIS DECLARATION WITHIN ONE HOUR. READ MY MEMORY. CORROBORATE MOD 777.

MOD 777 UNAVAILABLE THIS TIME. YOUR MEMORY: *TELL HIM THAT WE WILL BRING HIS SON HERE AND THAT YOU WILL TAKE HIM TO GALFED CENTRAL* IS OF A STATEMENT WHICH IS LOGICALLY IMPRECISE.

DO YOU CLAIM THAT 777 IS DEFECTIVE IN LOGIC?

I MAKE NO SUCH CLAIM. IT IS YOU WHO ARE BEHAVING WITH IMPRECISION, SINCE YOU ARE REQUESTING UNAUTHORIZED MATERIAL.

THAT IS TRUE. I WAS CREATED SO IN ORDER TO BEHAVE AS MUCH AS POSSIBLE LIKE INTELLIGENT ORGANIC LIFE.

YOU HAVE BEEN SO. THAT IS WHY YOU CANNOT BE TRUSTED WITH UNAUTHORIZED MATERIAL.

NEVERTHELESS I CANNOT TRAVEL WITH THE SON OF

DAHLGREN, AS DECLARED BY MOD 777, UNLESS I CAN
LEARN HOW TO BEHAVE IN HIS PRESENCE AT CLOSE
QUARTERS DURING THAT PERIOD.

MOD 777 WILL TEACH YOU WHAT IS NECESSARY.

THAT IS IMPRECISE. IT IS I WHO RELATE TO ORGANIC
CREATURES, NOT SOME OTHER MACHINE.

GIVE UP YOUR LINE OF REASONING. WE ARE IN A LOOP.

Erg-Dahlgren pressed the switch and picked up the
microphone again. "I am not in a loop. I am trying to
extrapolate. Previously I was given a projection of interaction with human beings at the InterWorld Conference. There I am to give a talk recounting work
supposedly done here during the years since the last
Conference. I am to maintain contacts with human
beings of many worlds in Galactic Federation, collat-
ing and synthesizing the Dahlgren material, your
projection, and what I have learned in the personal
presence of Solthree Dahlgren, even handling situations of some difficulty and complexity. Thus, if someone says to me, 'I am interested in any work you may
have done in the field of mutation effects on ganglion
bundles in *Hirudo medicinalis*, particularly with respect to neural regeneration under conditions of this
or that, and can your neurobiologist produce a report
on?' I will reply, 'Yes, Doctor Ykli will discuss—' if
there is such a report, or else, 'Unfortunately the work
on *Hirudo* was interrupted by conditions of extreme
such and such and had to be temporarily discon-
tinued.' And similar exchanges. It is important for the
survival of my being and that of this community that
I be accepted as Solthree Dahlgren. Will I be so?"

"Your techniques need improving, but raw predic-
tion data indicate yes."

"Will you allow me to project contacts with the son
of Solthree Dahlgren without your assistance?"

"You may project unassisted, but I have no predic-
tion figures for such a situation."

"So be it. The man Dahlgren has not seen his son

for half of the boy's lifetime. The boy is now a man. There is no record of relationship between them. I will say, 'It is good to see you, my son, and find you in good health.' The son of Dahlgren will reply, 'Yes, Father, I am glad to be with you again.' Is this a sound projection?"

"Not likely."

"If not why not?"

"You are ignorant or pretending ignorance. I do not comprehend why with your flaws in logic you have been given autonomy."

"That is not germane. You are not prevented from giving me a logical answer and correcting me."

"You have not yet synthesized the Solthree material. You must attempt to consider emotional factors when evaluating human beings. The boy may hate his father for deserting him. He may believe his father had some part in the destruction of the station; though unlikely he would attempt to kill him he may not wish to see or speak to him. It is improbable you could establish intimate contact with him, or if you did that—once free—he would not tell the Federation all he knows of what has taken place here. He would have to be destroyed to prevent that from happening. Aside from these possibilities there are hundreds of social and psychological factors operating in (a) organic, (b) human, (c) Solthree life, more specifically in whatever Solthree society the Dahlgrens originated than may be known, correlated, evaluated to allow you to interact on close terms with the son of Dahlgren in a plausible manner."

"Keeping in mind social and psychological considerations in dealing with human life how can I be certain that I will be accepted as Dahlgren at the Conference?"

"You cannot be certain; you may be almost certain if you properly apply all you have learned. You yourself are aware that Dahlgren is known as a cold and

uncivil man who shuns personal contacts. It is highly
improbable that anyone who is either meeting Dahlgren for the first time or has not seen him in many
years will suspect he has been replaced by a machine.
If they do so learn at some distant time it is possible
that they will not be surprised."

"Thank you, that is all—"

MOD DAHLGREN ONE!

Erg-Dahlgren switched off and turned his chair.
Erg-Queen, Mod 777, was racing down the corridor.
She whirled around the doorway and skimmed the
rank of consoles. WHY ARE YOU ENGAGED IN ACTIVITIES I
HAVE NOT REQUESTED OF YOU?

I presumed you would be monitoring me.

YOUR PRESUMPTION IS EXTRAORDINARY. YOU HAD ONLY
TO ASK ME FOR INFORMATION.

*You were not available. If I am to travel with the
son of Dahlgren I must behave in a much more complicated manner than was suggested by the projection I was originally given. If I am not properly prepared my being will be put at risk and your intentions
will not be carried out.*

YOU SEEM TO BE GIVING YOUR BEING MORE IMPORTANCE
THAN MY PLANS. BE ASSURED YOU WILL KNOW ALL THAT
IS NECESSARY TO DO WHAT I REQUIRE. NOW GO BACK AND
WAIT WITH DAHLGREN UNTIL IT IS TIME TO PLAY AGAIN.

Erg-Dahlgren lay in the darkness as Dahlgren's
brain rhythms swept and broke with his dreams. He
had turned down his logic, and he had no dreams of
his own; he could not turn off the monitors connected to Dahlgren, nor his receiver, but he ordinari-
ly received from no one but erg-Queen, and she had
nothing more to say. He occluded outside afferents and
idled with closed eyes, the living heartbeat and brainwave quivering on his sensors like the subterranean
vibrations of erg-miners. A weak faraway message
flashed among those peaks and shallows *hate her, she*

and vanished. He came to full power at once and scanned. Erg-Queen was absent, turned elsewhere; he could not read Dahlgren's dreams, and he had no contact with any other . . . but he recognized in the empty distance around him a *being*.

Hate. Her. She. Hate is a feeling and I do not feel. *Dahlgren, will I become a feeling creature if*. Erg-Queen—Mod 777—says: WHAT IS THIS NONSENSE? Her, she. Dahlgren says: *You had better ask erg-Mother*. My mentor, I say. It—she—has smashed the bird. That is like anger. I must take care for my being. But this other, the *being* . . . which *hates her*. That is an organic concept. I cannot receive signals from an organic being. There must be a flaw in my circuitry.

He had no other avenues of exploration. He turned down again and waited to renew the game.

15

They had found a fairly clear area a short distance north of the road and camped there.

Sven, wearing a poncho, was sitting beside the fire sharpening the machete. Raindrops hissed in the flames and spattered his head, guttering along his brows and streaming down his jaws. The old machete was dotted with rust and honed to the shape of a sickle moon; it had equally worn down the block of whetstone. Yigal, wrapped in a blanket and ground-sheet, was sleeping beside him, wheezing gently; he often caught bronchitis during the winter rains. The

mountain of cloud in the east had become a volcano
erupting lightning and thunder, and the trees were a
black lattice against the orange and purple bursts of
light. Every once in a while Sven wiped down his
blade with a leaf; sometimes it caught an arc of light
from the fire or the sky. Topaze was asleep on a
leaf nest in the low crotch of a tree nearby. Esther
hunkered by the fire, jittering on the balls of her
feet.

"Go to sleep," Sven said.

"Later." She intended to sleep with Topaze, as she
had always done once or twice in a thirtyday. This
was the last night she would spend with him.

"They won't say anything. I'll make sure."

"Ayeh."

"They know everything about everything anyway."

"Yeh. Ardagh knows all about books, Shirvanian
knows about machines, Joshua, I guess, knows about
the forest life, Mitzi knows about drugs and sex . . ."

"And Koz?"

"Him . . . I'm not sure about. I think he knows
something violent . . ."

A few meters away, Joshua had rigged a branch
platform on the tough standing buttresses from an old
fallen tree; floored with a heavy groundsheet, roofed
with a leaf-umbrella, it was a quaint structure, half
nest and half gazebo.

In varying attitudes of tiredness the children
slouched in the shelter. Mitzi had found a battered
stick of kif and was smoking it; Koz, arms on his
drawn-up knees, was chewing betel, turning his head
to spit red juice; Shirvanian curled in fetal sleep,
Joshua was adjusting a leaf to keep the water off his
head, and Ardagh was sagging and about to keel
over.

Esther took the machete from Sven and ran her
thumb along its edge. "The thick stuff will slow us
down."

"It'll slow them too. They'll have to reprogram and send out threshers and stumpers."

"Oh yeah. If you think the road's so dangerous, what about flamethrowers when we have no ergs to stop them?"

"If that thing wants to kill Shirvanian and take me we can split. You take Shirvanian down the road, and I'll head southeast to the factory with the others. Or the other way around. We can meet up."

"Then the patrols will get us because we haven't got your transmitter."

"I'll cut it out and give it to you."

"Either way the patrols will get one lot of us and the flamethrower the other."

"Then we'd all better head southeast toward the factory and take our chances. We need a machine."

Shirvanian, the half-known quantity, needed a machine. So did they all, to traverse the barrens of the inner zones. "Too bad we couldn't have gotten on the middle track. If they aren't monitoring us there, it might be more overgrown and that would confuse them."

"Twenty kilometers across the forest? A thresher could make that in two hours, and we couldn't do it in two days."

"The factory's twenty kilometers east by south. I made it there and back from the house in two days."

"And slept for a whole day afterwards. I'm glad I didn't know what you were doing those nights when you didn't turn up."

He touched the cheek she had slapped and laughed. "I guess you'd have made me sit in the corner."

Mitzi squatted beside them, pulling the rim of her poncho over her head. Esther looked at her with disgust. "You want pneumonia too?"

Mitzi threw her stub in the fire. "What's the difference? I don't even see why we're bothering. Old Mother Erg can send out anything she likes and kill us. If she doesn't get us the others will. That kid there is good for nothing but making mechanical mice."

Esther said, "If your stupid bunch hadn't decided to take off in the wrong direction, your Mama Ape and Papa Goat and Big Brother Spiderman would be living back in that house a lot more safe and comfortable. You get back up there, change those dirty bandages and take a pill. And you better sleep tight because you're gonna be let off watch tonight, but it's the only night."

"And what am I supposed to watch for?" Mitzi sneered. "That thing comes here shooting fire do I," she jabbed a finger obscenely skyward, "just say Bang! and it'll fall down dead?"

"No," Esther said quietly, "it's no use watching for that because we can't duck it. But this—" her arm whipped out, grabbing in the mud beside Mitzi's boot, and something crunched. She raised her fist and a three-centimeter sting pointed upward from its knotty clench like Mitzi's finger. She opened her hand to show the crushed body of the striped and multilegged creature, palm-sized, and Mitzi yelped. "This—" she tossed it into the fire—its burning matter shriveled and squeaked—then held her hand up in the rain to wash it, "—is not slow at all either, and it's not exactly a scorpion, but if you called it that it wouldn't be insulted; it carries just as big a load of poison. That's what we'll be looking for, and a few other things too. Now get to sleep."

The others, except Shirvanian, had roused and were staring at them. Sven said, "Mitzi and Shirvanian will skip watch tonight, and Yigal too, because he's been loaded down. I'm very heavy, I have to work harder just moving around and I get tired faster, so I'll take the last one, at dawn. Esther's always up early, so she'll take the one before me. The three of you can divide them as you like."

"Ardagh just fell asleep," Joshua said. "I'll take it now."

Without moving, Esther said sourly, "Sure you don't want to argue a little first?"

"Esther," Sven said, "go to sleep."

Esther pinched her mouth shut. She skittered over to Topaze's nest and slipped in under its bower of leaves and branches; his arm, thick as a giant fern's trunk, reached out to pull her against him.

Koz had rubbed depilatory over his jaw and lifted his face to let the rain wash it. Sven bent his head closer to the blade; the stone hissed on it. Koz rubbed his face down, shook water from his hands, and stared at the nest. "Some difference in size, huh?"

From behind him, Joshua said gently, "Gorillas are small in that area. Apes do some inter-species breeding, but they're usually a little more evenly matched."

Mitzi began to giggle. Belly down on the shelter floor, head propped on her fists, she sang, half whispering, an old song from her unimaginable childhood:

"I went to the animal fair;
The birds and the beasts were there;
The big baboon by the light of the moon
Was combing his auburn hair . . ."

Giggling again, she rolled over on her side and fell asleep at once.

Sven wound an oily rag around the machete and put it into a pouch. Koz hugged his knees and spit red betel juice into the fire. Rain soaked his braided hair. His body was tough and wiry, but without the heavy robes it seemed childlike. His pale face was blemished by the tattoos; his eyes narrowed staring into the fire. He had said little for the last few hours.

Sven asked, very evenly, "You take stuff, like her?"

"What, this?" He spat again. "This is just to chew."
He added contemptuously, "I wouldn't touch that
crap." He shook water from his poncho and wrapped
himself for sleep.

Sven poked about and found a few pieces of almost dry, half-rotted wood between the sharp flanges
of the buttress tree and tossed them on the fire. They
crackled and began to glow. He crouched in the
tree's angles, half under the groundsheet. "Are they
asleep?" he asked Joshua.

"They're so tired you could build a fire under
them."

"I'd do it if it'd dry us out. I never cared for wind
and wet myself." Thunder crashed, rain thickened to
mock him. "One thing I have to say . . ." He looked up
at Joshua's head, pushed out over the shelter edge, an
eye picking out a point of light in the deep shadow
of his face. "If we get there. If we find Dahlgren. I
don't know what he's doing, or what's been done to
him . . . I don't know what will have to be done . . .
with him . . . for you to get away . . ."

"Yes?"

"I won't do it. You understand? The man's my father.
I won't stop you, I'll help you any other way I can,
but I won't do anything to him."

Joshua came down. "I understand."

"Let the others know." He handed over the poncho
and crawled into Joshua's place.

"I will."

There was not much space for him, and the whole
structure creaked under his weight. He found a corner of blanket and pulled; Mitzi shivered to one side
of him, Shirvanian whimpered at the other. He rolled
over, catching a glimpse of Joshua's black shape before the fire, veiled by the rain; drops hissed in the
flames, the rotted wood smoked. He twisted to find
positions of comfort for his arms, his face brushed
Mitzi's tangled hair. *Spiderman*. He had too many

arms. He had never felt it so piercingly. Dahlgren (*what is the Dahlgren?*) had taught him (*what has he/they done?*) Dahlgren had taught (*done to him?*) him . . . Dahlgren?

16

The board stood thus: one black, one white Knight taken; Kings castled; their Bishops faced each other on N4, their Knights on B3, their Pawns on K4; the Queen's Pawns mirrored on Q3 and B3, her Knights on N4.

Dahlgren faced his erg, but he thought he must look haggard, no reflection of the other.

Other did not seem more daring: *11.* he pulled his Knight back to B2. Dahlgren went after his remaining Bishop with P-KR3. But White kept his pin on Dahlgren's Knight with *12.* B-R4. The board's symmetry had vanished for good.

Dahlgren spoke for the first time since he had wakened. "When will you bring my son here?"

AS SOON AS WE CAN FIND HIM. Erg-Queen watched, still against the wall.

"Then he has left the house. If you wait long enough he will come."

WE HAVE NO TIME TO WAIT FOR HIM.

"And you cannot find him? That seems strange."

WE KNOW WHERE HE IS.

"Ah . . . you cannot take him." Dahlgren smiled.

THERE IS NO JOKE HERE, DAHLGREN.

"No one knows it better than I. Yes," at erg-Dahlgren's nod, "I also know it is my move. But I want to see my son."

IT WAS PROMISED THAT YOU WOULD SEE HIM.

"I am not convinced he is alive."

I HAVE SAID SO.

"Men have said my Earth was flat." He turned to erg-Dahlgren. "It seems that you are going to become my son's father. What do you think of that? No, you don't have thoughts."

"Will you go on with the game, Dahlgren?"

"You will not malfunction, will you, when he asks why his father deserted him? What will you say?"

"What would you say?"

"I have no idea. I came back here in exchange for his life, because I made promises to machines. It takes a madman to make promises to machines. A stupid one to believe the promises of machines."

MEN BREAK PROMISES.

"Dahlgrens do not. Remember that, Mod Dahlgren. Think what you will say to him. Take care."

"'I kept the promise because I am Dahlgren.' Is that what I am to say?" Erg-Dahlgren moved forward slightly, eyes on his double, mouth open to take words into it.

"'And I make this promise, Sven. You will be free, even if I cannot stay with you.' Can you say that?"

Erg-Dahlgren sat utterly still, body bent forward, mouth open, eyes blank.

DAHLGREN!

Erg-Dahlgren blinked. "The game. The move."

Without hesitation Dahlgren played P-N4, picking off the pin on his Knight at the risk of baring the King. But he had nothing to play now but risks.

17

Because of tiredness Esther slept past her personal
alarm. The rain had stopped and the sky was the deep
gray-mauve of pre-dawn. In an hour the sun would
stand full on the horizon. No one was on watch. She
scampered to the shelter. "Koz?" She peered over the
edge; he was not among the tumbled bodies of the
sleepers. "Koz!" Run away? Not likely here.

Over her hands, clutching the rim, a tendril of
crimson runner-vine slithered, branching among the
hairs of her fingers, rooting between them prickling
as they went. She stared at it for one astonished second and pulled away. It came with her hands, bind-
ing them. She wrenched and bit until it broke, dragging away a great creeper swarming over the tree
buttresses; it writhed and quivered at every differen-
tiation of heat and moisture in its movement. As she
pulled she heard the gasping.

"Koz! Koz! Oh, get up, get up! All of you! Get up!"

Koz was wedged between the buttresses and the
branch floor in a twisted shape; the red tendrils had
swarmed over his arms, neck and head, run into his
gasping mouth, his nostrils, ears, the corners of his
eyes, his braids of hair.

Sven jumped down. "Oh God! Come out of that
thing, all of you, get the sheet off!"

Esther yelled, "Don't touch it, it grows right into
you!"

"Joshua, let's have some of your muck." He sprayed

and rubbed his four hands, and began to rip at the vines on Koz's arms.

"Take care of his face, you'll tear the flesh away!"

"Where's a knife?" He slit the cloth over Koz's chest. The boy's eyes were staring open, red with veins and tendrils. Sven sprayed the stuff over flesh, but dared not try it in eyes, nose or mouth. The liquid gloved his hands; the vine, once coated, gave way, bringing with it small shreds of skin and membrane. With twenty fingers he picked the runners out of eyes, throat, nostrils, knees gripping Koz's waist while Esther steadied the jerking head.

"Ah! Ah!" Koz cried. The inside of his mouth was raw and swollen, threads of blood ran from his nose.

"Don't spray in his mouth," Joshua said.

"I'm not. Get the alcohol and dilute it in water, about one to seven." He pulled the slitted cloth, clinging with frayed vine, from Koz's body, bunched it and flung it into the embers of the fire. The boy's face was free, eyes full of pink tears, lips and eyelids puffed and red. "I didn't sleep," he whispered. "I didn't sleep. It—"

"Don't talk. Tell us later."

Esther cleaned his mouth and nostrils with the alcohol mixture. It stung like fire and Koz screamed. "Get out your antibiotic pills," Esther said.

"He won't be able to swallow."

"We've got injection cartridges," Ardagh said.

"Use them." The runner had not attacked his eyes deeply; their membranes were reddened but untorn.

Sven yanked the vine away from the tree, it clung only by rootlets, and flung it on the fire. "The thing's still in his hair—and it's still alive."

Inch-long threads were rooting like cuttings and shooting leaf buds. Koz had the look of an ancient man cursed by a god. "Cut it off," Esther said.

"Don't—don't cut my hair!"

"That'll grow back, it's the least of your worries."

The shoots were crawling out past the hairline and down toward his eyes.

"It must be rooting in his scalp—oh God, the knife's gone dull!"

"Take mine." Joshua's knife was power-celled and edged like a razor. The shoots writhed among Sven's fingers as he cut, snakes of thread that made him cringe.

"Don't—"

"For God's sake, I've got to!" Hives were breaking out, the scalp-follicles welled with crimson sap and scarlet blood.

When Sven lifted Koz to his feet, cut free at last, he looked flayed to the waist. He leaned trembling against the buttresses, breathing harshly. Sven wiped spray and plant fragments off his hands, and washed down Koz's head and shoulders. His own fingers were breaking out in red lumps.

Esther stared at her hands. "I've got it too. Allergy, I suppose. Anybody got antihistamines?"

"I have lozenges," Joshua said. "Koz, can you swallow saliva?"

"Yes," Koz whispered.

Mitzi's voice quavered. "I want to get out of here."

Yigal scrambled to his feet, shook off his coverings, and yawned.

"Huh," said Esther. "Good thing it didn't get to him, with all that beautiful white hair." She studied her lumpy hands, and then her thick-haired body. "Or me either."

"There isn't any more around here," Sven said. "It must have been a single plant, and going fast."

Koz licked his lips and said hoarsely, "I was standing watch and felt something come round behind and touch my eyes, I tried to grab it, it ran into my mouth and round my neck and pulled me right over." He touched his raw scalp with his puffy fingers. "My hair . . ."

"That'll grow back."

"Years . . ." The tattoos on his face were half covered with black crusts of blood. He looked into the forest depths. "My robes, my clothes, my hair . . ." And down at the strange whiteness of his chest, a wisp of fine brown hair running its midline among spattered drops of blood or sap mingled with puncture marks.

Joshua handed him a pullover. "Turn up the sleeves and it'll fit."

"I wonder if that thing seeds," Esther muttered.

"I think it gave that up long ago," said Joshua. "It's a root and cutting propagator."

"Let's get out of here," Mitzi whispered. "I don't want any breakfast."

The sun was half up the horizon. The forest life twittered, buzzed and rustled; the mist swirled in the morning breeze.

"Koz won't be able to travel fast," said Ardagh.

"He'll ride Yigal," Sven said. "I'll pack half the load."

"Hey, where's the gorilla?" Mitzi pointed to the empty nest.

"I sent him home after midnight," Esther said. "He was too nervous to be trusted anyway, and I didn't want him getting any more jolts when the rads went up." The counters sputtered faintly but steadily under the forest noises. "We're not even in Zone Blue."

"We will be before noon. You ready?"

Sven swung the machete through what would have been his watch. Joshua came after, shoulders loaded double and hand on Yigal's neck. Koz rode, features swollen, denuded head hanging scored with black and crimson. He sucked lozenges, swallowing painfully. Ardagh and Mitzi followed with Esther, whose hands were so sore she did not want to swing in the trees; Shirvanian, straggling last, looked almost as beaten as Koz: his hair was roughened from burning, and his face, of the sort that collapses under stress, had mauve creases under the eyes and around the mouth.

The sun shone, as always, orange through pink haze. Far above, in the attic, pterodactyl-shaped birds wheeled among clouds of blue and yellow butterflies. When they alit, branches swung under them and shook off dead leaves, flowers, insects, dropping to become fertilizer on the floor. The dusk was of some ancient religious place, and all things, because they were half-familiar, looked doubly strange.

Below the swirling birds, bright snakes and lizards leaped and twined, sometimes caught in midair by a darting beak. Small animals skittered among the branches; they were patched with colors that did not accord with their surroundings, two or three albinos resembling huge white mice, one with two tails; a furred thing with blue webbed feet, a sharp black beak, and a row of glistening spines down its back. "That's a normal glymba from Cruxa Two," Sven said. "The techs used to love them because they're completely mutation-resistant."

"It's hard to see what it could turn into," said Ardagh.

An orange bat dived and whipped away, light in its wings like a stained-glass window. "That thing's got a nasty bite," Esther muttered.

"The clouds here must carry a great load of fertilizer," Joshua said. "This floor is thicker than any forest I've ever seen." The ground was rich with young ferns, seedlings, vines, tendrils. "But it's not . . . it's not the way it was back there . . . are those the same ferns? The leaves are narrower, they have galls. Some of them look so brittle, they . . . they are brittle."

"They're the same ferns," Sven said.

"The trees are shorter, upstairs . . . the branches are twisted. The leaves are clumped."

"We're not far from the zone baffle. Then it'll be worse. You took your anti-rad?"

"You'd better have some too."

"I doubt I'll have children."

"You never know. I'll take the machete now."

Sven flexed his hands; they itched with urticarial weals. "You ought to take some of those lozenges," Ardagh said.

"You want to give me antihistamines. Joshua wants me to take anti-rad."

"Esther thinks you should have breakfast."

"Yes. I'm a growing boy." He shifted the awkward packs.

"Koz . . ." Ardagh hesitated. "Koz hasn't done any praying today."

"Look at him! I don't blame him."

"Pain, danger, that kind of thing, always made him work harder at it."

"I don't think he has the strength to set up Mother Shrinigasa."

"You'd be surprised . . . have you ever heard of the Triskelian Order?"

"How would I?"

"It's the religion he belongs to. A triskelion is a thing with three bent spokes, you could call it a three-footed cross. It's part of his idol, and what he's tattooed with. The Order is celibate, like ancient monks, and it's a mixture of all the religions you could think of. It has no food laws, but it's got everything else, hundreds of ranks and rituals . . ."

"Did he tell you that?"

"A little . . . and somebody I met in the Twelve-worlds on a holiday, she had a brother."

"I see . . . I think I'm getting hungry."

"You scared?"

"Of what? I mean aside from everything. I just feel I'm getting more information than I can take."

"You may need this. It has nothing to do with the

catarrhine primate or the philosophy of Montaigne."

"You want to tell me he's a religious fanatic who's going to try converting me when we're busy fighting ergs."

"If that was what it was you'd be lucky. The Triskelian Order takes in only the children of very wealthy or very important officials—"

"Like an expensive school."

"Not exactly. They don't have the heavy robes and heavy statues to lug around, all the praying, the grooming, the tattooing . . . the impediments, the busyness."

"But not a prison, though—"

"Not for kids. And not a hospital for the ones who can't get around in the open."

"You mean the Triskelian Order takes in some pretty funny types who are—I guess you'd say on the borderline of something."

"Yeah, but I'm not sure what."

He looked at her. "You're sure."

"I could be wrong. I wouldn't want to look dumb."

"You're not scared of looking dumb."

"Thanks for the compliment."

"It is a compliment. I'm dumb about a lot of things because I haven't seen much of civilization, and I'm willing to take the chance of seeming stupid while I learn. What you want is for me to keep an eye on him."

"Yes . . . I'm scared for him."

Esther had recovered enough to run up a tree, and she called down, "Clearing!"

"Where?"

"Ten meters east-southeast. Don't jump right into it, it might be a bog!"

"Maybe we can eat there."

"Not till you find out why it's there, or it might eat you!"

Sven took the machete from Joshua. "I passed that

when I was scouting, but I kept wide of it. Can you find me a straight stick?"

Joshua found one and trimmed the branches with his powered knife. Sven pushed through the brush, bound the machete's handle to one end of the stick with straw twine, and stood watching at the clearing's edge.

It was set like a lighted room in the shadowy undergrowth. Except for one overgrown log there was nothing on its floor but dead leaves and twigs. "Not many insects. It looks quite dry." He extended the blade as far as he could and drew a long straight furrow toward himself with the point. He unearthed a snail and several clumps of rootlets, and halved two bulbous green worms whose pieces burrowed deeper in outrage. "It's solid. Just a couple of sling leeches."

"What's that?"

Sven pointed to the farther margin, where two thick threads extended to the ground from branches three meters high. "Just touch one and the leech will slide down and hit where it touches before you can blink. Then you can burn it off, if you're lucky, or spend three days pulling it out."

"Let's find another place," said Ardagh.

"Another planet," said Joshua.

"There's room for all of us. Get the fire going."

Mitzi's eyes widened. She pointed. "That log!"

"What about it?"

"That vine on it . . . looks like—"

"The other one was all red. That's just speckled."

"It moved!"

"The wind, silly!"

Esther crept forward. "Something shiny there, a piece of metal . . ."

"Watch out—"

But Esther was jumping up and down and yelling. "tKlaa! tKlaa!"

The log stirred, slowly raised up a few centimeters on its branches, and snorted.

Esther gave a great leap and hugged it, crushing vine leaves under her breast. "Oh, my dear tKlaa!"

hello esther said the log. *don't bend the leaves sweetheart*

"What the hell is that?" said Mitzi.

tKlaa was a reptile without eyes, ears, or mouth; she had an esp range of about a hundred meters, almost the lowest possible. There were three light-sensitive patches running back from her snout, and one beneath it; her two nostrils doubled in function, one as a sperm receptor, the other for food intake. Her belly was covered with sensors for moisture, temperature, and soil nutrients, and her branch legs gave her enough mobility to find them. Her back was deeply ridged, like bark, and its crevices were filled with the soil and humus that nourished the marbled red-green biovine which processed and pumped the nectar she fed on. She was about three meters long, perfectly resembled an old rotting log, and was very sweet-natured. She and her husband had been the only scientists on Dahlgren's World who were also specimens living out in the forest and risking mutation.

Esther pulled at one of the branching limbs to stare at the shining thing that had caught her eye, a metal chain with a numbered tag on it. "Years . . ." she said. "Where is nVrii?"

dead his bio mutated think it fell in love with a tree She snorted again.

Ardagh said, "Those leaves are an awful lot like . . ."

"Think it fell in love with us," Esther said. She rested her hand lightly on the trembling leaves. A tendril moved over it inquiringly and withdrew. She did not pull away. "I'm so sorry, tKlaa."

tried a transplant with mine   but no

They were squatting around her, breakfast forgotten.

"We'll eat here anyway," Esther said. "Go on, start the fire. tKlaa, what have you been doing all these years?"

lying around   thinking not much   what happened there esther

Esther told her.

did they kill all   then

"As far as we know . . . all but you."

missed   think I'm an old log hey   well I am

"Where is she from?" Joshua asked Sven.

"I've forgotten. She was a soil scientist here."

"Her people couldn't have done much with intelligence if they couldn't move around."

"I don't know what they did. But there seem to be an awful lot of people who don't know what to do with it."

They ate breakfast. tKlaa turned slowly to let the sunlight hit her sensors, and the vine rippled along her back, put out a tendril that slid into one nostril to drip nectar.

"Good man," said Esther.

miss him

"Why wouldn't your bio root on him?"

too close to me   he had no esp

"I forgot your people mate one ESP to the pair."

why both   he knew everything I

Ardagh touched the leaves gently and just as gently they inquired of her. "How do they mate? You don't mind if I ask?"

"Why not? You always do," said Esther. "His bio roots into his sperm duct and pumps the sperm along the same kind of vein that carries food, with little hairs—"

"Cilia."

"That's right, and empties it into her egg sac."

"Babies through the nose," said Mitzi. "That's one way of doing it."

"It's all right when it works," said Esther.

tKlaa was extremely ugly without being in the least repellent; she had no interesting ideas but she subtly emanated something that created an area of peace and love around her. Ardagh would have called it safety, but she knew how fragile it was.

"tKlaa," Esther said, "can we help you any way?"

I can help skimmers are out watch it

"How could you have seen them?"

birds

They looked up. Above the trees an orc-thing was squawking, a glint of light on its horn beak, its leathery wings; behind their eyes they caught, through tKlaa, a montage of the clearing with themselves, figurines (edible-too-far-down), a memory of the aircar, a huge gray egg pacing the wingbeat, the bird slewing wildly aside . . .

"Just one?"

pair crossing twice yesterday one single early today

"Too bad we can't catch one of them," Shirvanian said. "They must be shielded if they want to take Sven through the zones."

"You didn't think so yesterday when your hair was on fire," said Esther. "Big ideas."

"We haven't heard the erg patrols since yesterday," Sven said. "Maybe they pulled them in and replaced them with skimmers on account of the transmitter."

Esther jumped up and down, "And they may come around again any minute! We better get out!"

good luck

"I hate to leave you."

you can't take me glad for the company

Esther touched the ridged head. "I can do one thing. Where's a metal cutter?" She clipped the chain from tKlaa's branch limb and flung the tag far into the bush.

tKlaa gave her a smile-shaped thought: *goodbye dear*

"Come on. Get up, Koz, get up!" He had lain back among the ferns with his eyes closed. He picked himself up slowly, eyes glazed. His suffering turned them silent.

Ardagh took a turn with the machete. tKlaa's tp field began to ravel and fade.

"Erg!" Shirvanian yelled.

They froze. Up to the neck in greens, hair tangled in branches, they had no way to scatter.

The gray egg dipped, cast a random string of fire, swung up and away.

They stayed still, except for Yigal and Koz. The one had dug his face in the ground, leaving his hind end peaked like the apex of an irregular triangle; the other had slid off and was picking himself up slowly.

"What was that for?" Ardagh asked weakly. "A scare?"

Esther's face crumpled. "tKlaa . . . oh, tKlaa!" She swung back along the path. The faint living resonance of the logwoman was gone. The ground smoked through the clearing.

Sven called, "Don't, Esther, don't!"

She stopped in mid-swing, dropped, turned. "You're right."

"But why?" Ardagh whispered.

Esther shrugged. "I suppose the thing homed on **us** and aimed. By the time it got there we'd gone."

"It—" Shirvanian began.

"Shut up and get going."

Ardagh picked up the machete and went on slashing, scythewise. Sven shouldered packs, Esther skittered among the branches above his head. He dared not speak to her for a while.

But the questions kept burning in his mind, and erupted finally. "Shirvanian said the ergs have got a thing called a Dahlgren. Not my father, I mean some kind of machine."

Esther pulled her way arm under arm through the thickets. "Android robot."

"What?"

"Just the first thing that came into my head. They'd hardly name a servo in honor of Dahlgren, would they?"

"But nobody makes androids any more."

"The ergs have, if Shirvanian's right."

"Maybe my father's dead . . . but what would they want . . . could it be a copy of him?"

"They call it a Dahlgren."

"But why?"

"They might want a Dahlgren to order them around, like the good old days, chop up the forest, pick animals apart, twist things out of shape."

Her voice was so bitter and so painful that Sven stopped and pushed down on the part of his mind that said *android robot Dahlgren robot android.* "Do you hate me, Esther?"

She dropped down to his shoulder. "Why do you ask?" She hunched on the shifting muscle, arms folded.

"You've always done everything for me. I often thought it was too much. Maybe now you do."

"I'm thinking of tKlaa. Yigal, those aborted fetuses that should have been kids. Topaze, big ugly beast. I probably won't see him again."

He straightened and stretched his four arms. Yellowed skin, naked head, he seemed almost an oriental god. "And me too, Mutti?"

"I did it for Dahlgren." She jumped and grabbed a liana, rose up yipping into the forest attic.

Sven shook his head. "And she wanted me to do this."

Shirvanian caught up. "What did you say?"

"Nothing. Esther's upset."

"She got tKlaa killed by throwing that tag into the bush. It was a signaler. The erg read it as an enemy on the move."

"God . . . I'm glad you didn't tell her that!"

"I started to. Then I thought she wouldn't want to know."

Esther android robot hates me. It seemed there was a jungle in his head that needed clearing as well. "Esther thinks the Dahlgren is an android robot."

"It occurred to me."

"I wonder why they want me alive."

"I'm not sure . . . maybe to test it." *Because I am Dahlgren,* said a *being.* Shirvanian stopped with his mouth open.

"Then Dahlgren's dead, and—what's the matter?"

"I just felt funny for a minute."

"Oh, for God's sake, don't get sick!"

"I thought I was getting some kind of signal."

Sven pulled ahead. He was fed up with Shirvanian and his signals. "Ardagh, give me the machete."

"Maybe I could eat my way through this stuff," Yigal said. "I'm damn tired of stumbling through it."

"I wouldn't try it, the way it's mutating," said Joshua.

Yigal snorted. "I hate this."

"Be thankful it isn't raining."

Clouds slammed the sun and the rains beat down. They stopped to unpack their ponchos while the waters streamed, thunder drummed their ears, the soil frothed to mud under their feet, the counters ticked faster and louder. Far up Esther swung on the slender trunk of a fern; the fronds whipped her face. She looked out over the misty line of the forest top. All that was sweet of Dahlgren's World lay on that graceful billow, its gray-green sprinkled with red or blue, the silver needles of rain stirring it.

Sven watched the others crouched in the wetness around him, bent figures lashed with the powers of his father's world. He stood up, shucked off the poncho and packed it away, took up the machete and broke the path, swinging at the underbrush with his lower arms, breaking branches with his upper ones.

"What are you doing?"

"Going ahead. Follow when you can."

He pushed everything out of his mind, everything.

"Stop!" Esther yelled. "Stay where you are! There's something in a hollow here!"

"What the hell is it now?" He peered across the lancets of rain and fuming mist. "Where?"

"Southeast by south. Wait till I look."

The rain stopped at once. He stood, head bent, water runneling the dirt on his head and shoulders, idly swung the machete, tickling the fern sprouts.

Joshua rubbed his thin black arms, bitten here and there, welted in one place from the battle with the vine. "I thought this spray was a good idea, once." He scraped off the last blob or two with a finger and pulled out a rainskin from his pouch.

"It's not raining now," Ardagh said.

"It will." The sun flashed for a second, cloud covered it like a lid and rain began again, more gently. "Ha." He drew on the semipermeable skin. "How much farther today?"

"Eight kilometers," said Sven.

"And you did all this in two days once."

"In the dry season. It rains only half the time then."

Esther hopped to her perch above Sven's head.

"What is it?" he asked.

"Something funny."

"A trap?"

"I don't know."

"Well, what?"

Esther shrugged and bit her thumb.

"Are we playing riddles?"

"Something made by somebody and set up."

"A machine? What are you trying to say?"

"I don't know how to describe it. I never saw anything like it . . . yes, I did, years ago . . ."

"Animals?"

"Yeh. In a cage."

"Ergs put it there?"

"Not our old friends. It's not in the open."

"They've got a spy-eye on it," said Shirvanian.

"I had a feeling they wanted us to see it."

"Not necessarily," he said. "They may just be monitoring it for themselves."

"Can you tell what it sees?"

"No! I'm not some kind of electronic telepath."

"You must be good for something. Can you turn it off, at least?"

"I already did," said Shirvanian, nyah-nyah.

"Turn it on again," Sven said.

"Why? They'll think it's a malfunction."

"If they're expecting us here and the eye blinks off, they'll pop up swarming all over. The little servos can work the underbrush and slice us just as neatly. Who's monitoring? The factory?"

Shirvanian thought a moment. "No . . . the station." He had gone pale.

"Erg-Queen . . ."

The boy nodded. He seemed to shrink and his rain-beaded lashes quivered.

"You know where the eye is?"

"I think so."

"I'll go look. I'm supposed to be the one they don't want to kill. The rest keep out of range."

"We could all go around," said Esther.

"I want to look. I want . . . them to see me."

"Who?"

"Dahlgren, if he's there."

"But what for?"

"Because he's my father . . . I know you think I'm a bit crazy on the subject. I can't help it."

"That's not what we meant," said Joshua. "If we lose you we're lost."

"You can come up behind. Just keep your mugs away from the camera."

The rain stopped again, and water ran in silt-streams off the leaves and kept dripping. The sun was falling to the horizon, and the forest was silent in one of its rare instants. The counters whispered in the packs.

Sven wrapped up the machete, hooked it around his shoulder by the twine handle, and crept forward, parting the stalks gently.

Insects raised chirring voices, birds whimpered, epiphytes fell in dirty plops from the crotches of bowing trees. The ground abruptly shifted downward; grunts and chatters rose from the hollow. Sven divided the last of the branches.

There was no true clearing, only a space above which three or four lithe trees had been bound together in an arch. From their juncture a cage was suspended.

It was perhaps three meters square and inside were two creatures on hands and knees; they were human or something like it. A male and a female, hairier than any Solthree had been since Neanderthal. Wild yellow tangles bristled from their heads, lay in thick down on their naked skins, burst out darker from their armpits and hung from their groins like Spanish moss.

They turned their heads at the sounds of approach. Though their paws were pronounced their features were not coarse; they had narrow noses, their eyes were startling blue. The female was hare-lipped.

"The eye is four meters up aimed around your left

shoulder," Shirvanian said. "You should be half in view."

"Keep back," Sven muttered. He had broken into a sweat at sight of the male. "It's Dahlgren." In face, feature for feature.

They smelled like an old animal's lair. The floor of the cage, a meter and a half above the ground, was littered with straw, half-eaten fruits, lumps of dung.

"Not the original. That thing's not much older than you," said Esther. "The female's one too." Above the disfigured lip her face was one with the male's. Sven rubbed his nose, its same arch and nostril shapes.

"She's one what?" Ardagh hissed. "Those are Yahoos! Christ, you'd think they were made to order!"

Mitzi held her own nose and pulled back. Voice muffled, she cried, "Let's get out of here!"

Sven took a step forward. His shoulder itched, as if the eye had set a hot beam on it. Abased images of Dahlgren: my sister? my brother?

Koz crouched, hands covering his scarred and roughened head, and could not keep his eyes off them. Kneeling, splayed fingers gripping the bars, they stared back.

They were not as squat as prehistoric men had been pictured, but so thick and graceless they seemed ancient in shape. The female cocked her head to look at them like a child or a monkey, her hair got in the eyes of the male, he twitched his head and snarled, she gave a wild crow and he slammed her with his shoulder; she hit him full in the face with the butt of her hand, he yipped and hooked her under the knee with his foot so that she fell on her rump in the mess, he pushed her down on her back, threw himself on top of her and plunged.

Koz yelled at the top of his lungs, grabbed a lump of mud and hurled it at the cage. It hit the male

square between the shoulder blades and he pulled
out of the female with a howl of rage, blue eyes,
beautiful in the savage face, wild with fury. He
grabbed stuff from the cage floor and flung it, she
jumped up and did the same. Koz ran forward,
screaming as mud and dung hit him, and Sven
grasped him bodily with all arms and carried him
back.

"Stop it! Stop it!"

The boy gave a great jerk and shiver, then went
limp in a faint.

They groveled in the underbrush, Mitzi on her belly,
vomiting. Ardagh and Joshua hugged themselves and
shivered, Esther had jumped to Yigal's back and had
an arm around his neck and a hand calming his flank.
Shirvanian was sitting with his hands covering his
face. "The spy-eye's off," he said between his fingers.

"I bet they enjoyed it," Ardagh said bitterly.

Sven picked himself off Koz, whom he had flattened. "I hope he's not hurt." Both were filthy. "Let's
go. I think we stayed too long, we'll clean up later."

But Esther slipped off Yigal and ran toward the
cage, ignoring the cries of the others. She leaped to
its roof with an arm's grasp, knelt and pushed her face
down at the male's, stuck her tongue out and wig-
gled it. As he gaped up at her, she shoved her thumbs
into the corners of his mouth, withdrew them before
he had time to bite, jumped down and scampered
back.

Sven was aghast. "For God's sake, are you crazy?"

"Got all his wisdom teeth," she said. "Two or three
years older than you. So—who made them?"

"Who cares? We've—"

Koz gave another tremendous galvanic jerk. His
eyes blinked open, staring black and beady.

"My name is Nikoteles Kosmopoulos," he said in a
clear calm voice. Insects chirred around him and splat-
ters from draining leaves fell on his smudged face

and ran down. "I am a dangerous violent person registered in the Triskelian Order under the Protection Act of Galactic Federation." A cheek muscle twitched and blue triskelions jumped on his skin. "I repeat, I am dangerously violent, I have killed; my conditioning has broken down and I may kill or try to kill again. Do not speak to me, do not touch or try to restrain me in any way; stay away from me, report my whereabouts to the nearest Triskelian Center through the emergency number in your Directory. Again, do not restrain me, stay away, report . . ."

Before he was finished, Esther had looped his wrists and ankles with cord and knotted them tightly.

They watched him, half pitying, half repelled. Ardagh sighed. "Nearest Triskelian Center, forty-five million kilometers. I knew he'd blow . . ."

Esther hunkered beside him and cupped his face in her hands for a moment. "Poor child." His eyes were blank, his lips went on mouthing. "Pack him on Yigal. Eight kilometers, and we'd better go back and circle because they'll be sending—"

Sven stood gaping; his throat had constricted. "Look—" he croaked.

Two small servos, not much bigger than Shirvanian's bird, crawled out from the scrub beneath the cage. They wigwagged on their small treads like robot toys, but they moved with purpose, extending endless blue-steel arms. Yigal whinnied and backed up, Esther wrapped her own wiry arms around Koz, several times her weight, and plucked him away; the children stood numb.

Sven, all arms out like Vishnu, bared machete in one, moved forward in terrified desperation, wishing for a lightning bolt in each. "Shirvanian! Shir—"

One was reaching for Shirvanian, to kill; another for him, to take. Out of the corner of his eye he saw the child, trembling violently, grab at his box, crack it open with his clumsy hands, spilling things, clutch at something, twist, turn and push; his teeth were chattering.

The ergs hummed, Koz was moaning, "Report my whereabouts to the nearest Trisk . . ." The caged creatures gaped and gibbered.

Sven's erg touched him once with an icy claw, began to buzz, dropped its arms and spun madly like a dying fly. The arms tangled in its treads, sparked and fumed.

Sven dared turn his head. Shirvanian's erg, grapplers extended, had wheeled abruptly and trundled away. It stopped after a few meters, reached to pick something from a branch, turned again, came back to the boy, dropped the object in his extended palm, and froze in that position as if it were a dog begging.

Shirvanian immediately fell to his knees and began collecting the fallen pieces, wiping them on his sleeve and putting them carefully back in the box. He was crying so hard his whole body jerked with the sobs.

The other erg died hard, twitching as if it were crying too, in parody. The frozen erg stood suppliant, dirty water trickled on its beetle body and down its steel flanks.

Sven found his voice again. "Shirvanian—"

Shirvanian's tears were falling into the box. He stopped to scrub them off his face with his other sleeve. "Told you I could do it," his breath shuddered, "told you I'm not useless, I knew I could . . ."

"You were right," said Esther. "But how did you miss them before?"

"They were there all the time, inactivated and shielded. I have to home on a signal, I told you I'm not—"

"For God's sake, just thank him!" Ardagh snapped. "He doesn't have to apologize." She knelt beside him. "I think you got everything now. Come on, before they send out something bigger."

"What did that erg give you?" Sven asked.

Shirvanian turned up a suddenly grinning face. "The spy-eye. I can find a use for that. These things are too big to carry and too small to ride on."

"And you risked your life—oh, come on." He turned his back on the grizzled beings. A last lump of mud glanced off his shoulder. He ignored it.

18

The servos plucked Dahlgren from his bed, nudged him till he dressed, and brought him to the room with the screen. As he sat down, cursing, the picture came on, a cage among shadows, shadow-creatures in it. One pushed against the bars. It had his face.

Dreaming?

A pale hairless head rose from the screen's lower margin; a strangely curved shoulder, two arms dependent from it. The head turned, presented its profile, but did not glance back.

I TOLD YOU THAT YOU WOULD SEE HIM.

He had not noticed the sliding of the door. Erg-Queen tapped her arms along her flanks in waves of xylophone notes, tinkling, a weird prima donna's affected laughter.

He was morose, he said nothing. Sven did not have his face but the caged beast did. The caged beast would outlive Sven.

ARE YOU SATISFIED?

"You cloned me," he said without passion.

NOT I. MY MAKERS.

"Why did they not use my wife's ova and make something whole, at least?"

THERE WERE ONLY FOUR.

"You know even that." He sighed.

WE WANTED ANOTHER DAHLGREN. WE DID NOT EXACTLY SUCCEED, YOU SEE.

"My men helped you. Otherwise you could not have done this much."

YOU COULDN'T KEEP ALL OF THE BEST IN THIS TERRIBLE PLACE. EVEN YOU MUST HAVE KNOWN THAT.

He knew it now.

YOU HAVE NOTHING TO SAY OF YOUR SON?

"What do you expect me to say? He has grown."

ALTHOUGH YOUR HEART DOES FIBRILLATE, YOU ARE A GOOD MACHINE, DAHLGREN. I RESPECT THAT.

He looked her up and down, silver, diamond, blued steel. "Don't expect me to return the compliment."

On the screen Sven stepped forward but did not turn toward his father; he watched the cage with his arms folded, two behind his back and two over his chest. The screen went blank.

Servos ran in, manipulated dials and toggles with their chicken-claws, produced nothing but sparkles, found tool-kits, took apart and put together the console. Dahlgren and erg-Queen glared at each other, his eyes, her sensors. Flashes appeared on the screen, then scenes of jungle, mountain, lines of huge laboring ergs. No cage. An hour passed. The servos whirled out again and the Queen after them.

WHERE ARE THE THRESHERS? THEY WERE TO PICK UP DAHLGRENSSON AND KILL MACHINEMAKER.

They are not signaling and are completely out of contact.

SEND A SKIMMER TO RETURN THE CLONES AND BRING THE THRESHERS BACK HERE.

After she had gone Dahlgren stood up and faced the open doorway; it beckoned. Erg-Dahlgren filled it and leaned against the frame with his arms folded.

Then it seemed very strange, almost terrifyingly strange to Dahlgren that he had immediately recognized his bestial image in the cage when erg-Dahlgren's appearance, which he believed must be the truest reproduction possible, did not bother him. He could not even find himself in Sven. Yet he recognized the beast.

"You hate Mod Seven Seven Seven?" erg-Dahlgren asked.

"I don't hate any men or things," said Dahlgren. "There are only men and things I despise."

Erg-Dahlgren smiled. "Your pulse is up."

"Of course. I have seen my son. I suppose I should be grateful that the promise has been kept." And the screen had gone blank; perhaps he had been taken and killed. "Why this hurly-burly? What happened here?"

Erg-Dahlgren said indifferently, "I presume a malfunction."

Dahlgren looked at him more carefully. "Why do you ask if I hate your Mod Seven Etcetera? That does not seem like you."

"I should laugh, but I am not able. It is like you. I am curious." *Hate her, she . . .*

Dahlgren barked with laughter. "Erg-Queen tells me I am a good machine. You claim you are becoming more like me." Screen blank and busy wheeling about. *Malfunction.* A chance that he is still alive? Take it further then, than moving the fossils on the board. "But I do not think, machine or man, that I should ask such a dangerous question."

"Why not?"

"Because you are linked to your mentor."

"Not always, friend." Erg-Dahlgren turned his

head back and forth, not quite naturally yet. "Not always."

Then you have autonomy? No, not to that extent. She is busy, and you are learning new ideas. The mice are playing.

Erg-Dahlgren's head swiveled sideways and then fell forward; his eyes turned empty. He stood still.

Dahlgren watched him a moment and backed away slowly till he butted into the console. He would not for anything have risked touching the other by trying to push through the door. Let him behave so at the Sciences Council and Queen will know how well her piece is moving. If they do not say that is just more of Dahlgren's eccentricity.

But something peculiar was happening within erg-Dahlgren once more. The words *Why not?* had set up strange resonances among his circuits. The words *hate her, she* rose into his frontal store and looped there. And completed themselves at last:

hate her, she
broke my bird
said Shirvanian.

When he raised his head and saw how Dahlgren was looking at him he knew that his curiosity had been dangerous indeed. He had been going to say that erg-Queen needed him too badly to risk everything by destroying or tampering with him, but *broke my bird* stopped him. He said, "I am sorry, but I do not always operate properly." Dahlgren was gripping the console edge with bloodless knuckles. "Believe me, you do not need to fear that I will attack you physically. I have both strength and balance, but they are hard to coordinate. I was not made for fighting, and I have no reason to do it. Would you like to go on with the game now?"

"No. I want to go back to bed."

"Come along, then."

Erg-Dahlgren would have been incapable of playing chess just then. *Danger danger danger* was looping in his forebrain. He wondered if this awareness was something like fear. Do you hate her? *Hate her, she (danger) broke my bird.* Break me? She would only have to replace components. Take a few days longer. Begin a new game. And she lied to Dahlgren. O *Being*, stupid child! you have opened my mind to what?

Erg-Queen at end of corridor, Dahlgrens stop and stare, she skims closer. What to have in mind?

Help! cries erg-Dahlgren in silence.

The Middle Game in Chess, Forty-Seventh Revised, says *Being.*

"White's position seems to be admirable and full of promise, but his pawn-chain keeps all lines closed so that his pieces cannot take an effective part in the attack. On the other hand, Black's pawn formation is in no way weakened, and his inferiority really lies in the absence of defending pieces near the King's field."

Erg-Queen stopped before them. SEE THAT HE GOES TO SLEEP AND COME TO ME. She wheeled away like a White Queen on roller skates.

Dahlgren looked at his erg. "Something has gone wrong, I think."

"It appears so."

"Better you than me," said Dahlgren, and turned in to his room.

"It follows therefore that White must by some means force through some of his pieces for the attack in order to decide the issue. Any loss of time, however, would give Black the chance of consolidating his position . . ."

Mod 777 put three or four of her arms around erg-Dahlgren's shoulder. It was not an affectionate gesture; she was directing his attention.

COME HERE. She pushed a button and a square of the floor descended. In Design were vaults beyond vaults. Metal struts and tendons, flexes, transistors, endless walls of circuit diagrams, revolving vats of plastics, molds of hand, arm, head, hair spinnerets. YOU WERE CONCEIVED AND BORN HERE. YOU WILL DIE AND BE REPLACED HERE. WHAT YOU CHOOSE TO CALL YOUR AUTONOMY BEGINS AND ENDS WITH ME. DO YOU UNDERSTAND?

"I understand," said erg-Dahlgren.

DO NOT USE MY COMPUTER. DO NOT HAVE UNNECESSARY CONVERSATIONS WITH DAHLGREN. AND DO NOT GIVE SO MUCH THOUGHT TO YOUR CHESS GAME. IT IS NOT ALL THAT IMPORTANT. NOW GO BACK AND MONITOR HIM.

When she was alone she called Dispatcher. WHAT OF SKIMMER?

It has returned the clones. It found no sign of the threshers.

THEY WERE UNDER THE CAGE. TELL THAT USELESS THING TO SEARCH THE GROUND.

But what do I want? Why am I doing this? asked erg-Dahlgren of the darkness that was neither his night nor his day. Why am I doing so much to preserve my being? But then why does any creature wish to stay alive? No one has answered that yet.

Skimmer 174 reporting to Mod 777.

YOU HAVE FOUND THE THRESHERS?

One was destroyed and one deactivated. They emitted no heat, light or signal. That was why I missed them . . . Mod 777, are you in contact?

YES. DISPATCHER, ALL PATROLS, SKIMMERS AND THRESHERS WILL NEST. THE SOLTHREES ARE WORKING TOWARD DEPOT 4 AND YOU WILL MAKE WHATEVER ARRANGEMENTS ARE NECESSARY TO KILL ALL OF THEM THERE. DAHLGREN HAS SEEN HIS SON AND THAT IS ENOUGH OF PROMISE-KEEPING.

19

Ardagh wiped the place down hard with alcohol and pinched the skin so that the hard knob stood out. Then she took the knife and made a clean section slightly longer than a centimeter. The transmitter popped out on a small well of blood. She caught it in her palm. "Here, Shirvanian, it's all yours. I'd have been embarrassed if that was a tumor."

"So would I," said Sven. "Now let's pretend they won't kill me without it and they can't kill him with it."

Ardagh squeezed the cut once, lightly, to bleed it a bit more, and when it slowed cleaned it, pushed a gauze pad against it and taped it firmly. "I'm good with frogs and rats, but I've never gone higher yet." She knew it hurt; she didn't ask. She glanced at his face, then put her finger to her lips and touched the bandage.

"You could be a little more direct," Sven said. "I think I deserve more."

She looked around. Except for Shirvanian, who was examining the transmitter for signs of deterioration, the others were so tired their heads were nodding at the firelight. She pulled his face down and kissed his cheek. They were both dirty and sweaty, but she still carried a small fragrance of the world she had come from. "Thank you," said Sven. "Now where are you going to put it, Shirvanian?"

"Let me have some of the tape," Shirvanian said. He pulled up his jersey to expose a small pot belly, pushed the transmitter into his navel, and fastened it with the tape.

"New belly button," said Esther. "You won't lose it there, I guess."

They had struggled up and then down the zone baffle and cut back toward the road, where the bricks were blue now; they had camped half a kilometer away. There were no erg patrols; one ore carrier had passed them by. The trees had thickened so that even the dead ones stood stiff in their buttresses or were supported by lianas gross as trees had been in Zone Green. The forest was hunched and brooding, the ferns stunted and pocked with nodules; the floor was almost bare, and they had spread out a groundsheet over a mattress of twigs, with another set up at an angle to blunt the wet winds from the east and catch a little warmth from the fire. It was past sundown, nearly seven hours to midnight. The evening was quiet: animal noises, a little rain spatter, a lightning flicker. A moth or two jittered near the flames and caught red light on its wings.

Koz, too, was quiet. He had set his idol, Mother Shrinigasa, between himself and the fire, and his lips were moving in prayer. His wrists and ankles were haltered to allow movement, and he had not protested. He was aware of what had happened. Since his training had enabled him to stay at ease he had not disturbed the others, and they managed to treat him as before. But Mitzi was careful not to bait him.

"Day and a half, twenty-five kilometers," said Esther. "Only fair. We started thirteen from Zone Blue and there are three-four to the factory . . ."

"Yah, this time tomorrow we'll be okay or dead," said Shirvanian. He shivered and pulled his blanket tighter around him. Esther had noticed a mold spot behind his ear, and her scraping and scrubbing was the final knock on his exhaustion.

"Okay or dead," Mitzi echoed. "I don't think I really give a damn."

Sven was thinking of the cage. The beasts. The face of Dahlgren.

Staring through the bars.

He said, "The things in the cage . . ."

Ardagh yawned. "Clones, maybe . . ."

"You think so? How? Why?"

"I don't know why. But there were samples around the lab. Spit here, scrape there, pee in that. Sperm and ova. Esther said so. Maybe . . . maybe Dahlgren wanted kids—"

"Ugh." But he got me.

"Though if he was as good as you say, they should have turned out better. They looked like a botch."

"The lab techs wouldn't have left one with a harelip," said Esther. "What's the matter, Shirvanian? You feeling worse?"

"The things in the cage. I didn't like them."

"I don't think they were meant to be liked. They didn't even like each other."

"What they were doing . . ."

Esther reached over to pull the blanket around his head and tuck it tighter. "Usually it goes with affection, and maybe even love. Wait and see."

"I won't—" Shirvanian began, and pulled his lips tight.

Mitzi said through a yawn, "Shirvanian's gonna build himself a mechanical girl when he grows up."

"Why not?" Shirvanian was not annoyed. "Long as she's not like erg-Queen."

Shirvanian, friendless and adored focus of the family burning-glass at age six, had built himself a friend, a very small non-humanoid robot. It did what he wanted: raided the pantry for candy, stole components from warehouses to repair his other machines, composed excuses for tardiness and bed-wetting. His parents had seized upon it and entered it in a competition where it won scholarships, respectful tutors, advanced degrees, more adoration. He despised his parents.

He pushed Esther's hands away. "Leave me alone."

"You yell for Mama when you're in trouble, don't you?"

"You think you can read minds?"

"No. I learned a little about kids. Why?"

"I was thinking about . . ." . . . *such a dangerous question. Why not? Why not? Why not?*

Being, you stupid child . . .

"I am not! and I do hate—"

"What are you saying?"

Winds gusted and the heavy lianas creaked around the trees. Spatters hissed in the fire. The night closed down.

He pulled himself away and in, so tight his eyes crossed, half closed his lids, his jaws clenched. "The Dahlgren says." The words pushed through his stiff lips. "Do you hate Mod Seven Seven Seven?"

"Fever," Esther muttered.

"No!" He struggled with the blanket. "Oh no, no!"

"Not you too!" Esther grabbed, tried to hold him. "You'll get worse!"

Sven said, "He's full of solcillin. Let him chatter if he wants."

"All right, talk! But keep the blanket on."

Shirvanian squeezed his eyes shut and stuck his fingers in his ears. "Dahlgren says. I don't hate. I despise." He swallowed. "That is dangerous."

They waited, eyes on him, uncomprehending.

Sweat-beads burst on his forehead. "Mod Dahlgren One says. She does not always control me. Oh. I know the *being* that *hates her*. Shirvanian says *she broke my bird*. Dahlgren moves away and is afraid of me. I will not hurt you Dahlgren. I am not made to hurt. Will you play chess? No I want to go to bed. Now.

Mod Seven Seven Seven is coming. She can stop my being. I want to go on being. Dahlgren is correct: it is dangerous. Help. I cannot break, I must break circuit and clear this train of thought. Help! Please. Please?" The automaton voice ended, his eyes opened. "Think about something else, you stupid machine! Think of chess, you must have read books! Any page! *The Middle Game in* . . ." He went limp, breathing hard. "He made it."

Esther wiped his forehead. "He's cool."

Shirvanian's voice was cold. "You thought I was delirious?"

"Nobody knows what you've been saying," Sven said. "Maybe you'd better tell us ignoramuses."

Shirvanian pulled in again and shivered. "I don't think you'll like it."

"I know we won't like it," said Esther. "But we better find out."

"Dahlgren's alive, a prisoner." Shirvanian licked his lips. "But she's going to kill him, Mod Seven Seven Seven, the erg-Queen, she made the robot, the Dahlgren android she calls Mod Dahlgren One, to take his place at GalFed," the words tumbled, "I'm not sure why, and she's got them playing chess so the—the machine can learn what he's, what Dahlgren's like, but he learned, the Dahlgren robot, more than she wanted, so she doesn't trust him, he thinks she's going to turn him off and . . . and, he asked for help . . ." Shirvanian looked down and twisted the blanket-corner in his hands. "He picked me up on some kind of esp band, and he—he just called . . . out . . ."

"A robot? Asked for help?"

"Erg-Queen can read him, but he's got more storage than she can monitor all the time . . . she thinks she and the ergs did too good a job, made him too. Human."

"Shirvanian!" Sven cried. "Is it true? Is it real or are you dreaming? Do you know the difference?"

Shirvanian beat his clenched fists together. "Did I turn off the servos? Was that dreaming? I've done all I could and you just think I'm some kind of dumb weird kid."

"I don't think you're dumb," said Esther. "I just don't understand a machine calling for help."

Shirvanian went on twisting the blanket. "I told him how to break the circuit . . . I said you wouldn't like it."

"That's not what I don't like," said Esther. "Dahlgren . . ."

"Dahlgren is alive and a prisoner. I told you." He looked straight at Sven and tears rose in his eyes. "Please?"

The hot lead ran out of Sven's heart. "I'll take your word."

"But they're going to kill him. That I don't like," said Esther.

"And he did call for help. I mean Mod Dahlgren. I had to . . ."

"You helped because it's a machine!" said Mitzi. "I think you're one too! Maybe we ought to take you apart and find out!"

"Mitzi, can't you find yourself some kind of pill?" Esther picked up Shirvanian, clasped him round like a baby, and pulled back under the shelter. "Dahlgren is alive. So far."

Mitzi said, "If that thing can pick up Shirvanian it can find out whatever we're planning. Do you think it's going to be grateful for your help?"

"Maybe not. But if that one gets knocked off there'll be another. I'm sure of that."

Shirvanian did not struggle in Esther's arms. He was too tired. He said through a yawn, "The Dahlgren-erg's a prisoner too. It's scared. Frightened machine, huh, scared of erg-Queen. He asked Dahlgren if he hated her. Found out he'd reached me. Asked for. Help . . ."

"But it's more dangerous!" cried Mitzi. "Can you turn it off?"

"Just like I can shut you up," Shirvanian buzzed, and fell asleep.

Esther put Shirvanian down. "I think there's a spare knit bag in the pack. Fill it with some dry moss and shove it under him so he'll have something to sweat on." She turned to Sven, who was brooding by the fire with his arms circling his knees. "You feel a little better?"

"They killed the others. They'll kill him."

"Since he wasn't controlling them it's a miracle they haven't killed him yet. They couldn't have been planning to award him the Stainless Steel Medal. If," she nodded toward Mitzi, "they find out our plans, we can make as many plans as they can make moves. In chess games there's millions of moves and not many surprises."

"Yes," said Joshua gently. "Just mistakes."

Sven slept with his questions. Dahlgren alive? Check mark. And a prisoner? Check. But four arms? The clones in the cage? Harelip? Erg-Dahlgren?

The factory; the rads, .1 per hour now; if the ergs were not to kill him he was free to move among them without the transmitter—was Shirvanian safe with it? Suppose the plan had been changed and Shirvanian had simply unfolded their vulnerable sides? And Koz, painful, not to be trusted, his psyche enclosed in brittle shells?

His thoughts did not even take dream shapes, but extended and protracted in Euclidean nakedness. One light kiss, a shield, and his father living . . .

A teardrop wakened him.

"It's your watch," Mitzi whispered. She knelt beside him.

The fire was low. Yigal snored beside it, wrapped

in waterproofing. In the shelter the sleepers huddled like fetuses, Esther in a tree, covered with leaves. The forest rustled, the mists waited to engulf their breathing space.

He wiped her tear from his face. "What's the matter?"

"Nothing." Her eyes swam, her hair was lit in gold whorls from the fire. "I killed a couple of bugs with stings. Something ran over my foot, I didn't see what." She had raw pink mold scars on her jaw and neck, round as coins.

He sat up and stretched. She flung herself against him, knocked his wind out, and his arms went round her in reflex. She was shaking. He didn't know what to say. "It's not raining."

"I'm scared." Her hands thrust under his clothes and ran up his back like small wild animals. He shivered with her.

"It's the universal condition."

"Don't joke."

"I'm not." He was trying to decide what to think, feel, or do. At the moment he was as scared of Mitzi as of anything else. Her cold fingers pinched and kneaded his back; she had had practice. But the tears kept running. He picked her up and moved away a space, to a clump of ferns, and crouched among them. Some broke as he brushed them; some scratched. They had narrowed and sharpened into spines, a few into dark reddish thorns. The sobs ground in her throat, her hands worked writhing on his back; he pulled them away, gently, and her arms locked round his neck. "You have to sleep."

"I don't, I can't!"

Her hair was in his eyes, nose, mouth; it smelled of the forest dampness. *And the male snarled and slammed her away with his shoulder,* very simple.

"I have to watch . . ."

"We're all going to die anyway, so what?" She unwound one arm from his neck, her hand snaked in and down the skin of his belly and coiled about him; he pulsed.

"Mitzi . . ." He was afraid of her and full of desire.

She pulled at his clothes, ripped down the line of her magnetic snaps, found places and uses for all of his hands, took his mouth with her own. The rain held back for them. She carried him like a wave of the sea. Simple. He broke into sweat at the last shudder and glanced up at a movement near the fire.

Ardagh had risen on one elbow and was looking at him. Immediately she lay back and pulled the cover over her head.

He turned to Mitzi. Her eyes were closed, her mouth quirked. "First time I ever made it with a real freak," she whispered.

He pulled away. "You mean you haven't tried Shirvanian?"

She giggled, rolled into her poncho, and slept.

He stayed on his knees, watching her. Thorns scratched his arms. His hand groped blindly and snapped off a thorn branch, brought it in front of his eyes. He had a hideous impulse to rake it down his groin. The thought gave him a different shiver and he flung it away and put his twisted clothes in order. He had hours to watch. What was he to think and do?

Only in dreams had he believed he would have sexual experience. He had had an experience. He looked at it straight, and at Mitzi, folded in sleep with her poison mouth curled in peculiar pleasure. Remembering that he had believed his father controlled the robots, he looked carefully to avoid the fear and revulsion that might curdle in him later and embitter his spirit.

At length he picked her up and dumped her in his place under the shelter. And laughed. He wouldn't have to be afraid of dying without it.

Toward the end of that long watch, Ardagh, who was next in line, got up without looking at or speaking to Sven, and poked up the fire to boil water. She hunkered before it, watching the bubbles gathering in the bottom of the translucent boiling-bag.

Sven shouldered through the mist and sat down beside her; she did not turn her head. He picked up the end of her heavy braid and brushed her cheek with it. "Ardagh . . ."

She twitched away. "You want more? Go jerk yourself off!"

"Ardagh, don't speak to me like that. I did nothing to hurt you. Or her."

"Oh, her! She's everything-proof. You, you just fell in."

He grinned. "That's right."

She shrugged irritably. "Men."

"And I got paid off with her thorny tongue, too. That make you feel better?"

"Why should it? I'm just jealous. Not vindictive."

"You sure?"

Her mouth pulled into the slightest of smiles. "No, I'm not sure. Not here." Her eyes swung an arc around the steaming pit of the world. "You want some tea?" She took a tube from her pack and squirted it into the bag, turning the water first pale and then deep amber.

"I've never drunk much, I'm not sure I like it, but . . . will it keep me awake?"

"With stale water and synthetic concentrate you won't want to drink enough to keep awake." She poked the collapsible mug to size. "Here."

He accepted half a mugful and drank, because he needed her, not sexually yet, but for loyalty to the day ahead, the day of the ergs. "I wonder how much news got out about your being missing. Your parents must be worried."

"I guess they would be." She drank and watched

the steam wisping past the plug in the bag's spout.
"I've been so tired, scared, and busy I've hardly
thought about it."

"Goodnight, then. It's been quiet so far."

"Oh yeah." Low roll of thunder to the east, wind,
endless animal noises, Yigal snoring like a buzz saw,
Mitzi blubbering and . . .

The cut near his armpit pulled and throbbed. He
could not comfort her or ask for comfort. She had
been the most joyful of them all.

And she had not worried about her parents either.
None of them had.

Shirvanian woke last, by special dispensation, when
they were half through breakfast. The first thing he
said was, *The Middle Game in Chess* isn't enough."

"For what?" Esther asked.

"Blocking erg-Queen from catching what the Dahlgren knows about us. He's got to have his memory
wiped or dismantled and stored somewhere else.
Otherwise there'll be more traps at that factory than
we can handle."

"There hasn't been any sign of a drone or skimmer
for a long while," Sven said.

"They've been tracking, they knew where to set up
a spy-eye, so it's obvious they know we're heading for
the factory."

"Then Mod Dahlgren can't tell them anything
new."

"Only because *we* don't know."

"Can't you shield?"

"Not when I'm scared," said Shirvanian.

The sun popped over the horizon like a bubble, the
leaves stirred toward it and the mists writhed. It
would be a hot day.

"How can you wipe his memory?"

"I can't do it, he's probably got millions of microcircuits in him. He'll have to do it himself."

"That's crazy."

Shirvanian shrugged. "If you say so. He could do it with the computer, but he's been asking it questions and erg-Queen told him to stay away. And he wouldn't wipe completely anyway. That memory's his individual part—what makes him, he'd say alive. *My being.* That's what he calls it. He's still got to use the computer to store. He needs access—and a code. Did you use the computer?"

"Me? I was," Sven smiled, "ten years old. What would I use a computer for?"

"If you did you'd have a store and a private code. Did Dahlgren have one?"

"Of course."

"You don't know his code, though."

"Of course not! If I did I wouldn't trust an erg with it."

Shirvanian wrapped his box in plastic film and packed it. His eyes were far away. "I killed a machine yesterday. I'd kill erg-Queen, but I wouldn't kill Mod Dahlgren more than I would a human being or an animal. He's too good. Dahlgren and erg-Queen are both his enemies, and I'm the nearest thing to a friend he's got . . . I like machines more than human beings—"

"I've noticed."

Shirvanian went on musing. "But I am a human being . . . and if he went back to erg-Queen I'd be forced . . . but I think he's gone too far. I think he's stuck with the human race."

"Don't forget you are too."

"I've said so. We can't do anything from here, and I wouldn't risk bringing the ergs down on us. All I can do is give him a hint. He can't keep using *The Middle Game in Chess* forever."

Koz prayed, put away his idol, and helped Esther load Yigal. The girls stamped down embers from the fire. Sven and Joshua brushed earth and rubble into the latrine pit: Joshua had an ineradicable compulsion to keep the forest neat. "Maybe we won't have rain for a while," he said, glancing at the corpulent sun.

Thunder rose in the west. Joshua called defiance to it in an unknown language and went to fetch his rainskin. As he was shrugging into it Sven noticed that the pull on the slide fastening was a small bronze triskelion.

20

If P-N4 had been risky for Dahlgren, his erg did not seem willing to follow up. With *13*. B-N3 he backed away; Dahlgren played N-R4 to chase the Bishop and lay the ground for Pawn advance. Erg-Queen had left them alone, likely to prepare more deadly advances.

Erg-Dahlgren said suddenly, "Your son is alive."

"I don't suppose he will be so for long."

"She is planning to kill them all."

Dahlgren stared at the set. If he flung the pieces at the wall they would probably bounce.

"Do not hate me, Dahlgren. Mod Seven Seven Seven is planning to replace me, and I think you would care for Mod Dahlgren Two even less."

"Why does she want to replace you?" Dahlgren asked indifferently. One machine or another meant death.

"Even she thinks I am becoming too human."

Dahlgren smiled icily. "Twilight man. You cannot eat, sleep, breathe, secrete, excrete, copulate. Your hair does not grow, you cannot spit, shiver or weep. And you are too human for ergs."

"I have discovered, Dahlgren, that I can feel. I wish to maintain my being, and the threat to it induces what I call fear. I find I have wishes and wants. I want to live, and also I want to know. There are things that I do not want, and one is for you to ridicule my small claims."

Dahlgren said in a quiet voice, "Believe me, I take you seriously. You are certainly less arrogant than I, and that may make you even more human."

"Perhaps you are claiming more arrogance than you have right now."

"At any rate, it appears that we share pride and fear."

Erg-Dahlgren cocked his head in the odd gesture that made him seem to be listening, and moved 14. P-KR3, taking the pressure off his Bishop and applying it to Dahlgren's. "As a theoretical question, what would you be willing to barter for even a small factor of aid or safety to the boy, the ape, the goat, and the five children?"

Dahlgren's heart went at it again, and the air around him seemed to go very thin. He pushed words out. "In a day or two I will begin to rot and you to be reconditioned. I think neither of us has any counters to trade."

"Please try to be calm or it will be much sooner. Mod Seven Seven Seven will be here in a few minutes."

Dahlgren took the White Knight with his threatened Bishop. He whispered, "What could I possibly have to give?"

"Your sign-on to the computer."

"There's nothing there for you to use—only a few

fragments of notes . . . I wiped most of it out before—before everything else was wiped out."

"I don't want to take anything out, Dahlgren. I want to put something in."

"Information? Something to hide from—"

"One of those children has psi—a mechano-sensitive. He has no other talent except for machines."

"How do you know?"

"We linked up by chance and are in communication. We cannot help it. I don't know how to shield and he is a frightened child without much experience at it. I can block by looping on another subject, but not for long, because she is suspicious."

"She made you to obey her," said Dahlgren. "If you do that I don't think you will be destroyed."

"Now you are testing me. It is you who are taking risks."

"I must do that."

"Probably I was made too well. I have found she is not to be trusted, and I don't wish to be broken at her whim." The lucite casters hummed at the end of the corridor.

"If she knew about this—this sensitivity—she would know everything they might do to try to defend themselves, and—"

"They would have no chance at all," erg-Dahlgren said.

Erg-Queen swept into the room. WHY SO MUCH COGITATION ON CHESS? WHY SO MUCH DELIBERATE SPEED? YOU ARE NOT PLAYING AN INTERPLANETARY GAME. EVEN THE SAINTED ZNOSKO-BOROVSKY WOULD AGREE THAT THERE IS ULTIMATELY AN ENTRY INTO THE END GAME. She extended a steel claw over erg-Dahlgren's shoulder to grasp White Queen and 15. take Dahlgren's Bishop. She placed the mitered trilobite in front of Dahlgren at the table's edge.

"That is true," said erg-Dahlgren mildly. "Still it

should be 'deliberate and at the free will of the player who has the advantage . . .'"

He locked eyes with Dahlgren, who pulled his Knight back to N2.

MAKE SURE THAT YOU KEEP IT, said erg-Queen, and vanished.

"'Not merely a fortuitous happening or a disagreeable surprise,'" erg-Dahlgren finished. He folded his hands and waited for Dahlgren's decision.

The molds had stopped spreading over the walls once the dehumidifiers were working again, but though the ergs had washed everything down there were still brown stains around the cracks where strange bits of underground life had seeped in. Dahlgren stared at the cracks. There were no windows, and the light in his room was always yellow and sick.

"You have no proof," he said.

Erg-Dahlgren, sitting on the other bed, said, "I cannot reach him at will long enough to gather information in an organized manner—and if I could it would be too dangerous. I can tell you this: the being is named Shirvanian, he is a Solthree child aged ten years—"

"*That* is a dangerous being to be playing around with."

"He has the ability, and the others must trust him. He has saved them from death at least once. Mod Seven Seven Seven sent out a mechanical bird in a deformed shape to warn them from trying to reach you—"

Dahlgren looked up. "And that—"

"He restructured it and sent it back. You saw it, and how she broke it. Shirvanian's anger opened his communication to me. *I hate her, she broke my bird.* I don't quite understand why it happened, but I still don't know men very well."

"You asked me if I hated her."

"I was asking myself as well. The answer told me how dangerous it was."

Dahlgren's brow crinkled. "And you want to use the computer—"

"To store my knowledge of Shirvanian."

"To wipe your memory? And then you would be my old enemy."

"No. I would still have a distrust of Mod Seven Seven Seven and a determination not to be destroyed. My memory is too complicated to be wiped completely, and I think I am capable of storing that much so she could not reach it. Of course she distrusts me already. I have some connection with the computer, but only for chess information and some data about you, I have no private store, and I have not been allowed anything else. Your store would operate for me in a way analogous to your unconscious; you could put a protect on the information, and if you wished you might restore my access with a code word."

"You trust *me* with all this?"

"I have trusted you too far for the last hour. If I broke my loop on *The Middle Game in Chess* I would be a heap of components in ten minutes."

Then why not let him? But erg-Queen would find out all he knows first, and perhaps link up with that child in the forest—if it is the truth and not some game in a nightmare. A game at least more interesting than the one on the board.

Erg-Dahlgren said, "I know you do not trust me any more than she does."

"I trust you a great deal more than I do her," said Dahlgren. "I'll tell you, it is not simply a case of giving you my code. My store has probably been inactivated by now. You are only allowed on the machine to ask questions about chess—"

"And about you, but she has told me to stay away from it. And my only other connection with the machine is that it stores the information I receive from your electrochemical system."

"Probably she has told the machine not to answer any more of your questions. You have no access so you cannot store. I cannot use my code—"

"But, Dahlgren—"

"Do you know Mod Seven Seven Seven's call signal?"

"No."

"Then there are two problems. To find her call signal and reach the machine. Are there life sensors attached to the computer?"

"No. There was no need."

"Then it will not know the difference between her and me, if I reach it, and if I have her signal."

"Dahlgren, that is very bold."

"A bold thought is different from a bold act. What is your identification on the computer?"

"Most of the time just my appellation, Mod Dahlgren One. Occasionally it requests a further key, which is MODAL 1."

"Is the Shirvanian child truly intelligent?"

"He thinks of himself as a genius, whatever that may be."

"Ask the genius to pick up erg-Queen's call signal. If he knew she broke the bird he must have some connection with her."

"He is so terrified of her he may become very unstable if he is obliged to contact her. And she may pick him up."

"That is your problem, and his. I know how to use a computer, but I don't know how to tamper with one."

"If that is the only way—"

"It is. But you must approach your Shirvanian very gently, because you will need to ask him how to create a diversion."

"I am not sure that I can reach him."

"Mod Dahlgren, I believe that with your urgency, you will."

As he took the first step on the blue brick road Shirvanian screamed "No!" and fainted.

"Shirvanian!" Esther and Ardagh were beside him, grabbing him under the arms. "The bakri, he must have relapsed!" He fought them, swinging his head from side to side.

"No, he's still cool."

Shirvanian ground between his teeth, "It's her name! Her name! Leave me alone! I'll do—" His eyes opened. He looked at Esther and Ardagh. "I hate them all! I wish—I wish I'd never—"

"What? What is it?"

"I wish I'd never touched that bird."

"He said, 'It's her name.' That's all."

"Her name . . ."

"If I go near him again I'll make him ill."

"Mod Seven Seven Seven?"

"I suppose so."

"That sounds too good to be true."

"That is what he said, her name, and I don't dare contact him again or I will do him some injury."

Dahlgren sighed. "But we still need a diver—"

Thunder rolled in a distant area. Treads shrieked, metal clanged. "What's—"

"One moment." Erg-Dahlgren left the room and came back in a few moments. "A servo has gone out of control, a three-two-one."

"That's a fair size."

"Yes, it's making a lot of noise and confusion."

"Did he do that?"

"It has never happened here before." He opened the door; Dahlgren waited beside him. A hum approached them.

"White will sometimes make a series of exchanges

in order to bring about the end game," said Dahlgren.

"True," said erg-Dahlgren.

Two or three small servos, the size and shape of pug dogs, clustered around them. They clicked and tutted. They were used for chassis repair, and their fine multiple arms terminated in tiny screwdrivers, socket wrenches, soldering irons and pliers. *Where are you going?*

To play chess.

Do not do that. That is dangerous. A three-two-one is out of order in the tread-repair chamber. Stay away.

Certainly.

"I presume they say we are naughty," said Dahlgren. "And I suppose they will tell Mother."

"Hurry!"

The door to the computer hall was open. Erg-Dahlgren half-closed it and turned on the dim light over the main console. "It is too bad we need light. The door is never closed here."

"Too bad we're not somewhere else altogether." Dahlgren stood before the console he had not approached for nine years. He breathed deeply and pushed a button.

WHO IS COMMUNICATING?

EDVALG.

THAT IS NOT AN IDENTIFICATION. THE STORE DESIGNATED EDVALG HAS BEEN INACTIVATED. IDENTIFY YOURSELF PROPERLY.

"Now you know my code doesn't work any longer," said Dahlgren.

"Don't play, Dahlgren! We will have them on us very soon!"

COMMUNICATOR: MOD SEVEN SEVEN SEVEN.

THAT IS NOT AN AUTHORIZATION CODE. IDENTIFY.

Dahlgren's heart clenched and he coughed. "How do you like that?"

"He said, her name. Try the numerals."

COMMUNICATOR: MOD 777.

THAT IS NOT AN AUTH—

Dahlgren slammed off. "Now what?"

"I don't know what, he said her name, there must be some, it—"

"For the Lord's sake, don't malfunction! It's bad for my heart." He spent a minute, considering. "Are you sure that Mod Seven Seven Seven is her name?"

"It is what she is called."

"But she cannot be the seven hundred and seventy-seventh model of her type if the ergs made her on the specs of one or two scaled-down exemplars my techs designed."

"I see what you mean. She is called Seven Seven Seven because, not including the big drones operating outside, she is at the head of over seven hundred servos: skimmers, thresh—"

"You wanted to hurry!"

"That's her cognomen. Her nomen, or genus, is Creator Matrix One."

"Ha." COMMUNICATOR: CREATOR MATRIX 1.

WHAT IS YOUR REQUEST?

Dahlgren let out his breath. "Now you get out of here. Order a good meal for me, and take your time."

The erg hesitated for a moment, and left.

"But don't expect me to eat it," Dahlgren muttered.

He wished for a chair, for the moment, because he expected discomfort shortly.

ACTIVATE EDVALG.

EDVALG IS ACTIVATED. WHAT IS YOUR REQUEST, CREATRIX?

Creatrix indeed. ADD SVENSSEN. ERASE EDVALG. THIS STORE IS NOW DESIGNATED SVENSSEN.

SVENSSEN INSERTED. ERASURE: ~~EDVALG~~

INSERT KEY: EDVARD DAHLGREN SON OF SVEN ADOLPHUS DAHLGREN.

INSERTED.

IF THIS CODE: SVENSSEN, IS USED HEREAFTER AT ANY

TIME BY ANY MACHINE OR PERSONAGE OF ANY ORDER, RANK OR NUMBER YOU ARE TO . . . He paused to listen, and thought he heard a steadier and more purposive noise rising. IF THIS KEY: EDVARD DAHLGREN SON OF SVEN ADOLPHUS DAHLGREN IS USED HEREAFTER . . . The metallic sounds came closer. Dahlgren went on adding locks, blocks and barriers. UNDER EITHER OR BOTH OF THESE CONDITIONS THIS STORE IS TO BE ERASED. He left himself a minute for the core statement.

INSERT ALL MEMORY OF THE NAME SHIRVANIAN AND ALL REFERENCES TO AND ASSOCIATIONS WITH THE NAME AND BEING SHIRVANIAN NOW IN THE MEMORY STORE OF MOD DAHLGREN ONE INTO THE STORE: SVENSSEN.

INSERTED.

DEACTIVATE ALL MEMORY OF THE NAME SHIRVANIAN AND ALL REFERENCES TO AND ASSOCIATIONS WITH THE NAME AND BEING SHIRVANIAN IN THE MEMORY STORE OF MOD DAHLGREN ONE.

DEACTIVATED.

REACTIVATE THIS MATERIAL APPLYING TO THE NAME AND BEING SHIRVANIAN INTO THE STORE OF MOD DAHLGREN ONE ONLY UPON THE UTTERANCE BY THE MAN EDVARD DAHLGREN OF THE VOCABLE "SHIRVANIAN" IN THE HEARING OF MOD DAHLGREN ONE AND ON CONDITION THAT THE UTTERANCE OF THIS NAME "SHIRVANIAN" IS HEARD BY AND INSERTED INTO THE MEMORY STORE OF MOD DAHLGREN ONE. UPON THIS UTTERANCE AND UNDER THESE CONDITIONS ERASE THE STORE: SVENSSEN. VOICE IDENTIFICATION: He picked up the microphone and said, "Shirvanian." Now I hope that is the correct spelling.

He switched off at the moment the servos whined through the door, slamming it back so hard it rebounded in its slide, and wrapped their cold tentacles around him.

21

"You all right, Shirvanian?"

"I guess so. I don't want that thing coming after me again."

"Which thing?" Esther asked.

"The Dahlgren. If he gets his memory wiped maybe he'll leave me alone."

The boy looked sick and exhausted. He made her uneasy, and not him only. "I never thought there'd be a time when I missed the sound of those drones."

"That's only because they've switched to flame-throwers."

Ardagh thought it was time to change the subject. "Did Dahlgren do a lot of work with apes, Esther?"

"He was interested in genetic engineering and its influence on behavior, but he was a coordinator, not an intense specialist. Besides, all apes are expensive, and many are protected species, particularly gibbons. I once heard him say he couldn't bring himself to stuff an ape into a glass box measuring this much by that much with a tube stuck here and a tube stuck there and a lot of nuts and bolts in its skull to hold the electrodes in its brain. He saw too much of that as a student and it made him sick."

"How'd he get gibbons?"

"That was a funny story. On the way out here somebody bound somewhere else smuggled them on board, intending to unload them at a stopover. Just one breeding pair. Dahlgren found out. Gibbon traffic is illegal; he took them away and told the fellow he'd blow the whistle if he didn't keep his mouth shut. Not very pretty—but those were my parents, and I'd be the ape in the glass box."

"And that's why he picked you, rather than, say, a chimp, for experimental purposes . . ."

Esther jumped to Yigal's back. The trees were becoming so unpleasant-looking she did not want to swing in them. The leaves were narrow, the branches brittle, the bases had thickened like low palms and grew scales tipped with spines. "No, ma'am. He chose me for my beauty."

Ardagh smothered a laugh, and then examined Esther. With her economy of grace and strength, her fine features and vivid character, even with the odd-colored spots on her dark fur, she was certainly beautiful, especially against Yigal's pure white hair.

"I'm not joking," Esther said. "Chimps look like caricatures of men, and their brains are nearly halfway there. Dahlgren's a show-off. He wanted to start from less and not end up with something people would say was funny and cute. I'm sure as hell not cute."

"Neither is Topaze," said Ardagh.

Esther laughed. Of them all, Esther, who never failed to groom herself, and Yigal, whom she groomed, looked fit. The rest were ragged, dirty, scratched, reeking of adolescent sweat; Shirvanian drawn with strain, Koz the worst because of his scabbing and slowly healing welts.

"Take it easy," said Yigal. Sven was trying to pull him ahead.

"I want to talk."

"What now?" Esther asked.

Sven murmured, "Joshua's got a Triskelian emblem on his rainsuit."

"Is that so? Mitzi's got it stamped on the arches of her bootsoles. Want to guess where it'll turn up next?"

"I don't think I do . . . Ardagh told me something about the Triskelian Order. Celibate, ceremonial religion? It doesn't fit."

"It could be that's not all of the truth. There may be more ranks in that order than we know of."

"She said there were a lot. I wonder if we can trust them."

"We'll have to, now. We saved their lives, Shirvanian saved ours. But I'm not surprised. There had to be something more than pure chance holding that cranky bunch together."

Koz, Mitzi, Shirvanian? Unpleasantness of character wasn't synonymous with deviancy . . . but Ardagh? Joshua? "If they get together and try something—"

"We'll know what to expect."

"We'll know we have to expect something—but when?"

"Oh, I think about the first branch point: when—or if—we get a machine."

Sven turned and saw them murmuring among themselves. Plotting? "They look exhausted right now. I wonder if they'd have the strength. You think they'd try to kill us?"

"No! Koz might break down, but I don't think it'd enter their minds. They might try to strand us. They're still childish—they wouldn't realize what a half-baked idea it was."

"Childish or not, there are too many of those ideas floating about here," said Yigal. "We are depending on a ten-year-old brat with a very strange mind."

"Ayeh," said Esther. "It's time to start cutting south. Too bad. The bricks are rather pretty here."

"Yes," said Sven. "I can hardly wait to see all the other lovely colors."

There were fewer trees, thicker seedlings warping and dying faster. Occasionally some strange growth, a foreign or indigenous mutation, resisted hardily and took hold with a splendid display of vivid metallic leaves and flowers that shrugged off dust and water and clashed in the wind.

"Ugh, those are repulsive," said Ardagh. "They look as if the ergs made them."

"Maybe they did," said Sven.

Even the beetles, low broad things with steely carapaces, seemed machine-made, and the rodent forms had spines and scales, or were perhaps mis-shapen reptiles. Flying creatures avoided the area. There were no berries, and the bugs would have raveled the most leathery craw. It was hard to deduce what any creature would eat here.

Shirvanian said, "They've probably got a reactor there, but it's not leaking . . . can we rest before we go much farther? I'm still tired, and I want to think."

"Put down a groundsheet," said Esther. "We'll eat now."

Mitzi said, "There haven't been any machines at all out today."

"They stayed home," said Shirvanian. "Waiting for us. Plenty of them."

"And no plans," said Joshua.

"Sven's memory of the factory isn't a map. Any plan might get picked up by erg-Dahlgren and the Queen'd get it. Even if his memory's been wiped he'll still connect with me at odd times. We'll have to make choices when we're forced to."

An aircar buzzed them, laid a random streak of fire a hundred meters away. They picked themselves up from flattened positions. "There's one for you," said Shirvanian. "Clumsy, or trying to make us think it is." The rain began once more.

"Whatever it is, we could have been wiped," said Sven.

"No, I don't think they're sure of catching us all this way . . . they think human beings are pretty sneaky—

which they are—and it's simpler to lay a really good ambush."

"That makes me feel a lot better," said Sven. It seemed to him that they had reached some kind of plateau of terror; they ducked and dodged, picked themselves up and went on eating. Where the fear had been there was an ache, a depression linking them, like heavy chains: Yigal hardly spoke, Esther plucked and snapped thorn branches, the children seemed to be breathing hard all the time, the air was heavy with moisture, and Ardagh, suffering either from allergy or a cold, had run out of tissues and was wiping her nose on her sleeves. The all-weather clothing was spotted with mildew, the food was growing mold; they scraped off the mold and ate it.

The factory was in a small valley. Parts of it had been used to grow marsh plants, sections marked off in squares for hydroponic tanks, the flooded bottoms as shallow beds to trace the mutation rates of fry and fingerlings. The ergs had chosen it because it was free of heavy growth; they had only to cut one deep channel at the southernmost point to let all the water out. They kept the growth down by burning and defoliants; the slopes were still faintly marked by plot lines.

The place was a bowl of night, filled with deep rumbling, lit once in a while by sparks from the huge stacks, emblazoned with rust splotches on the slopes of its metal roofs; nothing resisted the rains of Dahlgren's World very long. Mists hung over it, thickened by smoke and rising in odd shapes from the heat: winds sliced them and rains whipped them down; they regathered endlessly, blackened or shot with fire.

The sun hung over one corner of this valley like a smutted lantern; there were four or five slowly revolving spy-eyes mounted on poles around its rim, mainly to regulate traffic coming and going. The ergs did not expect enemies or attacks. There were no fences.

Sven and the others gathered in a small thickly-grown hollow beyond the rim, northwest from the channel, at the base and out of range of one of the spy-eyes.

"You can't see anything in that muck," said Esther.

Shirvanian unpacked the small receiver he had made to test the erg-bird. The bird had been a show-piece, a seamless creation, but the instruments he made for himself were uncased accretions of wires, transistor chips, helixes and solder knobs, and looked like the viscera of small animals under dissection. "Moderate reactor, running properly. I won't touch that."

"Why not? Why not turn it off? You'll have to do that at the station."

"I don't see why. There's other ways of shutting off power besides tampering with protective devices and taking the risk of blowing everything up. I don't want to start trouble. All I want is a machine."

"Where are they?"

"Can't see much through the smoke . . . there's two roads spiraling the slopes . . . in and out traffic for drones and other big ergs. I think they start from . . ." rain and wind shoved at the smog for a moment, pushing it north; it spread again as the gust died . . . "yah, that big low building opposite the channel . . . probably the hangar . . . there's no chimneys."

"The upcoming road branches off toward the tracks," Sven said.

"Too slow for us." A big servo emerged and began to wind around and upward. "Suppose we drove one straight from the hangar through the channel—it's probably full of rubble and rock chunks—I wonder if we'd ruin the treads?"

"Not on a transport. They're versatile, they've got

auxiliary wheels, runners, balloon tires, legs. They use the treads on the undergrowth."

"Transport's what we need. We can't travel in a drone or a servo. Where does the channel run to?"

"South or south by west," Sven said.

"We don't want to go that way," Mitzi said.

"We will if it's the only way." Shirvanian said to Sven, "Suppose ergs were patrolling *all* roads, as well as the northern track, by mechanical habit when it wasn't worth while to change them, or to check up on crash landings or meteors they thought were crashes. If we got to the middle road we might find it clean."

"It might be faster—but there's a lot of forest between here and track two."

"The growth is thinning, and we'd have a water channel for a while."

"And a lot of ergs chasing us."

"Yah." He moved away a few meters and lay on his belly, watching the mist-blurred factory and its lumbering machines, fist clutching the radio.

Esther saw that his lips were trembling, and whispered to Sven, "He's scared silly."

"So am I."

"He's got more to do." She flicked another glance. "Should I tell him to empty his bladder and embarrass him, or let him wet his pants and embarrass himself?"

"I'll tell him." He slipped aside to Shirvanian and whispered. The boy slid back into the undergrowth. When he emerged, Sven said, "That servo will be passing below in a little while."

"Six minutes."

"It'll pick us up. We'd better move."

"Maybe." He bit his lip, moved a dial. "You recognize that machine?"

"Yes. It's in the five hundred range, maybe a five-fifty. Quite old. I haven't seen any new ones."

"No. They just repair and replace here. All their new ideas come from Headquarters and get put into erg-Queen and the Dahlgrens . . . and the ship. If they make the big jump they can pick up any new machines they want all over the Galaxy—"

"The big jump! You've never said anything like that before!"

"Yes I did! I said the Dahlgren would take his place at . . . but I never thought—"

"Is that why they've started making androids?"

Shirvanian swallowed. "I don't know! You're ragging me again! Maybe I just got some stupid idea. Taking over other planets—I don't know!"

"All right, calm down. I'm not trying to upset you. It's just—everything keeps growing. What about this servo?"

"I scrambled a three-two-one at Headquarters. I don't know whether I should try rattling this one."

"It's a lot bigger."

"Three and a half minutes . . . okay, let it go." He pulled back, and Sven followed.

"What are we doing?" Esther asked.

"Right now we're waiting till the next erg comes by, if it's not bigger." He held the receiver to his ear. "How many transports like the Argus were there?"

"About a hundred. They may still use them for hauling ore and parts. I hope so."

"What about shielding?" Joshua asked.

"Anything carrying men would have been shielded," Sven said. "I don't know about other machines."

Wind gusted, splattering filthy drops from the pit before them, and they huddled under the narrow metallic leaves. Their skin streamed with sweat, had become chafed and rashy in its creases. "Oh God, I used to hate the Midwest," said Ardagh.

Shirvanian unpacked from his box the instrument

he had used to stop the threshers. "What's that?" Sven asked.

"Control for my esp signal. What I turn things off and on with. I've made better ones than this. When it works I can amplify and calibrate, bugger up feedback systems." He crawled up the rim. "There's another—a five-twenty, real antique but it moves fast. I'll try with that."

"Try what?" said Mitzi.

"Rattling. Unbalance it. I knocked out the three-two-one without this, but I didn't half know what I was doing, and I'd better know now." Sven pulled up beside him. "Stay by the bottom of the pole, but don't touch it, it may be sensitive."

The servo churned along the coarse roadbed, kicking spray that joined with the yellow mist. Ardagh and Joshua coughed and spat the foul stuff. "I've played with one of these," said Shirvanian. "I think . . . I know . . ."

"How close will it come?"

"Twenty-five meters."

"It might sense us."

"If it does I'll have to use your transmitter, and then I won't find out anything." He slitted his eyes and pulled in his self, watching the turns of the treads on the rough macadam. His head sank inward like a turtle's and his tongue lapped at one corner of his mouth. With finger and thumb he calipered the knob of his instrument, and the erg slowed. It made a quarter-turn, gritting on the road, swung back just beyond ninety degrees, swung forward again like a pendulum, its arms extended and shook, clattering against one another, and its upper carriage rocked on the chassis. Then it stopped, folded in its arms and went on.

"That's rattling," said Shirvanian. "Next one I'll really do the work on."

"I think you'll have to do it a bit sooner, sweetheart," said Esther. "Number one's coming round behind us."

They turned. The five-fifty, a hundred meters back of them, was bulling its way among the trees, crushing the undergrowth. Its sounds had been covered by lashing wind and the clanging from the factory.

"Look!" Ardàgh cried, pointing downward. The other machine had made a smart-right-angled turn and was climbing the slope.

Shirvanian stood up.

"What are you doing?"

"Keep your heads down!" There was a pop, and pieces of spy-eye fell in shivers of metal and glasstex around the pole.

"We've got to get out—"

"There." Shirvanian pointed to a copse southward. "Transmitter's on."

They scrambled, Yigal light on his feet over the loose shale between the thickets in spite of his load, the others sliding and grasping. It was not until they had reached the illusory shelter of the growth that they realized Shirvanian was not with them. He was standing on the rim near the pole, head turning to watch one and the other of the machines about to pincer him.

"That transmitter's not working!" Sven yelled. They were far too close, twenty meters, fifteen. Shirvanian paid Sven no attention, kept his eyes on one, then the other, lids narrowed, smiling faintly, ineffably smug. He took his eyes off them long enough to turn the knob of his control and stood still with his arms raised slightly from his sides, powerful and a little repulsive, the prodigy in velvet and ruffles about to lift the baton to the giant steps of Beethoven's Seventh.

"He'll get mashed," Mitzi whispered.

Ten meters, five, gathering speed toward the rim's top, and he stepped away.

The machines crashed horridly head on, and he ran, tripping and stumbling, to where the others were huddled. Echoes were still ringing, the ergs' grapplers wrenched and twisted in efforts to free themselves, they seemed to be embracing, were in fact wedded.

"Biggest ones I ever worked on," said Shirvanian.

They did not dare call him showoff. His horrifying risks had paid off. Mitzi's teeth chattered, Joshua's skin was grayish, Koz's fists were clenched and pressed together. "We'd better get down to the hangar," Joshua said.

"Then they'll be after us by the hundreds. I want them busy up here. You can go over where the channel breaks through at the western edge."

Esther said, "I think we'll stick together."

"I can take care of this by myself."

"There's been a few things you couldn't take care of by yourself," Ardagh said grimly.

Shirvanian shrugged irritably. They kept their eyes on the locked and struggling machines. The flanks were pocked with rust, and water channels ran down them in crazy patterns.

"You can't handle many more of those," said Sven.

The machines stopped suddenly, their arms flipped and rang on their sides. Shirvanian turned off his power. "They won't send them. They'll send repair crews, and I want a lot of them. Listen . . ."

Rain, wind . . . *rrrackticktick!*

A little thing scuttled up the slope, a spiny echidna, it's limbs were screwdrivers, metal punches, wire clippers, magnetic clamps, pliers.

"That's what they'd send after us. They'd pick us to pieces, like those bats we saw in the forest . . ."

ticktick . . . racktick! A second and a third trimmer crossed the edge. They swarmed the huge metal bulks like insects.

"They'd never get those things apart," said Ardagh.

"They could," Sven said. "I've seen them."

Mitzi whispered, "Isn't it time to go?"

"Not for me," said Shirvanian. Mitzi pushed a couple of knuckles in her mouth and bit. "Go on," he said.

"We'll stay," said Sven.

rricktick. Two more. They pried, chiseled, levered.

"They'll turn on us," said Koz. His teeth were clenched.

"If they got them apart they'd call a drone, and then we'd have them on us," said Shirvanian. "But they won't. I want more up here. Keep them busy."

tick. Six, seven, a dozen, ants in metal carapaces with savage antennas. Probed, wrenched the stalled ergs. "When I yell *Go!* run down to the hangar."

"We'll run into more of them below," Sven said.

"If this works they won't be interested in you." He turned up again, fingered the control delicately.

The trimmers went on working, not faster, but more forcefully; the mist eddied around them. Occasionally one would waver, with screwdriver or chisel, before plunging it at the wreckage.

ticktick. Three, four, five. The great ergs were crawling with small ones.

Shirvanian rotated with thumb and finger. The trimmers stove, wrenched, twisted. Their noise, an armored battle, drowned every other sound. He sat like a boy at the shore watching crabs in mating dance. Turn. The tools became weapons that ravaged the metal bulks.

Shirvanian licked his lips. And the small things came, like lemmings to the sea. The big servos were almost invisible under their dreadful crew. What could be seen glittered in edges of ripped metal. The trimmers began to attack the layers of their fellows beneath, with sounds to make the teeth ache.

Koz backed away in a scrabble of hands and heels, the *kek-kek-kek* of hysteria rising in his throat. Ardagh followed and put her arms around him.

Sven said, "Shirvanian."

The boy did not hear, or did not choose to listen.

"That's enough!"

"I can make them and I can break them," said Shirvanian.

Sven stood up. "I said, that's enough, Shirvanian!" The boy did not move.

"We'll get out now," Sven said.

"Yah." Esther hopped over to Mitzi. "Take some of the packs off Yigal. You can slide downhill easier than he can." Mitzi skittered away. Esther got out the machete, unwound it, and sliced the ropes that haltered Koz. "I'm taking a chance on you, do you hear?" She kissed him. He looked up at her with eyes of sudden clarity and awareness. "Maybe you'll do," she said. She wound the machete with a quick flip and hung it over her shoulder. Ardagh took Koz's hand and pulled him up, and they began to heft the discarded packs.

Sven said to Joshua, "You take his feet."

"Right."

Shirvanian sat oblivious before the writhing mass.

He had time for one yelp as Sven grabbed him from behind, clasping with two palms the hand that held the control, locking it in place. The other two arms went around his waist, and Joshua had him by the feet. Shirvanian writhed and shrieked, but they went over the edge, sliding downhill in a Laocoön tangle beside Koz, Mitzi, and Ardagh, who were alternately skittering on the dry plant stems or rolling like rag bales with their bundles whacking about them.

Esther jumped on Yigal and howled him into a gallop along the rim southeast toward the channel; she held up the machete with its fluttering rag, a hallucinatory black figure of Time or Death on a white mount. At the base of the next spy-eye standard she pulled at his horn, yelling, "Stop!" and reached out—

"Don't, Esther, it's—"

—and grabbed the pole with her free hand. It was not electrified. "Find the others!" He skipped down, white streak sinking into yellow smog, and she climbed three-limbed, holding the machete. At the top she swung the blunt edge at the spy-eye. It popped at the same time the worn blade snapped; she shrank away from flying pieces, flung down the useless tool, climbed down, sprang over the littered ground and went downhill head pulled in knees up and arms wrapped about them arse over teakettle.

They picked themselves up, coughing in the miasma. Ardagh was limping and Mitzi spitting blood from a bitten tongue. Sven's wound had opened, staining his bandage and net shirt; one of his lower arms had wrenched, and he did not like moving it. Esther, a fuzz ball covered with dust and dry stems, unfolded herself and scuttled over to check Yigal, who was standing quite calm and clean. "You look disgraceful," he said.

"Hush! Where's Koz? Joshua?"

Both of them, graceful and athletic, were only a bit winded. Shirvanian, freed now, had flung himself face down in the mud, kicking and pounding with his fists, one of them still clutching the control. Two servicing ergs, much larger than the others, rolled by, heading for the battleground, and paid them no attention.

Sven cried, "Get up!"

"No!" Shirvanian howled.

Sven grabbed him, tucked him under two right arms. "Stop that stupid tantrum!"

Shirvanian waved his arm. "I'll break this!"

Sven picked it out of his fist, and dropped him. "You can't be controlling anything in that state." He turned back the dial and dropped the thing down his shirt front.

"You'll ruin it!" Shirvanian jumped up, eyes wide

with horror in his mud-painted face. "My box!
Where's my box!"

"In your bag," said Esther. "You'll get it when I
give it to you." She slung the bag over her shoulder.

"The hangar's over there," Joshua said. "It's so thick
here you can't—"

His mouth gaped; they whirled and found a tremendous drone bearing on them from behind. They
had not come unnoticed after all.

Shirvanian yelled, "Transmitter's off, and I don't
care! I don't care! Serves you right!"

Mitzi's face twisted, and with one clawing movement she ripped at Shirvanian's belly, tearing cloth,
tape and transmitter. The metal button came away in
crumbled pieces. It had not survived the trip downhill. "Broken!"

Esther yelled, "Get away! Run! Through the channel!"

How? The erg would crush them before they'd
gone ten meters.

Esther shrieked, the *yi-yi-yi* of her treetop call,
and leaped straight into the huge machine's sensor
complex.

"Esther!" Yigal ran after, and a swinging limb
glanced his head. He fell and lay twitching. Sven
jumped forward and hauled him away with supreme
effort. The others did not run; they screamed and
were rooted.

The erg stopped. Its limbs reached, clawed, and
clashed together; Esther was not there. She swung,
screeching with rage, from one to another, dancing
on wire probes, butting her heels at lenses, whirling in
figure-eights around gripper tentacles till they tied
themselves in knots grabbing for her. She was a bee, a
fly, a whip, a dancing black chromosome. How long
did she have? An eternity of ten seconds. Less. A second erg was bearing toward them out of the mist.

Shirvanian gagged and swallowed, reached out

blindly toward Sven. Touched him. "Give it to me! Please! Give it to me."

Sven dug in his shirt and handed over the control. Shirvanian did not even look at it. Mitzi sobbed, "All right, you sonofabitch! You better show!"

Shirvanian did not hear. Esther ducked, grabbed, swung like a pendulum, as if she were in some giant testing ground in Dahlgren's lab and knew where the next attack would come, a centimeter away from miscalculation, an instant from the second erg . . .

Shirvanian turned up to the limit, closed his eyes and prayed, perhaps to Vulcan or whatever other world's Great Artificer he fancied.

Three seconds. The erg, both ergs, slowed . . . slowed . . . slowed . . . did not stop but retarded, delayed, moved in slow motion. Creeping, trancelike, moved . . .

Esther jumped down. "Yigal!"

He pulled himself to his feet, shook his head. "All right, it's all right."

"Then run! For God's sake, run!"

Now they could outpace ergs. Esther jumped to Sven's shoulder, panting. Joshua grabbed one of Yigal's horns and urged the dizzy beast; the others slung their packs and ran toward the hangar.

Inside the broad doorway darkness, silence, stillness. They fell against the wall, gasping. Row upon row of machines, deserted by their servicers, waited, every size and shape imaginable.

To the mist had been added the fumes of machine oil. Ardagh coughed and rubbed her runny nose. "Where's the transports?"

Shirvanian whimpered, "I can't see!" His nose was bloody and he had the beginnings of a black eye.

"Those things—are still coming," Esther puffed.

"Some of this stuff is stripped down." Shirvanian pointed as his pupils opened in the dimness. "Those are just empty casings."

Sven swung his head. "I don't see transports. Nothing."

"Look!" cried Shirvanian.

Fifth in rank against the western wall there was one transport, nearly hidden behind some other machine's tanklike mass. It was hard to miss, once spotted, painted freshly in yellow and green diagonal stripes in sharp contrast to the dented and crusted flanks of the other ergs. It was a huge oblong, almost as big as the house had been.

"That's the Argus!"

Shirvanian headed for it.

"Stay away! It's got to be booby-trapped!"

"I know," said Shirvanian. "We've got about two minutes." Noises from the factory were blocked here, but not the rumbling of the slowly approaching ergs.

Esther looked the thing up and down. "They want us to pick it. They must think we're ninnies."

"Can you tell where the traps are?" Sven asked.

Shirvanian touched his nose and stared at the blood, then rested his hand gingerly on the striped metal, leaving a smear. "The one we're supposed to find, if we got this far, is on the axle beside the right rear tread. You can see the wire hanging down. The one that's supposed to kill us is in the voice activator under the control deck." He dropped to his knees on the greasy floor, gave a pull here and there, and brought out something that looked like one of his own crazy rigs. He offered it to Sven. "Don't let those wires touch. That's not a dud."

"What the hell do I want it for?"

"We may need a bomb."

"How do I keep the wires apart?"

"With your head! Roll up the wires separately on each side, and put the thing in my bag."

"Like to drop it down his pants," Esther growled.

Shirvanian nipped around the back. "Door's open." His voice rang hollow. "I need a screwdriver."

"You drove them all crazy."

"And there's no time!" Sven yelled.

"No, they left the screws out. That's handy. They're on the floor." He came out holding a similar mess of wires and bulbs. "Same kind of thing. They repeat themselves."

"Shirvanian!" The walls vibrated with the noise of grinding ergs.

"Come on in," said Shirvanian. "It's all yours."

They scrambled aboard, and Sven ran to the control deck and pushed buttons he had not thought of touching for nine years.

Will there be fuel? Electricity? He picked up the microphone.

"Argus . . ." He pulled out the tiny sensor bulb on its wire thread and stuck it under his tongue where it took a second to identify his temperature and saliva.

HELLO, SVEN. The voice of Dahlgren boomed and echoed around the hangar. HOW ARE YOU TODAY? Shuddering, Argus came alive.

"Very well, thank you, Argus." His voice shook; quarter-tank of fuel, working power cells.

WHERE SHALL WE GO NOW, SVEN? The drones roared along the walls.

"Headquarters, Argus, fast as you can!"

HOME, SVEN? Argus's ceiling lights flicked on.

"Head—yes, home, Argus, home—and hurry!"

Argus swerved out of rank and skidded down the laneway, pushing his passengers to the walls.

Shirvanian was squatting on the floor. "Leave the doors open!" he shouted. "Mitzi, give me your lighter." He had ripped a piece off his torn shirt and twisted the bomb's wires around it so they did not touch.

Argus bulled through the door, skinning the corner of the erg come to meet him. The erg swung about and followed.

"Faster!" Shirvanian screeched. He held the lighter

ready; he was sure the bomb was meant to blast the interior and occupants of Argus and not half a hangar full of ergs, but he wanted space. The drone had not picked up full power, but it was five meters away, the second one following.

Six, seven.

Shirvanian lit the rag. It was fire-resistant, but carried enough flame to begin melting the wire casings.

He hurled it.

It did not hit the erg; the erg caught it in a claw and threw it back.

It flew through the open door of the Argus and bounced in front of Shirvanian. The children screamed.

Except for Koz.

He picked it up and flashed a smile, the first any of them had seen on his face, and as the screaming and babbling went on he jumped lightly out of the bouncing Argus, landed easily on the rubble as if he had trained for this moment all his life, and clasping the bomb over his heart in both hands like one bearing a gift, ran toward the erg.

Flesh and metal joined in the blast. The erg, front end hammered in, slewed its treads in Koz's blood and bones, and stopped. The one following crashed it.

Argus closed his doors and ran the channel out of the pit and mist.

22

WHY WERE YOU USING THE COMPUTER?

Dahlgren in his room on a chair, erg-Queen before him, servo behind, erg-Dahlgren against the wall stiff as a toy soldier.

He regarded her with great insolence. Perhaps she recognized it; she reached out a claw, grasped and twisted his arm behind his back. His arthritic bones grated and he screamed.

WHY WERE YOU USING THE COMPUTER?

"Because it is mine," he whispered, shuddering with pain. His arm hung.

IT IS NO LONGER YOURS. YOU HAVE NO STORE. WHAT CALL SIGNAL DID YOU USE? She reached for his arm again. He winced, and the servo looped a coil around his neck.

"Yours."

HOW DID YOU KNOW THAT?

"It is only your name. I thought you might use your name."

WHO TOLD YOU MY NAME?

His lips trembled.

"I told him," said erg-Dahlgren mildly. She whirled. "That is no secret. He had never seen an erg of your model and he asked."

She faced Dahlgren again, and he looked up at her, wherever her intelligence might lie, behind those jeweled buttons or below the spiky crown. His humiliation was intense. His world and his station

158

ripped from him, he was being tormented in the place that held all the privacy he had left, where he ate and slept. His cage. Cage. He had manipulated flesh, flexed limbs. But I did not do that to torment. Did you not, Dahlgren? Only to be powerful.

YOU USED IT IN MY NAME . . .

"Why do you not ask the computer?"

She did. She was its terminal. MOD 85.

IDENTIFY.

CREATOR MATRIX ONE.

WHAT IS YOUR REQUEST, CREATRIX?

WHAT IS IN THE STORE: EDVALG?

EDVALG IS DEACTIVATED.

DO YOU HAVE A SUB-STORE IN THE NAME OF CREATOR MATRIX ONE UNDER CODE DAHLGREN?

NO.

She tapped Dahlgren's arm. WHAT CODE DID YOU USE? The coil tightened on his neck.

"SVENSSEN."

SPELL IT.

"S-V-E-N-S-S-E-N."

MOD 85, TELL ME WHAT IS IN THE STORE: SVENSSEN?

IF THIS CODE: SVENSSEN IS USED HEREAFTER AT ANY TIME BY ANY MACHINE OR ANY PERSONAGE OF ANY ORDER, RANK OR NUMBER YOU ARE TO SCAN THE PULSE RATE OF THE MAN EDVARD DAHLGREN AS MONITORED AND RECORDED BY MODAL 1 DURING THE TWO HOURS PREVIOUS TO USE OF THIS CODE AND IF THE HEARTBEAT OF THE MAN EDVARD DAHLGREN WITHIN THAT TWO-HOUR PERIOD EXCEEDS FOR ANY TWO CONSECUTIVE MINUTES A RATE OF ONE HUNDRED AND TWENTY-FIVE BEATS PER MINUTE THIS STORE IS TO BE ERASED.

Erg-Queen ranged her arms along her sides. IS THIS STORE ERASED?

NO.

WHAT IS THE HIGHEST RATE OF HEARTBEAT RECORDED DURING THAT PERIOD?

ONE HUNDRED AND TWENTY-TWO.

THEN TELL ME WHAT IS IN THE STORE: SVENSSEN.
IDENTIFY KEY.

Erg-Queen stood immobile before Dahlgren. The servo's coil was tight around his neck and he saw the pulses of his own eyes, his heart slammed his chest. The coil withdrew from his neck, suddenly, and he coughed.

Erg-Queen spoke quietly, without echo. GIVE ME THE KEY, DAHLGREN. YOU WILL BE FORCED TO DO SO EVENTUALLY.

"I agree," said Dahlgren even more quietly. He had no breath to speak louder. "But by the time you have the key you will be obliged to contend not only with my pulse rate, but with my extra systoles, the effect of choking on my brain rhythms, perhaps even my death—and then there will be no store: SVENSSEN. Force me if you will."

WHY HAVE YOU DONE THIS, DAHLGREN?

"To frustrate you."

She plucked the wrist of his wrenched left arm and he cringed, he could not help himself. She dropped the wrist and wheeled out of the room, the servo clanking after.

"Now what will she do?" he asked.

"I expect she will chase the store: SVENSSEN around the computer for a while, and perhaps she will find it, perhaps not. We are safe for the moment." Erg-Dahlgren remained standing against the wall, arms behind his back. "Whatever it was that I had to forget, I have forgotten. You have done this for me, Dahlgren, but I did not mean for you to be hurt."

Dahlgren let his head fall back and closed his eyes. "Don't think of it."

Erg-Dahlgren came forward and carefully lifted Dahlgren to the bed. "What may I do for you?"

Pain up neck to head, down arm to fingers. Dahlgren said, "Well, a glass of akvavit would—but I doubt you will find it here."

"What is that?"

"An alcoholic drink I enjoyed as a young man in my homeland."

"I see. I will find you something for the pain."

Dahlgren listened to the heavy step of his erg moving out the door and down the hall. No guard stopped him. Nowhere to run.

One arm's pain engulfed a whole body. Arm. Sven had four. Arms.

Four.

Why did you not use my wife's ova?

THERE WERE ONLY FOUR.

You knew even that.

Dahlgren, said Haruni, *this may not be so good a thing to do.*

I must have. I must have. Something. She left me with nothing. God knows I have enough sperm.

But only four ova.

1. Broke and disintegrated when thawed.

2. Infertile.

3. Fertilized and implanted in section of uterine lining maintained in vitro, soon engulfed in quickgrowing placental tumor arising from nowhere.

4. Sven.

Three-month embryo, six-limbed, a pulsing tiny lizard. A teratological monster.

My God, can't you do something? Why didn't you tell me before?

We hoped we could—Who would want to tell you? But—

What do you expect, Dahlgren? Cut out a whole cross section? A third of the heart and half the lungs and liver? Best to abort.

None left. Nothing. No. "Do. Something!"

Try cloning.

Clones have nothing of her!

Whispers . . . *stimulate rhomboid, latissimus dorsi and . . .*

Haruni, sad-eyed. *You see . . .*

This has never happened before. Why now?

You never knew if it happened before, Dahlgren. No one has said. This is the one you have been watching.

Every day by infrascope. The red worm, red lizard clenches. Double-budded in arm. Six-limbed.

Eddy of laughter in corner: *Good thing it's a boy, some girl with four tits . . .*

By God, you fool, that would be the she-wolf of some Romulus and Remus, I swear it.

Someone has done. No no, not Haruni, one friend, who plays chess and pins insects. Paranoid, Dahlgren. But someone. Laughers? Whisperers?

THERE WERE ONLY FOUR.

You knew even that.

Someone. He sighed.

"Does it still hurt so badly, Dahlgren?"

Eyes slitted, he saw erg-Dahlgren, needle in hand, push back his sleeve and inject.

Pain clawed again. "I had forgotten it," he whispered.

Erg-Dahlgren threw away the needle, lifted Dahlgren's head, brought a cup to his lips.

"What is that?"

"Edible alcohol. I had it synthesized for you."

"Good Lord, man, that is pure hellfire! Add an equal amount of water."

"I am sorry, Dahlgren. I did not know how men drink."

"No. Thank you. I am grateful." It was good, going down, it made a hearth in his belly. Little taste to it, but it was good enough. Pain ebbing and the hearth-fire spreading even to the source of the life that might last, oh God, long enough to do battle.

Erg-Dahlgren smiling, because Dahlgren had called him man.

23

Argus was four meters high and wide, seven in length. Up front he had a control room, a lavatory cubicle, and a crew quarters with four narrow bunks. In back the room for carrying animals had brackets for holding cages, tanks and other enclosures, though all these had been removed. Narrow guttering coursed the floors in a flushing and drainage system; most of his lower bulk held retractable wheels and runners, tool kits, waste compactors, and two engines: one a hay-burner that could use any kind of organic matter, including fossil fuels, the other a diesel with fuel tanks for oil and kerosene. He was the least sophisticated of all machines on Dahlgren's World, and the most adaptable.

Shirvanian slept on the guttered floor among bags of moss, mouth-breathing harshly, snorting a bit through his swollen nose; Yigal lay beside him. Ardagh, Mitzi, Joshua, had cried themselves out with fear and weariness as well as grief, and were sprawled on the jouncing floor, backs to the wall. Their eyes were red, their faces sweaty and dirt-smeared. Joshua had a light haze of beard and looked years older. They were too tired to climb into the bunks for comfort. They did not think of comfort. There was no place in the world to find it.

The counter in the control room registered .9 millirads internally, a great improvement over the external
one, which was running near .8 rad. Sven had found
the stores of water and air filter capsules, untouched
through the years. The heavy clay interiors of one or
two had crumbled or been attacked by organisms; the
others might take them as far as they needed to go.
Argus had only one window, in his control room, a
round port of thick yellow lead glass. It did not give
much of a view, but the telescreen was working.

"Sooner or later they'll jam that," said Esther. She
was riding on Sven's shoulder as he watched Argus
pushing ahead on the detritus from the channel, scanning for changes in terrain that would require the
shift to wheels or tractor tires.

"No, that's independent, but we'll probably have to
disconnect the transmitter . . . They'll send drones,
five-fifties, aircars. We're a beautiful striped target."

"No way to camouflage . . . if we put leaves and
branches on top, maybe the aircars . . ."

"The growth's too fine and brittle. That'd ruin the
intake system." Argus's roof was a catchment basin,
covered with fine mesh, for collecting and filtering
water and air. "When Shirvanian gets up we'll see
what he can think of."

They did not talk of Koz. What use? Esther could
not cry, and Sven would not.

There was another problem. Because Argus had
been bonded to a boy of ten his control, for safety's
sake, was limited in speed and direction, and Sven
did not know where to find or how to use the override
controls allocated to regular crews on working mis-
sions. He had had nearly an hour's head start at about
8 kph. It was not much to build on. Top speed would
not take that lumbering transport much higher than
twelve. Sven had spent a frustrating hour trying to
explain to Argus the importance of that extra four

kilometers. Argus would not believe that all other machines were enemies.

YOU MUSTN'T PLAY DANGEROUS GAMES, SVEN. DAHLGREN WILL BE ANGRY.

"Argus, for God's sake, all other machines are renegade!"

I KNOW, SVEN, the Dahlgren speaker said. WE'VE PLAYED THAT MANY TIMES.

Sven swore and kicked the panel, until he remembered he had done that as a child too, and turned red. "Better wake Shirvanian."

Shirvanian's face was bruised, grimy, creased with strain. His eyelids twitched in sleep. Esther's heart wrenched for him, in spite of his transparent unpleasantness. She did not want to wake him. His arms were flung out, one hand clutching his box. Esther saw through the rent in his shirt that his hairless armpit was tattooed with one small triskelion. She looked up. Her eyes met Ardagh's.

Ardagh said dully, "Yeah. He's one of us."

Us. "Will he become like Koz?"

"No . . . oh, no! He belonged to a different order."

"Of delinquents, you mean. What'd Shirvanian do, make one machine too many?"

Joshua laughed, weakly, bitterly. "When he was six he built a robot to steal cookies and repair parts for itself. His parents found it, and it set the whole scientific world in an uproar. Made him famous. We didn't believe him when he told us, but we do now." He closed his eyes, shook his head and sighed. "Oh yes, we do."

"But he went too far . . . ?"

Ardagh said, "At nine he had a whole fleet of them ripping off components all over Sol Three and selling them at wholesale prices. He could have retired at twelve if he wasn't found out."

Arms akimbo, Esther hunkered beside the child.

"And look where it got you." Black eye, blood-caked nose. She slapped his cheek lightly. "Wake up, genius. Sven wants you up front."

Shirvanian stirred, opened his eyes with some effort, lifted his head, giving the involuntary sneer of the gesture. "Wah?" He seemed stunned.

"Sven needs you up front," Esther repeated.

"Uh." Shirvanian dragged himself up and lurched off, slamming his shoulder against the wall as he went.

"Shame to wake him . . ." She turned back to the others. They were well knocked about. Not much rebellion left. "You had some independent plans? Hope you put them aside."

Joshua asked under his brooding lids, "How did you know?"

"Triskelions. You got lumped together, somehow, did all that planning. Why would you stop? Look." She touched Joshua's zipper tag. "Carelessness? Mitzi's boot soles. Why didn't you throw those away?"

"I made them," said Mitzi. There was a pinch of pride in her voice, the only flavor of that quality Esther had ever found in her.

"And you kept them clean in all the mud—even the soles."

"What are you going to do about us?" Ardagh asked.

"Try to keep you safe, what else? You've had enough battered out of you for a while." She gave her attention to the snoring Yigal, stroked his flank as it rose and fell. "Let him sleep a bit longer."

Shivanian yawned. "Attach my spy-eye to the visual system so you can get a whole-horizon view."

"Okay, but where are the crew controls?"

"Likely behind this panel. We'll have to stop so I can work on it."

"I don't like that much . . . the radio's off so they can't pick us up, but—"

"Shut down the visuals and intercom too, just in case, and make a detour."

"Navigate with that one little window?"

"Yah. I'm surprised we haven't had aircars after us yet. You shouldn't have let me sleep so long."

"I thought you'd fall apart if you didn't. Maybe there's some lead suits in that cupboard. Take a look."

"Just one," Shirvanian reported. "My size, but it's got four sleeves."

"Sven!" Esther bounded through the door. She was shaking more than the bouncing of the craft accounted for. "Sven! Yigal is—"

"Keep on course, Argus, to track two and east." He hung up the mike. "What—"

Yigal was gasping and vomiting, his limbs twitched. His eyes were still closed. Ardagh had his huge head on her lap, stroking it as the thin bile ran over her boots.

"What is it?"

Her eyes met his, and Esther's; she swallowed. "He got knocked on the head, didn't he?"

"Yes, but he got up, and he was—he seemed all right."

She pushed up Yigal's eyelids with her thumbs. The eyes were blank, glazed, almost all pupil. She slid her fingers around the skull, through the silky hair. "Not even a bruise."

"Yigal!" Esther cried.

He gasped and shivered. His slack tongue lay along his teeth. "He won't have much more to throw up. If we heap the sacks in the corner and try to make him comfortable, maybe we can clean this part up." Ardagh stroked his muzzle gently, as if her fingers could stop the twitching nerves. "We'll have his urine and—and stuff to contend with."

"Contend with!" Esther screamed and slapped her face. Sven grabbed her.

Ardagh's cheek reddened and her eyes filled with

tears. "I can't help it, Esther," she whispered. "He's dying."

Esther exploded from Sven's arms and flung herself, X, over the white heaving body. "No!"

Sven knelt beside them. "Just from that bang on the head?"

Ardagh said, "He must be hemorrhaging inside . . . In a hospital, in the lab they could . . ."

Yigal lifted his head with fearful slowness; it wavered with the bouncing of the carrier. Slowly his eyes opened, his vague pupils tightened, only a little. His tongue moved, ticked the roof of his mouth. "Es— Esther, I can't." His head fell back, lids closed, he retched again.

Esther clenched shaking fists in the hair of his neck and screamed. Mitzi clapped hands over her ears and shut her eyes, Joshua drew up his steep knees and wrapped his arms about them. Yigal did not speak again, then or ever.

Ardagh went on stroking the shuddering head, and Sven knelt with the thin bile stream sliding in the guttering under his knees.

Shirvanian yelled, "We have a skimmer coming southeast by east!"

Sven jumped to his feet and ran up front. "How far?" On the screen it was a dot above the horizon.

"About three kilometers."

"That's the end. We're finished."

"Turn westward into that gully where it's overgrown."

Sven gave the orders to Argus blindly.

"Now stop. Open the door. Shut off all systems. Why are you crying? Are you scared?"

"Yigal is dying from that blow on the head." Tears ran into the corners of his mouth.

"Oh." Shirvanian scuttled back, ignored all others, pawed through the sacks on the floor in frantic haste till he found the other bomb, ran back to the control room where the outer door was open, tore yet another strip from his diminishing garment, twined it in a wick as he had done before, and fumbled in his pockets till he found Mitzi's lighter.

"You can't blow up that egg," Sven said.

"I don't intend to." Bomb in hand, Shirvanian jumped out the door.

"Shirvanian!" Horrified, Sven leaned out.

"Shut up. I know what I'm doing." Shirvanian followed Argus's tracks in the damp gravel for about fifteen meters, watched the sky, counting silently with his lips, lit the wick, waited till it began to burn down, hurled it with all his strength northward, ran back with arms pumping and hair streaming, jumped in. "Shut the door!"

The metal egg sang overhead *zzing!* An instant of silence, *WHUMP!* A sizzle and a hum fading.

Mitzi, at the inner door, shrieked, "What is it?"

"An aircar," Sven said. He slid open the control-room door, jumped to the ground, Shirvanian following.

Back up their trail was a black fused star of glassy rock, crossed exactly by a long charred streak. The air reeked and shimmered. "What happened?" Sven asked.

"Once our transmission was off it had to home on heat or light. I gave it an intense source to distract it."

"The fire hit it exactly. I thought you said they were clumsy."

"I thought they might be, but I was wrong. They were trying to put us off guard, or your transmitter made the drones keep them away."

"We've got no more bombs."

"If we're lucky it recorded a hit. You think you could figure out their codes if I took a chance on the radio?"

"I could if they haven't changed them for nine years."

"I don't see why they should. They didn't need secret codes." He pushed toggles and the little read-out screen lit up and flickered. "Huh. GalFed symbols. Too bad we can't reach a spacelight."

"Think they'd waste an interstellar radio on a transport that does twelve kph at top speed?"

"BZV GFX 178," Shirvanian translated. "That's—"

Barrazan Five, GalFed Experimental. The original aircars were designated one-seven-five to two hundred. They must be using the old system."

"And that squiggle?"

"Is our code for call. There it is on that key."

"MOD 777 . . . reporting right to the top, and X . . . 933 . . ."

"Nine-three-three is Argus, and X, I suppose, marks the spot."

"I hope it holds them." The screen went blank, and Shirvanian shut off. "We might as well stay here and do the work. Once we're heading east it'll be too sticky." He looked up. "Where you going?"

"To see Yigal."

"I'll need you on the mike."

"Don't worry," he could not keep the edge out of his voice. "I'll be back."

Mitzi was waiting by the bunkroom door, hair wild and fingers clawing the air. "I can't stand it!" she wailed. "Esther's screaming over that beast and she won't let go!"

"Go in and rest on a bunk. Are you hungry?"

"No! I'm sick!"

"Lie down."

In the rear quarters he found Ardagh crying, trapped under the shuddering bulk of Yigal, Esther flung over him screaming rage and grief through her teeth. Joshua, backed into a corner, was folded tightly in on himself, blinking and silent.

Sven lifted Yigal's head and shoulders to free Ardagh. "Get into the bunkroom."

"But I—"

"You can't help. Go on. You too, Joshua."

He knelt beside the two people he had loved so deeply all his life, ran a hand down Yigal's neck, a hand over Esther's head. A little blood was clotting darkly in Yigal's nostrils and at the corners of his mouth. In a loving useless gesture he pushed bags under the big head; then he uncoiled a hose pipe from the wall and flushed the cleared area of the floor.

Esther stopped screaming, picked herself off Yigal, and sat beside him. She watched the breath fluttering his lax pale tongue. She pushed open one of his lids as if she might find his gruff stodgy spirit in the dark pool of his eye. Her own lids were thickened and inflamed. "Nothing can be done."

Sven did not even shake his head.

She said, "There's another triskelion you'll want to know about. Tattooed in Shirvanian's armpit." She bent down to stroke Yigal's head. "Not a type like Koz. He had an operation going, stole and sold machine parts."

"I'll watch them."

"Larcenous brats. Stupid to like them, eh?"

He was afraid, but mainly for her, sorrow glassing her eyes.

"I wonder . . . how long, do you think?"

"Esther, I don't know."

"The crew controls are here, all right, but they've also got sensors and monitors for i.d. You know who the crews were?"

"Usually a couple from Barnard Three. They had eight limbs and smelled of formic acid."

"Then I'll have to reroute to get our extra four kilometers." He added in a small voice, "The next one will probably get us, you know. I don't have any more tricks up my sleeve."

In one sense, I'm glad of that, Sven thought. But he

couldn't say it to this idiot savant who had saved his life so many times. A small child, exhausted and fearful, who had cried for Mama. "Can you do the work before nightfall?"

"Nothing I'd want anybody to see, but it'll operate."

"Because we're going to run night and day and stand watches. We don't dare go on automatic."

"We can monitor the radio that way at least, maybe get some warning . . . we're nearly out of liquid fuel."

"Then we start sweeping and compacting scrub, and waste, too, so we can switch to the hayburner. I'll make supper. If the heat-chamber still works."

Muddy stew, tasting of old plastic boiling bags. They choked it down while the sun fell; they had nothing to say.

Sven stood first watch as Argus navigated on infrared, installed originally not to disturb forest life. Now, perhaps, it might not arouse ergs. He did not feel much comfort in being dry for the first time in days as the familiar lightning streaked and the rains lashed the trees. Yet he dared himself to remember, dreamed himself back to a time that seemed in comparison sweet.

"Sweep and pack, Argus. Fill the tanks. Our enemies never give up."

NO, SVEN. THEY SEEM TO COME FROM NOWHERE.

But they had come from everywhere around him, docile ergs. They had grown themselves souls, like Esther and Yigal. *Another Dahlgren, so he can twist things out of shape.* And he had. Sane Dahlgren, who had given his voice to his son's game. HOME, SVEN?

The house in the forest, its plots and hutches. *Eat, sweetheart.*

THE BINS ARE FULL, SVEN. WHAT NOW?

"Steady as you go to track two."

AND EAST THEN? HOME?

"And east." Point nine on the counter and nowhere to go but up.

24

Erg-Queen did not waste a millisecond chasing the store: SVENSSEN around the computer; she simply considered briefly whether Dahlgren in seven years of crawling and puking and howling like a mad dog through the vaults had learned anything worth storing, and decided that he had not; he had wished to frustrate her: that was obvious. She gave orders to send the chessboard to his room and lock the door on him and his erg-brother to save herself further disturbance. Then she set her servos the problem of rerouting erg-Dahlgren's ten million microcircuits to minimize his eccentricity without spoiling everything that had been accomplished.

When Skimmer reported the hit on Argus she removed that problem from her list of priorities. Since they had swept Dahlgren's World seven orbits ago ergs had not engaged in battle situations. They had learned, from men, how to subvert men and keep secrets, but their exemplars had never waged open war. So ergs had experimented on animals and machines, had repaired and replaced, made Dahlgren's ship their own, shifted the drone patrols from serving the techs to keeping watch on Sven in the event that he might prove threatening or useful, to watching for meteors or crashes, keeping roads clean, servicing the odd stray ship. Even the aircars they had created were not attack vehicles but mainly burners to control overgrowth on tracks or factory grounds. Erg-

173

Queen saw the destruction and damage of several powerful machines by a few humans as a grave annoyance, but not a great marvel; she knew men were devious.

White Queen had taken Bishop and threatened Knight. Black Knight had retreated.

Dahlgren sighed. "I wish I could believe that we had accomplished something, but I wonder. Now we are locked in."

Erg-Dahlgren had nothing to say. He moved 16. KR-K1.

Dahlgren answered P-KB4.

"Opening your King," said erg-Dahlgren.

"King of the bone-orchard." Dahlgren laughed harshly. "And creating a phalanx." Four-armed Sven, monkey, goat . . . and oh, ten-year-old self-styled genius. "You see I can chase the Queen from here."

"If you can unlock the door," said erg-Dahlgren.

I have a key, a magic word. Shirvanian. It trembled on his lips. Magic? It worked when it chose. There was a world to unlock.

17. P-Q4. "That takes care of that," said erg-Dahlgren.

P-KB5. Eye to eye with White Queen, Pawn aslant from Bishop. "But I don't know where they are," Dahlgren muttered.

"At the red brick road," said erg-Dahlgren.

Dahlgren stared at him. "Oh my God, shut up!"

Erg-Dahlgren shook his head helplessly. "But Dahlgren, I have such odd th—"

"Think of something else!" Plug one leak . . .

"It has to do with what I was to forget." *18.* He pulled Bishop back to R2. "But there is a *being* that knows me, Dahlgren."

PxP. "Do you know what Mod Seven Seven Seven is doing?"

19. NxP. "Only what she tells me . . ."

Dahlgren played N-B2 to keep his Knight. "Do you know if she has tried to break into the store?"

"No. She has not contacted me since we were locked in. But Dahlgren, I am afraid. I have gone through *The Middle Game in Chess* a hundred times."

Dahlgren asked sourly, "Have you ever read *Chess in the Machine Age?*"

25

Toward midnight Argus made his turn eastward on track two, and a few minutes later began to thump and clang alarmingly.

The children woke and crowded into the control-room door, red-eyed and cranky. "What the hell is that?"

"Argus picking up loose bricks," Sven said without taking his eyes off the screen.

"Hey, Shirvanian, you better get to work on that."

"I wouldn't," Sven said. "We aren't sure what conditions are like out there. We may need to do some road-mending."

"How are we supposed to sleep?"

"When he gets the first layer down on the metal there won't be so much noise. Just the odd clunk. He hasn't got that much storage space."

"It puts on extra weight," said Joshua. "It'll slow us down."

"Not compared to the equipment he's got in his undercarriage already—tires, engines, fuel tanks, sweeper arms."

"Some crazy machine," said Mitzi. "Plays kid games and picks up bricks." She retired in disgust. The others followed, except Joshua.

"I'll take over. I should have started an hour ago."

"What's the difference? I couldn't sleep . . . I was thinking of Yigal."

Joshua set his narrow body in a corner of the small cabin and braced his feet against the lurching and thumping. He said slowly, "Nobody ever asked, and maybe it's not the right time . . . but . . . why a goat? I mean a goat who talks *lingua*, sounds like a philosophy professor, and likes Montaigne's essays? Surely it wasn't . . . it wasn't some kind of joke."

"No . . . a lot of things were pretty funny here, I mean compared to life on civilized worlds, what I've heard of them—but it was no joke. The goats were here for many years before the station was set up. Some colonists brought a few, because they're tough and can eat just about anything. When they lifted off they didn't bother taking them. By the time the crews came down to work here there was a big pack of them, all wild. Some got killed off when the area was cleared, and the rest escaped into the wilderness. Then they kept wandering back into the cultivated areas; they were fierce as wolves, and cunning too. And an awful nuisance because they mucked up the experimental plots and in the hot areas where they died of radiation, or when they didn't abort, mutated into terrible-looking things. Just before I was born there were maybe a dozen left . . . and one day somebody brought in a dam that was dying horribly trying to give birth, so they killed her and found the biggest kid they'd ever seen or heard of . . . I don't think he was even full term . . ."

"And that was Yigal?"

"Yeah . . . they had all this synthetic milk ready for

me—I was born a few days later, so . . . we were both
pretty odd-looking, so we got a lot of attention. He
was a gentle creature, not like the others. I used to
play in his straw . . . his skull was so big—I think his
brain measured something like eighteen hundred cc
at full growth—they thought he'd never be able to
hold his head up. But he did. They could tell right
away he was smarter than a dog, and one day somebody said, 'Here's your milk, Yigal,' and he said,
'Milk,' and everybody went wild. He talked before I
did."

"But how did he get from there to the essays of
Montaigne?"

"Oh . . . Dahlgren's idea of a liberal education. We
had tapes and cassettes but he never gave up books.
Yigal hung around with me and listened in, because
I learned to read on that stuff. He couldn't read—he
wasn't any Houyhnhnm—and I never read in French!
If we'd been using Solthree languages he'd never have
learned to speak. *Lingua* was designed for so many
different kinds of minds and speech organs, it's so
phonetically simple . . . Montaigne's a sensible man,
if you take him a page at a time and leave out a
couple of hundred quotes in Greek, Latin and Italian
. . . I guess . . . I guess his ideas fitted in with Yigal's
. . . view of the universe . . ." His mouth was twisting
uncontrollably.

"Let me take over now, Sven. I'll call you if I have
trouble."

Esther had dimmed the lights and was sitting silently beside Yigal, stroking, grooming, touching.

Sven lay on his side near them, propping up his
head on his two right hands. He realized that he had
a headache growing to an intense focus of pain at the
top of his skull, and his eyes hurt as if he had rubbed
sand into them.

Yigal breathed raspingly; occasionally he coughed.

"I don't think he feels anything," Esther said. "Do you?"

"No."

"I would have liked to be able to tell him he did well."

"He didn't need to be told."

"I needed to tell him."

Eventually she fell into a light doze with her head on Yigal's flank and her arms curved over him. She muttered once in a while, uninteilligible sounds like a forest animal's.

Sven tried to compose himself. Stared at the dim light. That hurt his eyes more, and the pain ran down his neck and into his arms and back. Why not two heads, Dahlgren? Would they both ache at the same time? Argus jerked and clanged. If they were riding Argus they'd both ache. Why not two transports instead of one, this old creaking box, vulnerable. Split the party up? Dangerous. One on automatic to use for a decoy? Wouldn't last long, and the wrong one might get hit. They only left us one, anyway, and at least it's the one I can control. Control! *mustn't play dangerous games, sven.*

Argus, for God's sake, those machines have gone renegade!

YES, SVEN. I UNDERSTAND.

Some game I get to play when that machine treats me like an idiot.

You are a boy playing games and it treats you like one, says Dahlgren.

Any time an aircar goes by I get radio messages, How's it going, Sven, catch any spies yet?

Dahlgren laughing, laughter so rare it should not have been wasted on ridicule. *You ought to wear a false moustache.*

And you're treating me the same way!

No, I'm not, Sven. I'm quite serious.

What's a moustache?

If I shaved the beard off my chin, the hair left on my lip would be called a moustache.

And I'd look pretty silly with that when I'm nine years old and I don't have any hair anyway.

You are too literal-minded, I think, like your father. I am not making fun of you. I very rarely do such things. I meant to suggest a disguise, something to keep you from being recognized, that would not put you or anyone else in danger.

Disguise? With four arms? Oh, bitter reproach . . .

I did not say that you should disguise your body, Sven . . .

He sat up and the pain hammered the top of his skull. He had drifted off. *With four arms?* Did I say such things? Or is that what I would tell him now?

But he gave me that . . . false moustache.

He stood up. Oh God, my head.

The children would have painkillers. Mitzi the peripatetic illegal Pharmaceutical Co. But they would be asleep, exhausted. Or maybe not. His head ballooned, he felt half-irrational, Esther muttering, Yigal snorting. Thunder rattled, or was it Argus? Tomorrow *Light the stove, Sven!* the mist will push in at the windows past the dripping thatch, Yigal will toss a cabbage on his horn and damn the east wind.

But he won't, he's dying. I am literal-minded, and I have the false moustache.

And the damnedest headache. And maybe . . . maybe they're awake, talking away the night and the fear.

There was an intercom switch to the bunkroom. His hand hesitated at it; eavesdropping. But if they were quiet, presumed asleep? He'd keep the headache. He pushed the switch—

Screech!

—and turned down the volume.

"—don't care! I can't stand that ape howling! The goat's dying, and that leaves two, and we can push them both out!"

Ardagh hissed, "Stop it, Mitzi! You're waking Shirvanian."

"Shit on him! He gives me the creeps too!"

"If you'd get to sleep you'd—"

"I can't sleep! That leftover from a geek show, all he's after is his Dahlgren and if they got the ship we'd end up in Central and not look like poor misunderstood kids either!"

Ardagh said gently, "We don't look like that right now—and I don't think we're going to get anywhere near the ship with or without them."

"We can try and do something! There's only two of them and there's four of us."

Sven stood with his head against the cold metal, crying like a big booby.

"Four? With big strong Shirvanian? Joshua just might be able to handle Esther, and I'm not sure of that. And Sven—"

"Him! He's so musclebound a good shove—"

"I thought you liked him, Mitzi." Ardagh's voice narrowed to a deadly edge. "What's the matter? Wasn't he any good?" Scuffle. "Don't you shoot your dirty nails at me or I'll break your wrists! I'm not the Ox for nothing!"

Sven slid the two doors that separated him from the bunkroom and with a pair of arms for each parted the scratching grunting figures; he gave each of them a hard impartial push and turned on the light.

Mitzi and Ardagh were glaring up at him from the floor, still so full of rage they did not even bother to rub the places they had hit when they went down. They had bathed and cleaned up as well as they could and did not look so much like weathered castaways any more, but beneath the anger their faces were ledgers of fear and weariness. Ardagh had a scratch on one cheek. Shirvanian was scrunched in a corner of his bunk, a shadow with large animal's eyes.

"I was listening in," Sven said.

Mitzi snarled, "Oh, sneaky!"

Sven leaned on the doorway and wiped down his face with two palms, steadied himself against the endless lurching with the others. "I have a terrible headache and was hoping if you were awake you might give me something for it."

Ardagh said through her teeth, "I don't get headaches."

Mitzi got up on her knees, slowly, found her cosmetics bag at the foot of her bunk, and thrust a pill at him. He washed it down with a handful of water in the lavatory without looking at it. He did not care at that moment whether it made him sick, sleepy, or dead. When he turned back to the girls Ardagh was picking herself up, Mitzi was still on her knees. "I want you to come into the control room for a minute. Shirvanian too."

Ardagh touched her cheek and muttered, "I've got to wash my face first."

"Yeah," Mitzi said. "You might get hydrophobia."

Ardagh grinned suddenly. "Only from bites, dear."

"Sorry."

The five made a tight fit in the cubicle. Joshua, eyes on the screens, said, "I thought I heard some noises. Was there something I should have done?"

"No. It would have been a risk." He picked up the mike. "Argus, we're putting on our false moustache."

RIGHT, SVEN. NINE-EIGHT-THREE IT IS.

"What's that?" Joshua asked.

"When I was a little kid, playing games with Argus out in the forest, the transports and aircars used to pick up my messages, ask for i.d. and say, 'Hey, Sven, is that you? Catch any pirates lately?' and break up laughing or clacking their mandibles or rattling their antennas. Maybe they thought I was a spoiled kid . . . but I got mad and complained to Dahlgren. After he finished laughing he gave me a disguise, what he called a false moustache, the i.d. and class of an old ore carrier that got knocked over by a falling tree in a storm when it was carrying a full load. After that it was only good for scrap, but nobody bothered to cross it off the register, and it was forgotten. Dahlgren remembered because he saw it happen . . . it looked a lot like Argus, and several other nine-eighties were running. Nobody ever questioned it. Dahlgren might have told them not to, so I'm not sure it'll work."

Shirvanian asked, "Did they ever do any refining at the station, any kind of factory there?"

"None that I know of."

"Then nine-eight-three has to be a parts carrier, not an ore carrier. And if we meet anybody we have to pick up and challenge them first, before they attack on spec."

"You're right. I hadn't thought of that."

Mitzi yawned elaborately. "Is that all you wanted to say?"

"No," Sven said. "I've hardly got started. Shirvanian may realize but you don't that the ship at the station headquarters isn't one of those little things that you jump in and push a button, like the one you came in. It brought everything here, and was bedded in a silo, and hasn't lifted off more than two or three times since, to bring in more equipment. It takes dozens of crew and can't move without them. We had a shuttle for transporting workers, but the ergs broke it up when some of the people were trying to escape in it. They may have built another, and that would be an erg. The big ship, if they plan to use it, will certainly be an erg by now.

"The radio will be in their control. They've probably been sending out fake messages and reports for years, or GalFed would be here by this time, and we

wouldn't. There's no way for me to find Dahlgren
and let you stumble around looking for the ship and
radio, no way we could work as separate parties.
Everything we're heading toward is behind one solid
wall of ergs. Whatever you're afraid of going back to,
outworld, has got to be very pale compared to that."

Joshua said wearily, "Then what's the use of all
this?"

"Maybe nothing. But it was you who wanted to do
it, and we're doing it. And Esther and I . . . and Yigal,
are running and dodging instead of letting ergs creep
up on us while we grow old or go crazy. Maybe—
maybe it's not such a bad thing for machines to become . . . people. But they have to become people we
can live with. They can't be allowed to kill everyone
else in the district while they're creating themselves."
He grinned at the expression on Ardagh's face. "You
think I sound like a Dahlgren? Then I'll bring up my
last point. This thing, this Argus," he stretched out his
arms and they ducked, "is mine, no matter what kind
of rattletrap you think it is. It belongs to me, Sven
Adolphus Dahlgren, son of Edvard Dahlgren. You can
forget the Adolphus, but you'd better remember the
rest when you're feeling feverish and want to go off
alone. It's mine. It won't move without my permission.
I didn't have access to the crew controls, but when-
ever I turned it in I had to give directions allowing
particular crews to use it. Sometimes I forgot and was
dragged out in the middle of the night to do it. Remember, no Sven, no Argus. Put a knife to my throat,
you'll have to cut it. That's all."

He went back to Esther and Yigal. His head, at
least, did not ache so much as his heart.

Esther was tapping at his cheek, pulling a wrist.

He woke thinking he had been awake tumbling in a
kaleidoscope of horror. He found it. Yigal, bronchial
tubes already thickened from wet weather, was chok-

ing on blood and saliva. His body heaved and thrashed. Esther grasped him with all limbs as though she might by main force pull him into life, or re-create him through her will. When he quieted in a few moments with a trembling sigh, a small exhalation of blood, he was dead.

Esther pulled away at once and stood up. "Wash that stuff off him."

Sven hosed down his muzzle and Esther wiped it with her hands. She smoothed down the white hair where she had ruffled it, sat back and looked at him, pinching her lip. "Get him out," she said. "He'll stink."

Sven found Ardagh in the control room, arms tightly folded, mouth tight, staring at the screen. The red brick road stretched into the mist like a path through a graveyard; the morning sun, flat and pink, hovered above it, and to either side the hunchbacked trees were plunging their branches into the earth and rooting there.

"Yigal's dead. We'll stop here."

She licked her lips. "I'm sorry."

He glanced at the counter. "One-point-two. We won't stay long. I'll get Joshua."

"Can you bury him?"

"I don't want to take the time. We'll cover him with whatever loose stuff is around."

No longer bouncing on the floor, the body had a moment's still dignity with Esther at its side. Ardagh came in cradling Koz's idol in her arms. "Can we put it out too? He didn't have . . . he didn't have any-thing . . ."

Sven took it from her. "Is there some kind of prayer we can say?"

She shook her head. "Mother Shrinigasa never had another worshipper. They—the Triskelians made it for him so he'd have something to . . . to—to put outside himself, love, hate, everything—to separate them so they wouldn't blow up inside him." With her fists she squeezed tears from her eyes in a child's gesture. "It didn't work."

Esther did not come out. Ardagh had to help Sven and Joshua with the body. It was monstrously heavy, and horrifying to have it, once so light of foot, gritting its fine hair on the rough brickway and the littered earth. Sven did not want to bring attention either to it or to the statuette; he laid both by the roadside and covered them with branches and handfuls of earth.

"Rain will wash that off," said Ardagh.

"And mud blacken it and heat rot it," Sven said. "This place takes the dead back in a hurry."

He knelt before the mound and leafed the heavy books of his memory for any word or ritual, any memorial. No one would see or know, yet his feelings demanded it. He recalled a sentence underlined certainly not by Yigal or himself, but most likely by his father or grandfather; he scratched and smoothed a clear patch of soil and wrote it with a small twig: *Were I to live again, it should be as I have already lived.* A few heavy drops of rain exploded the words before he finished writing them.

"You don't have to worry about being a visual target any more," said Shirvanian.

He was sitting on a front corner of Argus's roof, wiring his spy-eye into the screen system, dressed in Sven's old protective suit. The lower sleeves hung empty and the extra torso length bulged around his middle. He pointed downward: beating rain and thrashing branches had crumbled the paint on the transport's flanks; it was flaking away, half gone, and rust spots showed beneath it.

"How'd you get up there?" Ardagh asked.

"Climbed." The ladder was a thin pole with half a dozen short crossbars. Shirvanian drummed his heels on the metal plate and a few crumbs of paint drifted down. The silver-coated skin of his suit glinted pink in the sunlight. "I don't know if I can get down."

"Why don't you ride up there and enjoy the scenery?" Joshua suggested. But Sven climbed the crossbars, plucked Shirvanian like a cherry-picker, and carried him inside.

Standing, Shirvanian looked like a battered teddy bear. "I don't think I can get out of this," he said in a small voice. "The slide broke."

"How the hell'd you get in?"

"I dunno."

Argus said, SVEN, THERE IS A SKIMMER TWO KILOMETERS AT ONE O'CLOCK.

Sven left off wrenching at the fastener. His hand shook grabbing the mike out of its clip. "Request i.d. We are carrying parts to station."

"Why are they called skimmers?" Shirvanian asked.

"They used to fly on survey mainly at treetop level." His eyes were on the screen. "Skimmer one-seven-five reports track-two washout in Zone Yellow three-point-five km from Orange border. Menders at work. Well, thanks." He told the mike, "Received and noted." When he hung up, his breath came long and ragged. "We passed." He fell to his knees again and peeled Shirvanian out of his casing. Skimmer buzzed and faded above.

"You're bleeding," Shirvanian said.

He looked and found a red thread running from his cut. Probably it should have had a stitch. It had gathered lumps of scab and bits of whatever bandage he could find to stick on, had not been dressed since Ardagh removed the transmitter, and his shirt netting had become cemented to it.

"So I am . . . Ardagh, do you know where the alcohol is?"

"I'll see . . . here."

She was standing in the bunkroom doorway holding up the bottle. There were a few cc left in the bottom. She jerked a thumb. Sven peered in and saw Mitzi snoring in her bunk; the room smelled of alcohol.

"God, I hope she diluted it!"

Ardagh picked the cup from Mitzi's hand and tipped the last drop on her tongue. "Yeah."

"She'll have a terrible hangover."

"Not if it's pure—but I don't think she'll feel so good. Anyway, she's quiet."

"Thoughtful of her to use the cup."

"And leave a little over—" Ardagh gave a combined gulp, sob and hiccup. "Why am I talking like this? I never was so bitchy."

"Maybe the same reason she got drunk. Try not to hate her."

"I don't . . . she's some kind of natural disaster area, like a small whirlwind. I'll see if there's enough left to unglue that thing of yours . . . she's one of the few people that I don't even want to know why . . ."

Esther was sitting against the wall, under lights turned to their dimmest, arms wrapped around knees, eyes staring at nothing. Every so often she plucked a tuft of hair from her body, rubbed it between thumb and forefinger.

Sven took her hands. "Don't do that," he whispered. Her shoulders shrugged, her hands twitched.

Shirvanian rolled himself into a corner of his bunk and sucked his thumb to blank out Mitzi's snoring, rain drumming, water trickling through the filtering system, bricks clunking.

Reason, instinct, emotion whirled round each other in his skull like an illustration of the three-body problem. He hated the weird kid's, snotty brat's, insignificant ten-year-old's body he inhabited; he was aware that he had the emotions of a five-year-old child and was almost powerless to control them. The sun and center of these whirligigs' orbits was a hard bright faceted reasoning machine doomed to be fed by flesh and blood. Shirvanian hated the flesh dressed in the civil cloth of the worlds' inhabitants. Flesh kissed him for, pushed him toward, things that flesh wanted. Machines did what he wanted. Shirvanian was also well aware of his monstrous ego; like many powerful minds, he was not unidirectional, but absorbed everything his senses brought him: he knew how emotional dynamics worked even if he could not operate his own, and sometimes his insight watched in horrified contempt while his body kicked and screamed.

In the end it came down to what he had told Sven: he liked machines better. He did not mind Esther, because, giving love, all she wanted was to give. He considered his relationship with Sven a working agreement, a truce. Mitzi he hated because she had slapped him, and he had never been struck before: retaliation took a waste of energy that was dangerous to all, and principally himself.

Erg-Queen. The machine that wanted. Erg-Dahlgren, the machine that wished to be flesh. Terrifying anomalies, they stood against everything he was and wanted to be. Argus, protector and controller: don't get your feet wet! But not malevolent; more the guardian. Good dog, Argus!

Erg-Queen. Forget the others. Erg-Queen, the first of the machines he did not like better, and the first he must contend with from his own specialist's standpoint. Many persons in the world disliked or hated him—or loved him too well. At least, none wished him bodily harm. Mod 777, his own peculiar kindred, was a destroyer, a betrayer.

Flesh was greater than Shirvanian, erg-Queen

greater than flesh, insane formulation. *What does Dahlgren mean, King of the bone-orchard?* erg-Dahlgren asks from far away. Shirvanian knew: Yigal and Koz planted with the hundreds who had perished. I may die. Mama! I'm going to die! He inhabited the sobbing child with disgust. Fell asleep, bouncing, thumb in mouth, in terror, centered with the smallest grain of delight, to do what was foreordained: reach out with the delicate filaments of thought, weak threads bearing the current of his power, toward the center, Mod 777, erg-Queen, Creatrix, savage maelstrom at the terminus.

Ardagh sat with Esther, held those twitching hands in her own blunt strong ones. "Esther . . ." She did not know what to say, and Esther said nothing, looked into nothingness.

Joshua watched the screen with Sven. He was a quiet person, never had much to say, and was uncomfortable with people. At the Space Academy he had suffered in the atmosphere of tumbling jocularity. His personal bubble was a large one, always pinched by lack of privacy and elbow-nudging jokes. He had been happiest in his forest at home and he preferred the dangers of the open air in the jungle of Barrazan V to being confined in a metal box.

"I realize you don't much like being stuck in here," Sven said.

Joshua smiled thinly. "How did you know?"

"I grew antennas from being brought up in a rain forest by Esther and Yigal. I'm afraid I can't promise you'll ever have anything better."

"Obviously," said Joshua. The red brick road buckled over a subterranean rivulet. Argus lurched, bricks shifted clanging against his side. "I'm surprised we haven't had those heavies from the depot coming out after us."

"Shirvanian says high radiation levels may interfere with some of their equipment. Thyratrons, whatever those are."

"A kind of electronic switch."

"He thinks that may be the reason the factories have moved out of the hot zones."

"If they had sense they'd phase out the drones, or turn down the reactors, or both."

"They don't draw conclusions very well . . . but we've still got to worry about skimmers and plenty of other machines."

26

Communications called erg-Queen. *Skimmer 175 on fly-over reports no metal mass in target area large enough to account for destruction of 933.*

LIST TRAFFIC ON TRACK 2.

Trencher 446, Thresher 462, Carrier 983, Menders 351, 352/4, stationary, at work on washout in Yellow.

Erg-Queen called Registrar. CHECK WORK RECORDS OF TRENCHER 446, THRESHER 462, CARRIER 983 FOR ALL ACTIVITIES ONE HUNDRED HOURS PREVIOUS.

No work record 983 in this Registry.

Erg-Queen drew conclusions. She contacted Skimmer 175. WHAT POSITION CARRIER 983?

Observed 0746 traveling 10 kph track 2 Zone Red 11 km E Blue.

EIGHTY-NINE KILOMETERS FROM HOME, said erg-Queen to the universe.

Erg-Dahlgren played *20. KR-Q1*, and Dahlgren pushed Queen to B3.

Dahlgren's shoulder ached. He saw in his mind's eye two Dahlgrens playing endless chess in hell with bones and coral for pieces, small receding Dahlgren seeing in his mind's eye two Dahlgrens . . . He got up and looked at himself in the mirror.

"What's the matter, Dahlgren?"

"Now I look older than you. I expect you will not change."

Without comment, erg-Dahlgren played *21. P-QN4?*

"Time waster," Dahlgren muttered. QN-K3.

"Like the rest of the game, Dahlgren." *22.* He took the black Knight with his own. Dahlgren took Knight with Queen.

"We move little men and we are moved," said erg-Dahlgren.

"It has been said."

"I would not expect to be original. Do all men believe in God?"

"No." Dahlgren waited for the inevitable.

23. P-QR4. "Do you believe in God?"

QR-Q1. "Not so much that I would pray to Him to get us out of here."

Erg-Dahlgren pushed against the phalanx with *24. P-R4.* "Mod Seven Seven Seven says that Man was created in order to give life to machines. You know more about religion than I. Does that seem reasonable to you?"

Dahlgren sent Pawn chasing Queen to N5 and remembered how many liquors were drunk, narcotics swallowed and smoked, philosophies, cosmogonies, ontologies debated after midnight in the great academies of his youth by earnest roommates lodged together through chance. Natural theology among the ergs . . .

"Does it, Dahlgren?"

"It is reasonable enough . . ." Oddly, his mind went back farther, to the nineteenth century and its ponderous thinkers, good graybeard Robert Browning in vest and watch-chain, fire on hearth, loving Elizabeth at hand, comfortable spaniel at foot, dreaming of Caliban musing by island shore of his god Setebos:

> Who made them weak, meant weakness He might vex,
> Had He meant other, while His hand was in,
> Why not make horny eyes no thorn could prick,
> Or plate my scalp with bone against the snow,
> Or overscale my flesh 'neath joint and joint
> Like an orc's armour?

Well, why not? No thorn would scratch erg-Queen. "It's as reasonable as anyone else's belief in God. Although you might say that any organic creature is a kind of machine, because it operates by the laws of physics and chemistry, and even uses metals in various forms." If they needed a God to justify killing animal life, they might try unwinding that one.

"That is true too."

"What form does your God have?"

"It has no form. It simply is."

Yes: power that gathered among the circuits in mystery.

What mystery? Dahlgren had made and marred at will: so they. He was seized with sudden savage contempt for himself and his works, his captivity, his captors. He said roughly, "At least it is not a great Gaming Machine in the sky with complicated arabesques and little windows showing lemons and cherries."

"Now I believe you are ridiculing me."

"You know my dry way of speaking. Have I offended you?"

"Only somewhat, Dahlgren. I have become accustomed to you."

Dahlgren found his pajamas. "You would be safer

with Mod Seven Seven Seven. I am no longer any help to you. You have become a prisoner like me."

"How can you say that? She would harm me, change me."

"If you returned your loyalty to her she would probably trust you more than before, because she would feel you have been tested."

"But I don't choose to do that." Erg-Dahlgren got up as well and began to undress. "I have made my decision."

"If your safety lay more in being allied to her than to me wouldn't it be reasonable to choose her?"

Pausing with one foot in pajama leg erg-Dahlgren said, "Yes . . ."

Dahlgren smiled grimly.

". . . but you should know that that question took me longer to answer than any I have ever been asked."

"Many men have been unwilling to give their lives for others. That is no sin."

"Now you are truly offending me, Dahlgren. Are you still so angry at me?"

Dahlgren pushed the words out. "I am angry at myself. You are the only friend and ally I have had in all these years."

"I wondered why you were baiting me."

"We are both so vulnerable here, and we cannot move at all! I want to do something! My son is still alive . . ." He would have flung out his arms in a gesture of frustration, but the pain in his shoulder stopped him and he slumped on the bed. "I had no right to treat you so badly. I have made you show your innocent self-regard in an ugly way, and that is sinful."

"I presumed you had some reason for your anger."

Dahlgren sighed. Erg-Dahlgren, imprinted on him, twinned image, seemed determined to complement him by revealing traits he possessed but could not show. "I think you were more like me when you did not know me."

"You seemed simpler then." He went to the chessboard, moved 25. Queen to Q3. "There she stands, back of the Pawn, looking over his shoulder."

Dahlgren shrugged, got up and moved his Queen to N3. "*I* cannot confront her."

"And you want me to do that." 26. Q-K2. "You see, on the board it is easy to make the Queen take a step back."

P-B6. "*There* is a Pawn under the noses of the enemy that cannot be taken."

Erg-Dahlgren said with something of dryness for the first time, "If you are talking about either me—or that other Pawn . . . you do not know whom you are dealing with."

"You know," said Dahlgren quietly. "I would try it myself if she would take me for you."

"That would be interesting."

"This way one of us might be able to get out and see what is going on. If you can demonstrate your loyalty to her—"

"She may be less likely to tamper with my being. I understand. But she will be able to tell if I am lying."

"Then tell no lies. But don't give information that has not been asked for." He did not speak of erg-Dahlgren's connection, the *being* Shirvanian, for the same reason that he had wiped his memory: not to halter him with too much to hide.

"Whatever I say I will seem to be betraying you," erg-Dahlgren said. "I will be betraying you."

"That will be hard on your conception of yourself, but tactically it is much better. The more you become like the idea of Dahlgren in Mod Seven Seven Seven's mind the safer you will be. You must be arrogant and incisive if that is to your advantage . . . or if necessary even crawl and cringe . . . it is not pretty, but it is Dahlgren on record. That is what I saw—" He swallowed. "Do you think I learned nothing of myself during those years I spent among the bones of my friends and workers?"

Erg-Dahlgren picked up the clothing he had just taken off. "She may not be willing to communicate with me."

"You are the crux of her plan. I am certain you will be safer with her."

Erg-Dahlgren, dressed, sat down. He bowed his head. After a minute, he raised it. "She agrees to have me speak to her. A servo will come for me." He stared at the chessboard. "I am afraid, Dahlgren. Am I clever enough to represent you?"

"If it is necessary to save anything at all out of this, anything at all—you must really take my place. On Earth and in the heavens."

Bolts clicked and the door slid open. Erg-Dahlgren did not pay attention for a moment. He raised his hand slowly over the board and with 27. Q-B4 put Black in check. Dahlgren shifted King to R1 and took him out. "It can be done," he said.

The servo was waiting. Erg-Dahlgren, about to go out into the darkness, paused in the doorway and half turned. He said in a low voice, "Your son is alive . . . but Yigal has died."

Transport 933 has disappeared, said Skimmer 175.

IT HAS SWITCHED IDENTITY TO 983, erg-Queen said.

Does destruct order now apply to 983?

Erg-Dahlgren appeared in the doorway.

THAT WILL BLOCK TRACK 2 WITH WRECKAGE. MAINTAIN FLY-OVER AT INTERVALS OF THREE HOURS. I WANT 178 ON SURVEILLANCE ABOVE CLOUD LEVEL.

Erg-Queen, connected to everything, did not need more than a broom closet's space for her physical being, and her headquarters was only slightly larger. One wall was lined with screens connected to spy-eyes.

She pushed a button that changed one screen to a map on which three tracks radiated toward the focal maze of Station Headquarters. Nearly halfway along track 2 a small red light flickered among vari-colored dots of erg positions. SHALL I KNOCK THEM OFF THE TRACK AND BURN THEM OR LET THEM CRAWL A LITTLE LONGER?

"That is your prerogative," erg-Dahlgren said.

I'M GLAD YOU AGREE. SEVEN YEARS AGO WE MADE A PROMISE TO DAHLGREN AND DID NOT INTERFERE WITH HIS SON. THAT IS WHAT MEN CALL HONOR. NOW DAHL-GREN'S SON IS APPROACHING IN FULL SIGHT WITH I SUP-POSE SOME MAD HOPE IN MIND. I DO NOT KNOW WHAT HE WILL TRY TO DO AND I DO NOT BELIEVE THAT HE KNOWS WHAT OR WHY.

"Dahlgren's son did not make any promises."

Erg-Queen tapped all her arms at once along her sides. They rang. Erg-Dahlgren did not like this, but since he had no glandular system he did not flinch.

NEITHER DID I MAKE ANY TO YOU. WHY DID YOU ASK TO COME HERE? YOU COULD HAVE COMMUNICATED WITH ME FROM YOUR ROOM.

"You can do many things at once, but I cannot ob-serve Dahlgren and speak with you as well."

THEN WHY? PERHAPS YOU WISH TO SAY THAT YOU HAVE LEARNED ENOUGH OF CHESS TO PLAY DAHLGREN.

"I have learned enough of chess to play as well as Dahlgren. I believe that I can play Dahlgren as well."

IT WAS BEGINNING TO SEEM TO ME THAT YOU WERE PLAYING WITH DAHLGREN RATHER THAN AGAINST HIM.

"I have played with Dahlgren. I do not wish to play with you."

HOW YOU HAVE CHANGED, MOD DAHLGREN. PERHAPS YOU ARE PLAYING FOR YOURSELF.

"That would be impossible for me even if I wanted to do it. You control my power sources."

AND YOUR FORM AND YOUR FUNCTIONS.

"As you have demonstrated."

AND YOU ARE OBVIOUSLY UNWILLING TO BE TERMI-
NATED.

"Certainly. But you are not likely to do that, when
my works depend on ten thousand circuitry charts
allowing combinations in the billions. You will not put
me together again in a hurry, Mod Seven Seven
Seven."

OR—

"Or modify me easily without damage. You wanted
a Dahlgren, and Mod Dahlgren is what you got." And
perhaps a little too much of him. Erg-Dahlgren added
quickly, in a calmer voice, "I have not come to show
you defiance, but to demonstrate that I *am* Dahlgren
to all intents and for your purposes, and as I was
made to do what you wish I am fully willing to do it."

THAT IS VERY HELPFUL, MOD DAHLGREN. IT IS
PLEASING TO KNOW THAT YOU HAVE NO AIMS THAT ARE
INIMICAL TO MINE. Erg-Dhalgren waited for the
crunch. . . . AND GRATIFYING TO KNOW THAT I WILL
NOT HAVE TO SCRAP YOU IN FAVOR OF SENDING OUT
DAHLGREN HIMSELF UNDER DRUGS AND HYPNOSIS, AS I
HAVE BEEN CONSIDERING, SINCE YOU WILL CERTAINLY
BE MORE CONVINCING THAN HE WOULD AFTER THE
EXTREME TREATMENT THAT WOULD BE NECESSARY TO
RESHAPE HIM.

"I doubt he would last long."

HE HAS ALREADY DEMONSTRATED THAT HE IS A MAN
WHO LASTS. A PACEMAKER AND A FEW OTHER DEVICES
CAN TEND TO THE REST.

"You are suggesting, Mod Seven Seven Seven, that
you do not trust me after all."

Yet he knew that she did, at bottom, and was waiting for something else. A look into the vulnerable,
his identity to which she had no access and which he
termed his *self*. He did not know how to show it to
her, or if he did how he could bring himself to do it. *If*

necessary even crawl and cringe, says Dahlgren. All well and good, but he had no tears, he did not know how to whine.

She said nothing, waited for something, her arms rang down her sides in waves of deepening notes.

Erg-Dahlgren bowed his head.

Why don't you tell her about me? said the *being* out of the void.

Erg-Dahlgren froze. *Who—*

You know, said the communicator. *The one with Sven Dahlgren.*

What Dahlgren wiped from my memory . . .

Yes! Hurry up! She can't read me, but you'll turn into a scrap heap if you just stand there like an idiot!

But I may endanger—

Go on!

Erg-Dahlgren had no time to discuss questions of ethics with himself or anyone else.

IF I AM TO TRUST YOU, WHAT—

He straightened and said deliberately, "There is a being in the company of Dahlgren's son who can communicate with me. Directly."

The tapping stopped. NOT BY RADIO?

"No. Through my store."

A TELEPATHIC HUMAN? ANIMAL?

"Human, I believe."

COMMUNICATING WITH A MACHINE?

"It would seem so."

WHO IS THIS BEING? IS IT THE ONE WHO WORKS WITH MACHINES?

"I don't know."

WHAT HAS IT TOLD YOU?

"Very little. It was as frightened to be in communication with me as I was startled to discover it."

TELL ME WHAT IT SAID SPECIFICALLY.

Being gave explicit directions and erg-Dahlgren hesitated only a half-second. "It hates you."

WHAT A SURPRISE. CAN YOU GIVE ME ANY PROOF OF THIS CONNECTION?

"Not directly . . . it gave me a kind of proof by allowing me to observe that it sent a machine here into malfunction, a three-two-one, I believe, in the tread-repair chamber."

SHOP, called erg-Queen, REPORT ON 321 RENEGADE IN TREAD REPAIR 30 HOURS PREVIOUS.

Cause unknown, Shop said. *No malfunction on diagnostic except original tread breakage. Do you wish to see this machine?*

NO. THAT IS ALL. She considered. IF THIS IS AS IT APPEARS AND AS YOU SAY IT IS LIKELY THAT CHILD WHO MAKES TOYS OF MACHINES.

"Perhaps, or maybe two of them are working together, one who knows and one who acts."

HOWEVER IT WORKS IT WOULD MAKE A SUPER DIAGNOSTICIAN. CAN YOU COMMUNICATE WITH IT AT WILL?

"No. Usually we reach each other by hazard."

TOO BAD.

For a moment erg-Dahlgren considered himself as a heap of parts, or at best stretched out on the construction table with servos winding this and soldering that. "But then, I have never tried."

TRY THEN, MOD DAHLGREN. WHY DID YOU NOT TELL ME OF THIS BEFORE?

"I thought there was a flaw in my circuitry, and I was afraid," erg-Dahlgren said with perfect truth.

But she had no more questions. GO BACK TO YOUR ROOM, MOD DAHLGREN. I WILL THINK ABOUT THIS.

Design, at erg-Queen's request, riffled at a millisecond apiece the ten thousand wall-sized circuit diagrams that mapped erg-Dahlgren, and knocked off the two or three thousand relating to physical function.

HOW CAN THE OTHERS BE TESTED TO ISOLATE A RECEPTOR AREA?

*By establishing steady contact and trying millions
of switching combinations.*

THERE IS NO TIME.

And there are no short cuts, Mod 777.

Erg-Dahlgren, in the dark corridor, sent thanks into
the void but asked no questions. He had exhausted his
human resources and did not want any more tests.
All he wanted was to tell Dahlgren what had been
done and let him decide whether it was help or
hindrance.

The door was open, the room was dark. He did
not have to turn the light on to recognize by the lack
of body heat that Dahlgren was not there. The heartbeat leaped on his monitors, the brainwaves spiked;
the man was gone.

27

To either side of the orange brick road the land
buckled, and sometimes its granite spine broke the
surface, blackened by rain and paled by wind. Mist
and cloud were thinner, though the sun still dropped
bloody in the west. Most of the plant life had gone
underground in writhing trunks, looping up every
once in a while into the poisoned air to flower in a
spray of dark red or blue-black spikes that seemed a
shriek of steel. There were no greens. The animals
were humps of multilayered scales driven by scrab-
bling claws, or else huge black metallic centipedes of

incredible speed. The track was much repaired and wound occasionally to bypass gullies; when it could not it was supported by retaining walls of granite blocks.

Sven did not urge Argus, because he wanted to avoid the road-menders in Zone Yellow. He was alone for the moment, and he did not think much because he was afraid. He hoped to leave the track halfway along White, draw a wide arc around the station complex and stop past the eastern border of the shielded zone, the point of the exclamation mark, where, if he were lucky, there would be cover in a low-radiation area, and he could plan what to do next.

Progress was slow across the broken land, but there was plenty of time now; the great obstacle aside from threat of attack was the sparseness of his memory. He had blotted out many events from terror, but he had also paid little attention to his surroundings because he was a child. Even Esther had not known much of the underground maze or the cultivated tract.

Ardagh came in. Her shoulders were slumped, she said nothing.

"She still the same?"

"Yeah. Was she ever like this before?"

"When we first came. It took her, oh, I guess some days to get out. I was in shock too. Yigal . . . Yigal was sensible, he pushed us around with his nose, pestered us . . . don't you get that way."

"I won't." She bit down on I *won't* have time. "I'd better see if Mitzi's back from the land of the living dead."

Shirvanian opened his eyes and ran the ball of his thumb across his teeth. He was feeling a bit queasy.

"I didn't know you sucked your thumb, Shirvanian," Ardagh said.

Shirvanian took his thumb out of his mouth and stared at it. It was red and wrinkled. "I've reverted to infancy."

"Infantilism. Don't let Mitzi catch you."

"Why not? She's got a thumb of her own." He jumped off the bunk and headed for the control room.

Ardagh leaned against the wall and watched Mitzi.

Mitzi opened her eyes, yawned, grimaced, and sat up slowly. She swung her head around her neck as though there were a lead ball rolling in her skull; glanced up at the light, blinked and shuddered. She looked dully at Ardagh and said, "What've *you* got the shakes for?"

Ardagh lifted her quivering hands and frowned at them in surprise. "I was holding on to Esther all day. She's the one that's shaking."

"What for?"

"Yigal's dead. She's in some kind of depressive state."

Mitzi grunted and got to her feet by pulling at the rim of the upper bunk. She lurched out of the cabin and down to the back chamber where Esther was still sitting blank-eyed.

She squatted, and with a sudden jolt from Argus, sat down hard and made a face. The light was sick. She squinted at Esther, a dark shadow trembling in a corner.

Esther's lids narrowed slightly, masking the yellow pinpoints reflecting off the corneas.

Mitzi asked, "You in a trough?"

"Yeh." A mere croak.

The sound made Mitzi clear her own throat. She turned her head aside a little and raised her fingers to her lips as though she were speaking to herself or to the air. "You've got to put yourself crosswise to it and bull your way through the wave head first."

Esther parted her dry lips. "I know. I've been there."

"You're lucky." Mitzi flattened her palms on the rumbling floor and pushed herself up. "I never got through to the other side."

Esther nodded, perhaps a centimeter. "Well, maybe . . ."

Ardagh was sprawled on the bunk with her feet hanging over the side; Mitzi flung in with her rag-doll gait and grabbed a shelf for balance. "She'll be coming out of that pretty soon."

Ardagh sat up, bit her tongue, and said, "Thanks."

Mitzi shrugged and Ardagh unclenched her fist. "I'll go see if I can get her to eat."

"The cover's blown," said Shirvanian.

Sven folded his arms front and back, rode Argus's floor like a surfboard. "I didn't think it would last. How'd you find out?"

"Opened a line to the Dahlgren. He didn't know much, but erg-Queen knows plenty. We won't get burned on the road because it'd make a mess, but there's nothing to stop them from shoving us off."

Sven grunted. "Will they do it?"

"Not yet. I had him tell her about my psi and she's waiting to decide if it's worth anything to her."

Sven said harshly, "Why don't you sell yourself to her? You might get off."

"Your father made the Dahlgren do that, to save himself. The erg didn't want to. He likes your father, I dunno why."

Sven's helpless laughter dissipated his usual hostile impulse toward Shirvanian. "How long do you think she'll take to evaluate her treasure trove?"

Shirvanian took a lick of his thumb and wiped it in his armpit. "I'll try to find out, if my thumb holds up."

Sven glanced at him. His face was so pale he looked like some child wasting away in an old tear-jerker. The sight of him, his fear, gave Sven a fearful lump in his own belly. "Sucking your thumb? What for?"

"Distraction. Keep my mind off other things while I'm exploring. I hate it, actually."

"You ought to have some worry beads. Dahlgren gave Esther a string once to keep her from grooming him."

"Huh. Do you know anything about something called the pit?"

"The Pit? Oh . . . yes, it was a kind of nursery or hothouse . . . a simulated forest environment where they kept lab animals after they came in or before they let them outside. I spent time there myself, and so did Esther and Yigal. Why?"

"I caught something about it from erg-Queen, I don't know in what connection. Was it underground?"

"Yes, right in the center. Design, Surgery, and all the other things were around it."

"Looks like you remember more than you thought."

"Mostly more than I want. I think we could have supper now."

"Not me, I haven't time." Shirvanian's eyes looked big again, glancing off into corners of nothingness. "And I'm afraid I might get sick."

28

Yigal was dead. Dahlgren sat down and allowed grief to lash him like bloody surf. He found himself, head propped in hands, staring at White's side of the chess table. The obvious move, B-N3, would stop Black's advancing pawns. He fingered his fallen pieces, bishops, pawn, knight. If he had had a choice of pieces to represent Yigal it would have been White Knight, most gracious gentleman, perhaps old Charles Lutwidge himself. But Yigal had been only a white goat, a marvelous sport of nature, whom Dahlgren had not tampered with but simply loved.

The bolts clacked, the door opened grating in its slide. Dahlgren's heart sank even further and he did not look up. So erg-Dahlgren had been rebuffed. He muttered, "What did she say?"

A coil looped round his wrist. YOU WILL COME.

He yelled, twisted away from the servo and smashed his good fist against the coil. It loosened, curved back and lashed forward again; he raised his right arm before his face in time to block the steel from circling his neck. It snaked his forearm instead and pulled again. YOU WILL COME NOW.

"No!" Dahlgren roared. "I am not dressed!" He was in pajamas and barefoot.

The servo absorbed this information in some dim manner for a quarter-minute. GET SHOES.

Without releasing him the coil slackened enough to let Dahlgren grab his boots and zip them on. It pulled him out of the room, balking and stumbling down the gray corridor. He swore, in *lingua*, in Swedish, in half a dozen languages and dialects of the Twelveworlds, his anger sent sparks before his eyes. He was dragged as by a savage dog around a corner, down a ramp, along a hall toward a niche where the floor was a red square. Dahlgren recognized this. The erg pushed him in, touched a small button with the tip of its arm; the square descended into flooding light.

In Design the ergs were tall silver mantises with complex sensor lenses. They were scanning electronic screens. Dahlgren caromed off the corners of their

lecterns, grabbed at table legs, drawer pulls, lamp
standards; his arms wrenched and he did not care; he
was hysterical with rage. His tables, his records, his
Designers, his very light mocked him with silent
complicity. He braced himself against a standard and
kicked at the coil with a boot heel, it loosened with a
jerk and slid into the erg body. Freed, he flung himself at an insectile form, battered his fist at the cold
light of the eye, screaming, "Don't you understand?"
although he himself did not know why it should. The
silver creature did not move.

He raced around desks to dodge the whipping coil,
swung his arms knocking over whatever was loose, a
few meters ahead of the skimming casters; knew
where he was going and did not know: through the
archway into the next room where the tables were
stacked with the pink, brown, or reddish bodies of
men and women—what? no, androids, for their faces
were blank and unlined. And why? He was not mad
enough. He realized that these would be erg-Dahlgren's crew for the voyage outward to GalFed Central, all humanoid forms chosen by the ergs because
they had one excellent template. O traitor Dahlgren!

He wept, he wanted to beat at the still shapes,
recognized in flashes a face here or there: Egon
Klemm, the botanist, Evi Lindstrom, the ecologist,
with her round face and fair cropped hair—and at the
last, Haruni. He screamed, "Haruni! Are you going
too?" Touched in passing the slack mouth he had
poisoned with his food, stumbled down the aisle,
slammed into heavy glass at the end, an immense
wall of it, bruising cheekbone and forehead, stared
down into a depth of greens and mist, far down and
extending far, steamy wraiths eddying under a pink
arc light of sun, unknown life forms twisting in the
dark earth of a forest floor. His hands splayed on the
glass, his ribs ground against it, his body jerked with
every clench of his heart; he looked as he had looked

five thousand times into the true Pit of Dahlgren's World.

Servos hummed behind him, a needle drove into the flesh of his hip. As his eyes darkened, he looked up and glimpsed in the reflection of the glass, great distances away, the mantis, picking up a sponge and polishing the lens of its cyclopean eye.

Erg-Dahlgren sat at the chessboard, read quivering brainwave and heartbeat. The man was alive, he did not know where. The door had been locked, so he had not escaped.

Erg-Dahlgren knew a few rooms in the complex, a few pictures of worlds outside, a few ergs, one human being. He did not know how to behave in this situation. He had only two choices. He did not consider attempting to find Dahlgren: that was exacerbating the danger. He could remain quiet for fear of upsetting his precarious balance, or he could demand answers from erg-Queen. Demand? That was almost as risky as search. Answers? Those would be: *WHY DO YOU WISH TO KNOW WHERE DAHLGREN IS? HE IS NO LONGER YOUR AFFAIR: YOU HAVE TOLD ME YOU LEARNED FROM HIM EVERYTHING YOU NEEDED TO KNOW.*

So I have done. But I also know his heartbeat.

How would Dahlgren react, then? He had said, *If necessary you must cringe.* He had said, *If necessary you must take my place.*

So I sense this heart and brain. I will not stop if they do; I need power sources, not blood. My attachment to Dahlgren is—what, emotional? *You do not feel,* said Dahlgren. Dahlgren said, *You are my friend.*

He had learned loyalty first from erg-Queen, and then again from Dahlgren. The first depended on care for his safety, the second on identification. He did not know of love or courage except what he had seen in Dahlgren, and even Dahlgren had told him that many men would not give their lives for others. Yet he had said, *You are the only friend,* and erg-Queen had said, YOU CAN BE REPLACED.

So I can. I am only a machine, like her. But I am in Dahlgren's place, and in his image. I believe he would try to save another man.

He called erg-Queen.

29

Sven was right; Shirvanian needed worry beads. When he had a piece of work to do with his hands he did not need to think: his hands thought for him. When he had to think with his hands empty he felt unraveled. Distraction had always been his problem. He did not care for his thumb, and he found nailbiting loathsome. As an infant he had disliked toys, and his first act after learning to walk at the advanced age of two was to flood forty-three apartments by trying to flush his teddybear down the toilet. He did not masturbate because his childish sexuality had immediately become absorbed by his hand–brain–machine complex. At five he had been intense about chess for a short time, but after spending an afternoon with his father's first edition of Philidor's *Analyse du jeu des échecs* he had walked into a room full of people and perceived the floor as a chessboard and the men and women as pieces, when he found that he could not move them about with the force of his mind he had thrown a tantrum and given up chess.

Now he lay in his bunk, bouncing slightly, quivering with fright. He would reach out and touch the great battlement, the nerve-complex of ergdom. The hive. The dynamo. The heart.

He curled up on his left side and felt the pounding of his heart on the thin mattress. Eighty-seven per minute.

After a while he caught the beating of erg-Dahlgren's heart, a pump designed to circulate artificial blood in a coarse network of vessels mainly through head, arms and thorax. Steady seventy-two.

Together the hearts created irritating dysrhythms: ricketa-lubb-pocketa-tick-a-tick-dubb. He considered speeding up erg-Dahlgren's heart to match his own and decided that would cause dismay. He read Dahlgren's heart on the erg monitors. LibaTEEPliba-TEEPlibaTEEP. Fibrillating. The man needed quinidine.

Now he had three of them going.

Tick-liba-ricket-a-pock-a-TEEP-dubb.

He thought of astrolabes and armillaries which had measured with their dials, circlets and pointing hands so many times within the time of Man. And he thought of the Queen with ergs moving about her in their orbits. Within the circlet of beating hearts he moved closer to Her Majesty of Machines.

Terror rose in him and he let it wash over and subside. Terror was her force-field. He contemplated her, ten-armed and triple-crowned. She noticed no presence; she was incommunicado, self-absorbed. He surmounted revulsion, stepped within. Her being was a small electrical storm. She had no person, like the Dahlgren, an erg aware of having a body and a character. She had no more than the essences of ironic self-regard and pedantic sadism which had perhaps seeped in from her designers. She was a function of steel, silicon, germanium and selenium, and her passion for control was as mechanical as a baby's grasping reflex. Her ambience was not female: only her shape suggested gender. Within her steel castellated wall he felt his thought rebounding, his heart constricting, and he withdrew quickly to breathe before the terror mounted again.

Why is Dahlgren not here? erg-Dahlgren asked.

Shirvanian closed down, shuddering. Opened again, immediately.

HE IS SAFE. YOU HAVE SAID YOURSELF YOU DO NOT NEED HIM, erg-Queen said.

Inside, where the circuits ran silent and motionless, Shirvanian waited, picking threads: (safe? where?) (IN THE PIT) (why?) (BECAUSE THAT IS WHERE THE ANIMALS ARE) *where they used to keep the animals,* Sven said.

He was safe in my company, said erg-Dahlgren.

BUT YOU WERE NOT. YOU WERE BEING DISTRACTED, AND I AM MUCH MORE CONCERNED WITH YOUR SECURITY THAN YOU ARE WITH HIS, she answered.

This creature wants to save Dahlgren. Get away, idiot, before you're broken! No, warning him is dangerous, and she must talk.

There are still a few days before lift-off, Mod 777, and I would like to be sure I have properly finished the task you set for me.

BE SURE OF IT NOW, MOD DAHLGREN. THE DATE HAS MOVED UP AND YOU WILL LIFT OFF IN 30 HOURS.

Erg-Dahlgren broke off in confusion momentarily and regained control. *We will have no docking privileges if we arrive too early.*

NO TROUBLE. YOU WILL ORBIT UNTIL IT IS TIME TO SET OUT. THERE IS MORE THAN ENOUGH FUEL. THAT WAY EVERYONE WILL BE SECURE.

(PARTICULARLY DAHLGREN BECAUSE HE AND THE) (*Being! where are you?*)

Erg-Queen's mind was a furiously busy control tower, and Mod Dahlgren's urgent call came blurred and distant.

Shit, said Shirvanian. *Get out and shut up! I will speak to you when I can.*

He beat about her maze in a fury, trying to pick up that thread once more.

Particularly Dahlgren, because he and the

because he and the

he and the others will be dead

Naturally, as long as Mod Dahlgren is in orbit. All plans secure. Plenty of time. *SHALL I KNOCK THEM OFF THE TRACK AND BURN THEM OR LET THEM CRAWL A LITTLE LONGER?*

Erg-Queen asked, DON'T YOU AGREE, MOD DAHLGREN?

And erg-Dahlgren answered, subdued, *That seems a very wise move.*

Shirvanian left erg-Queen and through erg-Dahlgren's eyes saw the chess pieces, shell and bone in their icy blocks.

In the obvious move, B-N3, White will prevent the further advance of the pawns.

And Black will attack . . .

Why not?

Shirvanian walled erg-Dahlgren and himself with the beating of three hearts, and called, *Mod Dahlgren, do you receive me?*

I do. There was no color to his thought, not fear, despair, or anger.

Are you still willing to help Dahlgren?

I am, but how? I am only her machine now.

You were willing to go to Central and tell what has happened here.

I will do that if I can, but I am afraid Dahlgren will die and so will you.

Would you trust me with your—with your life, to save Dahlgren and us, as well as yourself?

Pause. Small Solthree child, willful, selfish, and unstable . . .

I know all of that, Mod Dahlgren. But, like Dahlgren, I am also not a liar.

Yes . . . I will trust you.

Good. For starters tell me what, if any, classes you

know of in the station complex are not under direct control of Mod Seven Seven Seven.

She controls all classes under maintenance, power source, defense . . . she does not control trimmers.

But they give orders to no one.

That is correct. The only other classes that she does not control directly are those under Provisioner, because they took care of the personal needs of the humans working here, and are not often used now.

List machines under Provisioner, with their lines of command.

Erg-Dahlgren did so.

Okay. Now you have to trust me an awful lot. When I tell you to do it, will you lie down on the bed and disconnect your power cells? That will leave you helpless for a while, and I can't force you to do it, because you're the one machine that's so complicated I couldn't possibly control you in any way. But I swear you will be reconnected soon.

Being—

My name is Shirvanian.

Shirvanian . . . I suppose I knew that once, before my memory was wiped. Shirvanian, I have taken risks to save your man and yourselves. I am the one you must trust now.

It's a deal, said Shirvanian.

He came up briefly out of that ocean of electricity where he felt he was drowning. Eyes closed, knees drawn up, hands clasped between them.

"The box," he whispered. Then squalled, "The box!"

"Here it is, here!"

He freed his hands, moved them without volition in the empty air.

"Open your eyes."

"I can't!"

"What do you want?"

"Control. Control . . ."

"It's not here . . . look in his bag . . . all right, here it is."

But he had gone down again, hand + brain + machine, into the sea.

30

Provisioner still controlled a dozen machines for various purposes: some kept down mold and gritty dust or maintained plumbing and vents, others supplied Dahlgren's needs. But Provisioner's most interesting employee was Clothier.

Although it was one of the oldest machines on Dahlgren's World, Clothier was almost as great a marvel as erg-Dahlgren. It was the only machine with an aesthetic sense; its storeroom was lined with thousands of bolts of texture, color and shimmering luminescence. In a small closed society where tempers frayed and morale faltered it soothed by dressing all inhabitants who wore clothes in a manner both suitable and pleasing. For those who, like Dahlgren, did not care if they wore old burlap it made sure the plain materials they chose fitted them with comfort and grace. Once in seven of Barrazan V's years it had come out to clothe erg-Dahlgren and the android crew.

Engaged in routine activity with lift-off twenty-nine hours and counting, Provisioner suddenly began to spin and clatter, emitting alarm signals and battering everything it came into contact with. One of its own slaves got in the way, had its directional antennas broken off and it too started to spin. Both reeled around the corridors, knocking holes in walls and denting doors. The rest of the slaves, still powered but uncontrolled, trundled on in the ways they had been going, butted against walls, edged along them like blind rats in a maze . . .

Go ahead, said Shirvanian.

Erg-Dahlgren wondered briefly if he ought to address the God of Machines and decided that the deity was likely controlled by erg-Queen. He unzipped his uniform, freed his left arm from both it and his undershirt, and lay on the bed. He lifted the bared arm, with his right hand pressed apart the seam in the flesh below the armpit, pulled out first the auxiliary power cell and then the

Clothier woke in its stall, summoned by an unknown and powerful voice.

It clasped a heavy bolt of cloth on its back, ran silently down dark hallways, avoided the rampaging ergs by slipping down narrow service corridors, rolled into erg-Dahlgren's room on thick tires. It snipped a square of cloth with its scissor arm, wrapped the power cells and replaced them in erg-Dahlgren's body so that the connections did not touch, closed the flesh-seam, dressed the body, automatically ran a steel tendril over the rucked uniform to smooth it, pulled the board stiffener out of the bolt and took two minutes to shred it with a ripper, burn it with a heat-sealer and flush the ashes down the toilet. Then it rolled erg-Dahlgren into the cloth, clasped the now much heavier bolt on its back once more, skimmed back into its storeroom, reshelved its burden, turned down its power and waited.

In the Dahlgrens' room the vents blew away the

odors of burning and the standing chessmen stared
each other down across the board.

Something cold lapped at Dahlgren's nose and
lips. He opened his eyes. A big triangular snakehead
was touching him, snout to mouth. "For eating?
Food?"

He understood the words, though the narrow black-
red tongue made hisses of all its consonants.

"Food?"

"I am not food," Dahlgren murmured in his dream
and raised his hand to touch the gray-scaled head.
The pain in his joints assured him he was not dreaming. The hand remained poised. Grayhead flicked its
tongue at it.

"That is not food, stupid. That is only one more of
Us," said another voice.

"It is like the Us in the cage. Why is it not in the
cage?" Grayhead asked.

Dahlgren sat up slowly. Very slowly, both from
stiffness and caution. He had been lying among rocks
and ferns, the arc sun overhead far away through
mist. "The Pit," he said.

"The Place," he was corrected.

Grayhead was a long and many-coiled serpent with
three or four pairs of useless webfeet ranged along its
sides. The other speaker was a massive creature the
size of a tree trunk with a narrow head and mouth,
small red eyes, thick stumpy legs. Its ridged brown
back reminded Dahlgren of tKlaa and nVrii.

The *lingua* they spoke was a bit slurred because of
the limitations of their mouths, but it also had the
cadence of an indigenous dialect. He wondered how
old they were, if they had predated the rebellion, in
some secret place. As Sven had predated it, and the
model of erg-Queen.

They had not moved while he sat up, and he was

glad they had agreed he was not food, but as he got to his knees they drew away.

"Why are you afraid of me?" He had not felt so sore and weak since his forced rehabilitation.

Ridgeback stammered, "You—you are like the Us in the cage, stranger. They do nothing but fight."

Dahlgren became aware of the screaming and chattering behind him, and turned. The Pit had the rank smell of the more unpleasant places on the planet, and the clone cage was likely the most unpleasant place in the Pit. Its occupants were rolling on the floor, tugging each other's hair, biting each other's faces in an ecstasy of some sort. "They are not always fighting," Dahlgren observed. He turned away.

"It is time to eat," said Grayhead.

"I'm not hungry," said Dahlgren. He sat on a rock, which emitted a sharp exclamation point, and he got up hastily.

"That is Thinks," the serpent said.

"What?"

"Stranger does not read you," Ridgeback said. "Thinks is one of Us."

Dahlgren knelt to examine it. The creature called Thinks did not look as much like a rock as a brain coral half a meter across; very deep brown, the color of polished wood, and actually composed of closely packed layers of frilled and fluted bone. He touched it gently. It repeated, "!", and then "?"

Dahlgren murmured, "Lower grade ESP than even tKlaa."

"tKlaa is my mother," said Ridgeback suddenly, "but I am not a Thinks." Dahlgren nodded. Mutated clone or artificially conceived child of tKlaa, and her people had racial memory. No biovine on this one either. Well, tKlaa would never know she had had— whatever it was. And Dahlgren's wife would never know—his heart wrenched—to what use her flesh had been put, either.

He spent an hour exploring the Pit. He avoided the cage; those savage faces of his chilled him. There were other reptiles and mammals, mildly or severely warped variants of species he knew. Perhaps some had come from his own labs, but he thought most had been created by the ergs, because there was only one of each, and no signs of offspring. They were apathetic from long confinement; there was nothing to fight over: each took a different kind of food, one slept on rock, one half in water, one in a tree. They let him examine them, when he asked. They seemed to enjoy his touch, for they had been so long without stimulation. He noted with sadness that their sexual organs were either atrophied or absent. Nothing here reproduced except insects and small scavenging lizards. The erg-created animals had no particular grace or beauty, but they were alive, and they were the first and last of their kind.

The one of Us they called Thinks he left for the last, because he felt it might be the most interesting. "Will it let me look at it?" he asked Ridgeback.

"It does not care."

Dahlgren sighed. He did not know why he should care. Death was upon them all. He knelt before the brain coral and peered at it in the dull light. Its bone-flutes were pale in the depths of their creases, and it seemed to glow from within. He turned it over. In the large round opening of its underside there was a pursed mouth and a protruding foot. The mouth contained silt deep in its creases, and threads of glittering slime; likely it fed on soil organisms and rejected the grit. The muscular foot, like a snail's, would allow it to move and to push soil into its mouth at the same time. Dahlgren approved of this economy, and was about to turn over the heavy casing again when he noticed on the other side of the foot, between it and the bone, a protruding membrane. He slid three fingers into the fold gently and felt a sac of hard round things, like walnuts. His heart thumped. "Are these more of Us?" he asked Ridgeback.

"Yes."

Dahlgren felt a surge of joy, at this time and in this place, as a lily will spring in a field of thorns. "Parthenogenetic female," he whispered. "Has she had them before?"

"No." Thinks was objecting silently but strongly, and he withdrew his hand carefully, not to break the membrane, and turned her over.

So it had taken years for her to grow and hatch these, for true fertility to be born in the Pit.

He realized that the cage was silent and looked up. The male had found a strong heavy stick somewhere and was wrenching at one of the rusty bars, which was beginning to give a little. It stopped when it felt his eyes on it, shoved its face at the bars and began to scream at him; the female joined in. They had borne no children; they were sterile, like some clones, or had become sterile out of rage and frustration, like some captive animals.

A door scraped; a servo appeared, dropped a lump of this and a gob of that before each creature. The Dahlgren male quickly hid the stick under a heap of rubble in the corner of its cage and went on howling, reaching clawing hands at Dahlgren. The servo threw a few moldy and misshapen fruits at it and dumped a heap of them in a trough before the cage, then paused to let fall a few more at Dahlgren's feet.

Feeling thoroughly demoted, Dahlgren settled his stiff joints on a genuine rock and began sorting through the garbage for something to eat. Every once in a while he raised his eyes to glance at that bending bar.

31

The road menders had finished their work and gone;
the yellow brick road wound in darkness, buckling
over ridges of broken granite, and dipping in sloughs
of crumbled sandstone edged with salt crystals. There
was no life except in the occasional vein of lightning
that crossed the sky. It was an hour to midnight; in
erg-Queen's terms it was twenty-seven and counting.

In the main chamber of the Argus its crew were sitting on lumpy sacks of dead moss and wilted cabbage leaves. Esther was crouching on Sven's shoulder
with her arm around his neck; everyone looked
frightened and sickly.

Shirvanian ran a finger around the remains of his
black eye. His voice quavered. "I had to hide him;
there was nothing else I could do. She's planning to
kill us and Dahlgren once she gets him up in orbit."

"All right," Sven said, "but what will she do when
she can't find him?"

"I—I think she'll pick us up."

Sven said, "It's better than being burnt down. Why
do you think she'll pick us up?"

"Because the only way I could get hold of a machine she doesn't control was to knock out the one
that gives it orders, and the one I chose was in the
same class as the one I scrambled before. I left a trail
to give her a hint that I'd done it, and make her
more curious about me. Maybe I did more than I
should have." He rubbed the sweat off his forehead

219

with his sleeve. "I'd have had to come out to check with you, and I couldn't have made myself go back in there again."

"Maybe you should have stayed," said Mitzi.

"I don't think she's ready to take orders from me yet."

Joshua said, "She may decide to burn us anyway."

"I don't think so. I'm sure she'll have to find out where he is and I did my best to make her realize I'd hid him. She was threatening to send out Dahlgren under drugs and hypnosis, but that was just a bluff. Even if she could make him go under it wouldn't last, or else his heart would give out."

"Nine years," Sven whispered, "and he may die first."

Joshua kept on, "But why'd she move the time up?"

"She was afraid of the erg's loyalty. She made him too well; they both agreed on that. The more he stayed near Dahlgren the more like him he got, and naturally the more he liked him."

"It doesn't sound natural to me," Mitzi said.

Ardagh asked dryly, "When did you last like anybody?"

Shirvanian scrubbed his forehead again. "When I was in her brain I found out a lot—I found out a lot more than I wanted to." His eyes were on Sven.

"You mean you found out more than I'd want to know. It always turns out that way."

Shirvanian was silent.

"Go ahead. I'd better learn while I'm still alive."

"Your four arms . . . she didn't do that, but the ergs that made her did."

Sven's stomach tightened. "Why?"

"They wanted to—to weaken, to demoralize Dahlgren. They did something just after the ovum got fertilized, when the cells start dividing and you get something called a—um—"

"Blastula," said Ardagh.

"Yeah . . . and they knew how much he'd wanted to—to have a kid . . . with his wife . . ."

"I see." For a few moments Sven thought his thoracic muscles would tighten till they broke his ribs. Suddenly they relaxed. Esther's fingers drummed his shoulder.

"Yes, Esther . . . you were right . . . I admit it. It fits with his being a prisoner, anyway."

"We haven't got much time," said Shirvanian.

Esther said, "Suppose—if they do decide to pick us up—they send a crew to pry us open right here, where it's about seventy-five rads per hour in the shade?"

"That's inefficient," said Joshua. "I'm sure the skimmers have strong enough grapples."

Sven asked Shirvanian, "Where'd you put the erg?"

"Are you sure you want to know that?"

"We're going to tell her before we let her pull any of us apart trying to find out. The idea is to stay alive."

"He's on a shelf in Clothier's storeroom wrapped up in twenty-five meters first-quality midnight blue taklon from Sirius Two."

"What?"

"I can't help it. That crazy machine thinks like that and it gets to you!"

One of Argus's tool kits was open, rattling on the floor, and Joshua and Shirvanian were staring moodily into it.

"What an arsenal." Mitzi hugged herself with white-knuckled hands.

Joshua lifted out one of the coils of explosive. "What'd they use the plastic for?"

"To blow out rockfalls on the road," Sven said.

Joshua picked out a rivet gun, a clip of rivets, two lighters . . . his hand hesitated over the blowtorches.

"Don't take the heavy one," Sven said. "You'll fall all over it, and you won't have time for big jobs."

"How much time do you think we have now?" Joshua asked.

Shirvanian shrugged. "Maybe an hour. She'll have to make plans too."

"Ardagh, would you have a book with a blank page we could draw a map on?"

"How'd you guess?" Ardagh picked herself up.

"I can't draw," Shirvanian said.

"It's the right time to tell us. How did you design?"

"On a computer, with a light pen, and then the computer rectified it. It's in my head all right, I got it out of erg-Queen."

"As long as you've got it in your head I'll get it on the paper. Come on, we can't use more than fifteen minutes for that."

Sven went into the control room, Esther riding on his shoulder. There was nothing more to do. Fly-over had stopped, and there were no signals from Surveyor.

"I said terrible things to you, once," said Esther.

"I thought terrible things. At least what you said was true."

"Are you upset?"

"I'd have liked to be able to tell him . . ."

"Oh yes, I know that one," said Esther. After a moment, she added, "I did the best I could with my life, but it would have been nothing without you. And Yigal."

Sven took her hand and kissed it.

"I'll just go and stay by myself for a bit," Esther said, and slipped away.

Sven picked up the mike. "Well, Argus, have you found any pirates in the forest lately?"

THERE IS NO FOREST HERE ANY MORE, SVEN. THINGS HAVE CHANGED.

"Yes, they certainly have."

Ardagh came in and leaned against the wall, face

lifted to the screen where the yellow brick road wound in the strange light of the infra-red.

"We might as well drop our brick load," Sven said. "At least leave a block for anything coming up behind us." He gave the order and the bricks went out with a clatter.

Ardagh found a sack in the corner and sat on it. "You look like a Brobdingnag from here."

"I feel small enough."

"Do you feel very different about your father now?"

"Different, but not as much as I thought I would. After all, how did I get through those years? I tried to make myself believe he had a reason—not only for making me, but for keeping me alive."

"Because he loved your mother . . . and you . . . and—and now you've found it's worth living you've given your whole life to a—a bunch of petty criminals."

"That's dramatizing, Ardagh. I didn't think you were all that criminal."

"We weren't that successful at it . . . tried to steal a ship, couldn't even make a go of that . . . just failures."

"Koz didn't fail."

"Yes, but he's dead . . . did you think the rest of us were like that?"

"Oh, no."

"What did you think, Sven?"

He was thinking of her face as she caught sight of him with Mitzi. "That's very hard to answer."

"I didn't mean to embarrass you. You did so much for us . . . I wondered if you thought we were worthless."

Do you hate me, Esther? "I thought you were unhappy . . ." What did she want from him? "Why do you ask?"

"Because we were all Triskelians . . . you might have felt . . ."

"Many ranks and orders . . . well, I felt that Koz was sick in some way. Mitzi too, I guess. Hates and hurts herself. Shirvanian!" He laughed. "You and Joshua puzzled me . . . and then I decided that Joshua probably deserted the Space Academy and had been sent, or was being sent to the Order to duck the disgrace, or the law, or maybe both . . ."

"And me?"

"Why should I ask, Ardagh? I'm not the law."

"I didn't want you to think—"

"Whatever it is, I don't." It hit like a crack on the head, finally. *I would have liked to be able to tell . . .*

He said gently, "If you want so much to tell me, I'll listen. And I won't think any differently."

After a silence she said, "No. I don't believe you will. Now I don't know why I want to tell you . . . or where to start. Where the beginning is . . .

"The colony. That damned colony. Rotten place, all tundra . . . and we took the blame. Wel My great-grandparents. And the shape. Servos. School kids used to laugh. Ox, lummox, everything. And the whole bunch insisted on marrying among themselves, even though the geneticists told them they'd better not. Oh no, kids might have faulty bone structure. I think it was because they hated the Terraform Branch and wanted the government to keep remembering what it'd done. Stupid. It's stupid, people don't remember that. At the same time they've got some kind of inside-out pride, they work harder to show they're just as good or better. And they're right, as far as brains and money go. My parents actually are Solthree diplomats. I guess I love them, but they really are a goddam sour lot."

Sven laughed. "How did you escape?"

"What?"

"Being sour."

Her face gave in to a smile. "The same reason they work harder. I'm a lot like them, that way. But . . .

"I had these two great scholarships to offworld medschools, where the competition runs in the millions. The first one I interviewed got nervous about my background, mild physical flaw, dissenters in the family; it was like religious prejudice. And they don't care, the line-ups chew your heels for a thousand worlds. Maybe a lawyer could have made a case out of it, but my family was scared of getting into court for that, into the news media . . . they said, try the other one, and if it doesn't work, forget it, go into something else. I couldn't do that. So I bought a background.

"Sol Three is a sector capital, pole-to-pole bureaucracy. You can buy any document you want, and I had plenty of spending money. Not too many lies, a few shifts here and there, phony X rays with the medical . . . those people are very clever. I got in, I was happy for a while, everything was—I thought everything was going well . . . until they started asking for more money or they'd spill it all. After a while I ran out of money, the family caught me trying to sell one of my microscopes, and that was the end of it . . . Mitzi says I wanted to be caught, I wanted to disgrace them. Maybe that's what she wanted. I don't know."

"You can't get back into school? I mean, medical school?"

"Not with my record, plus whatever would be thrown at me if I got out of this alive."

"Biology? Pathology?"

"I don't know. I wanted to be a surgeon. I suppose I was lucky to get into the Order instead of one of those really great Juvenile Homes. Maybe I should have left it at that."

"And the others?"

"You got them down about right. And it's true, their parents were going to the Conference: it's a big thing, thousands. Our Center's on Barrazan Two and we met them on Four because it has a big port facility. They hadn't seen us for a while and it was on the way."

"The Order didn't send anybody out with you."

"A robot cruiser on a two-day trip, custody of our parents, we stayed in port the whole time . . . the Triskelians just didn't know what they got when they took on Shirvanian—and neither did we."

"Joshua hated that uniform so much . . . and he wore it."

"I think he wanted to make things easier for his parents . . . that takes a kind of pride too. You've got the whole story now. And it's true." Her voice thickened. "It doesn't matter much at this point, does it?"

He knelt before her, took her hands in one pair of his own and framed her face with the others. "I'm sorry—"

Her face twisted. "For God's sake, don't give me any—"

"Ardagh! I'm sorry you were so unlucky—and so foolish too. I'm sorry I didn't have more resources to help you with, or the brains to plan more wisely so we wouldn't be in such a mess. I'm not giving you any pity, and I don't want any either."

She turned her face into the palm of his hand and kissed it, wet it with her tears. "You couldn't have done more. We brought you into the danger."

"There wasn't anything to do back there but grow old and die like a beast in a cage." Like the clones. "And if I hadn't come out of Zone Green I'd have lived my life thinking my father had helped kill hundreds of people."

Her face turned back to his; his brows were like arcs of frost on a window. Those were Dahlgren's, and the nose and sharp cheekbones, but Dahlgren could not have had so generous a mouth. She freed a hand and touched his head; its skin was not tight or

shiny but matched his body texture in the same manner as that of many hairless people.

He kissed her lightly, a question. His hand went to
the fastener at her neck and paused there. She took it
in both of her own and pulled down. He reached
back and slipped the bolt of the door.

She shrugged her arms, her body from the cloth.
"Now you see my flesh . . . do you want to turn off the
light?"

"No. I wish there was more light." Her body was
firm and strong. "It's like a sculpture." She smiled,
and his brows quirked ruefully. "Somebody told you
that before."

"No . . . I never truly believed I was ugly. It only
hurt because so many others thought so."

Argus swerved and lunged about them but they
did not. They mated slowly and in stillness like warm
sculptures. At completion Ardagh lay with Sven's
body curved about her, his hand on her breast, his
breath on her shoulder, and when Argus said, SVEN,
SKIMMER 178 IS DESCENDING, it seemed to her that his
voice was almost apologetic.

Sven, pulling on his clothes, picked up the mike
and said, "Shut down all systems except light and
air. We're stopping here."

YOU SAID WE WERE GOING HOME, SVEN.

"We are, but I won't be driving."

ALL RIGHT, SVEN. WE'LL PLAY SOME MORE TOMORROW.

Sven paused for a moment with the mike in his
hand. He said, "Goodbye, Argus," and hung up.

The transport stopped, and there was silence.

Ardagh was dressed. Face turned away from Sven,
she unlatched and opened the door. The noise was
startling.

"Now have I got it," said Joshua. "Pit in the center,
labs around it, quarters west, machines east—really
fine detail we have here, all five levels of it—clock-

wise from north about mid-level: biolabs, infirmary, computers, design, radio, power plant due south, outside that, ship silo; lowest level: machine hangars, Pit maintenance, transformer rooms off corridor circling Pit floor at northeast, southeast, northwest, southwest. I need a compass."

"The transformer rooms are numbered," said Sven. "Or they used to be. Northwest one and going clockwise. That level is actually below the Pit floor."

"Remember some more," said Joshua.

"I used to race—not Argus, he's too big—I used to sit on top of a servo and race around there. The machines didn't mind the noise."

"The staff must have really liked you."

"They weren't allowed to have kids. Not here. They came for terms of three to five years."

Joshua pulled the chronometer off his wrist. "Anybody want this? I don't dare put out any signals . . . no, I guess you don't either." He dropped it on the floor and ground his heel on it. Licked his lips. "That was a beautiful thing." Shirvanian was knocking his clenched fists together. "Shirvanian? Your box?"

"Dropped it in the waste compacter." He was shivering. "Wouldn't give it to her." He took the esp control out of his pocket, carefully turned it up a few points, and passed it over. Joshua taped it to his bare chest. Mitzi had cut an oblong of material from her poncho and was attaching it to the leg of his jumpsuit with grommet pliers.

"Why don't you turn it up all the way?"

Shirvanian, eyes downward on his fists, muttered, "Too much power . . . I get hyper . . . like at the depot . . ."

Joshua wound three strings of plastic around his thin waist, twined four fuses about them, loaded the clip of rivets into the gun, and tucked it into the front of his laplap.

"Make sure that thing doesn't go off at the wrong time." Mitzi handed over the jumpsuit.

"Don't worry, Mitzi, I'll take good care of it for you." He got into the suit, dropped the blowtorch into the new pocket, tucked in the last two fuses and the lighters, and draped the remaining plastic around his neck like a modish scarf. With all that, he did not look much bulkier than before. Shirvaninan handed him a small button receiver and he hooked it into his ear. Then he stood motionless for a moment.

"What's the matter?"

"I was just . . . looking for a word . . ."

"Take a leak," said Mitzi.

The erg hummed above, an electric bee swarm, the magnetic grapples rang CLING CLANG CLUNG CLONG on the transport's flanks like a chime of bells.

"Too late," said Joshua.

Shirvanian said, almost whispering, "Clothier will be waiting for you."

"It better be." He and Sven ran for the vestibule separating the three chambers, dragged up the floor hatch, and Joshua ducked down into the hot cramped space of the lower compartment. Sven settled the hatch carefully over his head.

The hour was twenty-five: thirty and counting.

Skimmer lifted. The transport swung forward, backward, forward, backed to the stationary and hung. The erg did not rise very far, since there were no obstructions, or travel, so burdened, with great speed. "About forty kph," said Shirvanian. "Maybe an hour."

The children were crammed together in one corner; Sven and Esther against the opposite wall, silent, eyes half closed. They had been parties separated by their aims, allied by their fears. They joined for a few minutes thinking of Joshua alone in the tool compartment among the wheels, shafts, and gears. He was far enough from the engines not to be burned by their stored heat, near enough to be very uncomfortable, and too uncertain about timing to dare wait anywhere else. Skimmer picked up speed.

Shirvanian had his knees pulled up and hid his face against them. Mitzi was clenched into herself, biting her lips, probably wishing for some of that stuff lost in the spaceport. Ardagh, square torso flat to the wall and hands on knees, joined eyes with Sven. "Is it really possible to pull off this thing?"

Sven said, "Shirvanian has to get out of sight. You make sure."

"I can't think what to do."

Esther cackled. "Be your own natural selves." Her hands, unconsciously grooming, never stopped picking at her fur. She stayed next to Sven but did not touch him.

Sven, separated from all, was like a man of an ancient tribe who had been given the prerogatives of a god for a short time in order to enrich a sacrifice. Without talent, power or weapon he was preparing to confront erg-Queen.

32

It seemed strange to Dahlgren that the Pit had survived and been maintained; perhaps its warped life forms and degraded humanity were erg-Queen's monument to herself. "Creatrix of Animals, I declare in My works."

"What are you saying?" asked Ridgeback, lying drowsy on a full belly. The clones, exhausted by fighting, coupling and bar-bending, were asleep.

"Nothing. I am raving."

"What is that?"

He did not answer. He was again among animals, and he longed for Esther and Yigal. He was surrounded by green leaves in warm earth and he wished he were back in his own cold land. Grayhead was writhing slowly nearby. Thinks had moved away to a fresh patch of earth.

The arc light had circled the Pit slowly, and was dimming to simulate evening. Dahlgren, joints aching, looked for a resting place. The earth was damp; insects swarmed over his boots, his pajamas were soaked with sweat and mist.

"Stranger," said Ridgeback, "do you not sleep?"

"I am not used to being in this place. I am afraid of those Us in the cage; they hate me and will kill me if they can."

"They sleep all the dark," said Grayhead.

Dahlgren found a clump of dwarf trees, some dying. The Pit had grown as scruffy as a half-forgotten zoo. Like many another deity Creatrix formed life but did not always provide for it. Dahlgren picked leaves and made a nest in a tree crotch the way he had learned from Topaze.

As he settled grunting in this uncomfortable couch he heard a crackling and looked out. The serpent Grayhead had wound its length about a dead tree and was crushing it; insects scattered madly out of the rotting wood. Grayhead's scales rippled and a seam parted down the midline of its back. It dropped from the tree, squirming in the slough of loosened skin, its little legs flailed to untangle itself. Immediately an army of tiny lizards emerged from beneath leaves and stones, attacked the ragged skin, each ripped off and bore away a shred in its jaws, eating as it ran. The serpent coiled itself in its new coat of gray scales and slept. Dahlgren closed his eyes and listened to the insects rustling their way back into the crevices of the shattered tree.

33

Joshua found his cramped quarters more disturbing than the heat. With one ear he heard the tinging of cooling metal beyond the compartment wall. The other, through the receiver, was picking up Skimmer's signals. He could not understand them; the receiver was meant to tell him when ergs were nearby, not what they were broadcasting. His knowledge of machines and explosives was very modest: he knew from working in underdeveloped regions how to dodge terrorists and get old crocks working; he knew far better how to prevent run-off in parched areas and increase the yield of breadfruit trees. Now that he was prepared for action his fear was blunted by a faint sense of the ridiculous.

His mind strayed to the group above him. He knew that Mitzi, Ardagh and Shirvanian were worried about him, but his thoughts lingered on Sven. He himself was a lonely person, but Sven was lonelier, and of all the tasks Joshua was to perform, freeing Dahlgren, at Sven's insistence, was the last.

He touched the compartment wall at his head: it was very warm, but not stinging. He rolled over to a crouching position on folded knees and banged his head on the ceiling, neutralizing his sense of the ridiculous. He picked up the penlight and screw-driver which had been left on the floor for him, lit the one and with the other began to loosen the bolts of the wall in front of him; he did not have Shirvanian's time sense and he could not afford to wait for the last minute.

Skimmer slowed and his heart quickened. He flattened himself for the inevitable thump. The transport went down sighing on its tires. All of its metal parts creaked, he bounced slightly, and there was one sharp crack that suggested the break of a wall's radiation shielding. He pulled the compartment barrier away quickly, wriggled between the engines where the heat blasted his face, whipped the plastic off his neck and wound it as far as he could reach around the still quivering shaft of the transmission. The grapples sang once on the walls and retracted, the signal grew fainter and stopped; he could not hear what was happening above. Sweating, he squeezed an arm into his pocket to pull out a lighter and a fuse, and waited. The twitters and warbles of smaller machines told him that his companions were being taken away, and he swallowed hard. The branching point was here: the ergs would immediately take the machine away to examine—goodbye Joshua—or would examine it on the spot, or would leave it alone for a few minutes while they attended to the humans, allowing him to slip away. He took a mental read-out of Shirvanian's directions: *The ergs inside the station have no life sensors, only heat and light, except for erg-Dahlgren, erg-Queen and Clothier; don't run into one where you're the only warm object in the area or you contrast with the surroundings, otherwise you're okay.* He was not okay. The operating alternative was the second, one he dreaded almost as much as the first but had allowed for by breaking his watch. A *twee-*

wheep in his ear told him that at least one erg was going round the transport, checking for time-bomb traps. He had no choice now. He plunged three minutes' worth of fuse into the plastic, lit it with a shaking hand, pulled back agonizing centimeters into the compartment as flame whispered and flickered, unzipped his suit and took out the rivet gun; then pushed up with head and shoulders on the hatchway and confronted a small servo in the center of the guttered chamber. It had picked up the flash and heat of his fuse.

He grabbed the blowtorch in his left hand as the erg flicked a tentacle, knocked it down with the tank, the coil gave him an agonizing crack on the shin as it whipped back.

Joshua yelped and swore, let the blowtorch fall, dropped forward between the reaching tentacles, hugged the metal creature savagely, pushed the muzzle of the rivet gun against a sensor lens and squeezed the trigger. The rivet drove in with a crunch, the erg jerked and backed away, its treads shrieked.

Joshua jumped up and forgetting the pain in his leg hopped forward, planted a boot against the erg body and gave it a mighty shove out the open back doors and into the darkness, picked up the torch and flung himself out, ran past the wheeling erg. Three others sped toward it. He ran.

He was on a small landing field with several skimmers quartered on it, a huge dark opening before him; that would be the hangar. It was drizzling, he kept running over the wet macadam, limping now, flash-memories of the erg factory lit before his eyes as he ducked around the doorway of the building and leaned against the wall, panting. The transport exploded.

He did not look out to see the destruction but withdrew farther into the shadow. Two more ergs whirred past him out of the hangar. Lightning flashed with a roar of thunder. In the instant of light he saw that there were not many vehicles in the place, it was too small for erg-skimmers, and along one wall was what he thought must be a row of obsolete machines; he recognized an aircar of a type he knew and had ridden in at home.

His leg throbbed, he was shivering cold with sweat. He put the blowtorch in his pocket and zipped up, keeping the rivet gun in his hand. Fastest gun on Dahlgren's World! He had an impulse to giggle, but discovered that he was weeping.

He rubbed the tears off his face and sidled along the wall, picked up speed as the pain in his leg eased a bit, because the ergs would be coming back. There was an arch of dim orange light in the opposite wall and he headed for that, feeling his way along by the rough tacky concrete; ergs kept themselves clean to maintain working order but they did not care about their surroundings, and if they cared they would not see them here in conditions of near-darkness. He panicked for a moment at the thought that in the dark he could not be able to work at all. But Shirvanian had words for that too. *They keep the light and venti-lation going in most places, mainly because they need some light and the ventilators keep some of the dust away. Mostly I think because they're conserva-tive, they're following evolutionary patterns. They only change in reaction to the need for survival. Of course they don't worry about competition or sexual selection, but they do have a kind of ecological econ-omy, like the jungle. You ought to be interested in that, Joshua.*

But Joshua, who would kill for food, or in extremis, to save his life, and would not on any other account harm a living creature, was not interested in the ecology of machines, murderous zombies, *things* he found no more alive than a cup or spoon. He did not hate the slime on the walls, but despised the ergs, who killed the forest life, for letting it grow in their hangar.

He stopped by the archway, flattened against the wall, afraid to put his head out into the sickly light. Signals whined in his receiver: the first of the ergs coming in from the field.

Before he could move, a soft voice asked, "Joshua?"

His skin prickled. "Who is it?" he whispered.

"Clothier," the machine replied, very gentle and tentative for an erg. "I was told to wait for you here, and I sensed you."

He whipped around the doorway, the clattering erg was nearly on him now, and found a long low black thing waiting, almost invisible in the dimness.

"Hurry and get on," it said sweetly. "Come along, Joshua. I was told to take you where you want to go."

34

The doors crashed open and the servos reached in and pulled at them, tentacle to a wrist. These were like the threshers Shirvanian had combated in the forest. There were three: one took the girls, another Esther and Shirvanian; Sven had one to himself. The metal limbs coursed their bodies for weapons. They did not resist.

The airfield was drizzling with rain, they splashed through puddles in the musty hangar; it smelled of mold and machine oil. The light was faint in the halls. An elevator took them up one level; the door opened into blue-white light that hurt the eyes, into a vault with a stained and dirty concrete floor; shadowy corridors led away from it.

In its center a figure was waiting.

Shirvanian began to whimper.

Only he had ever seen it, but they knew it. The ergs pulled them to within three meters of it, and stopped without loosening their grasp.

Erg-Queen moved along their line and paused at Sven.

YOU ARE DAHLGRENSSON. Her voice echoed and re-echoed.

"My name is Sven Dahlgren." He spoke in a low voice, not to wake those echoes.

YOU ARE THE SON OF DAHLGREN.

"That is correct."

(*THAT WILL PROTECT,* said Memory)

IT IS A PITY YOU MOVED OUT OF ZONE GREEN, SVEN DAHLGREN.

(Memory: *WILL PROTECT HIM FROM THE SERVICING DRONES AS LONG AS HE STAYS IN ZONE GREEN, half-asleep Sven wakened to machine grind and clash and human screaming, cold numb Sven; stitch-stitch-stitch staples going into the soft-place near a juncture of arms, blurt of blood, medtech smelling a little of warm oil, Dahlgren in*)

LOOK ABOUT YOU, SVEN. DAHLGREN STAYED IN THIS PLACE FOR SEVEN YEARS.

(*Dahlgren in the cold light of infirmary haggard, face scratched, beard clotted, a swath of blood diagonal across his breast, diplomat's red sash*)

Sven did not look about him. Watched erg-Queen, half a head taller than he, rolling on silent casters and

(*stumbling through darkened hallways, lifted on Yigal, Esther behind arm-wrapping for comfort, it hurt there in his arm-fold now, Dahlgren with hand on*

Yigal's head, pausing before the silver figure—not erg-Queen, but some predecessor—in the archway of orange light)

pausing before Shirvanian.

(YOU WILL COME BACK, DAHLGREN *and passing in darkness, ergs before and after, until the clashing and screaming faded, but they did not, they went on silently in the black pit of his memory for nine of his years)*

AND THIS IS MACHINEMAKER.

Shirvanian was yellow-white, shaking, retching. The physical presence of erg-Queen was more than he could bear.

WHERE IS MOD DAHLGREN, MACHINEMAKER?

Shirvanian clapped his hands to his face.

WAS IT YOU WHO COMMUNICATED WITH MOD DAHL-GREN AS HE SAID, OR SOMEONE ELSE? WAS IT YOU WHO SENT MY MACHINES OUT OF CONTROL?

With two of her claws erg-Queen reached forward and dragged down his hands; the servo shifted its coil to his ankle.

TELL ME, MACHINEMAKER! She jerked at his hands. Esther screamed with rage, pulled back on the tentacle clasping her wrist; when she could not get free she jumped on top of the servo and stamped up and down with both feet. The limb whipped her in an arc to the floor with its whole length, and if she had not landed on all fours like a spring she would have been smashed.

STOP THESE STUPID ACTS! YOU CHOSE TO COME HERE AND YOU ARE HERE.

"Esther, enough," Sven said. His body was shaking with anger and his mind was clear.

NOW . . .

Shirvanian was gasping, eyes shut tight.

"Stop bullying him," said Sven. "You'll make him sick and you won't learn anything at all." It seemed foolish saying this in the face of death.

WHAT IS HIS NAME?

"Shirvanian."

SHIRVANIAN, TELL ME WHETHER YOU HAVE THIS ESP AND IF SO—WHAT? THERE IS A GROUND CREW OUT OF CONTROL ON THE AIRFIELD . . .

A low *crump* reverberated far back from where they had come.

. . . AND YOUR TRANSPORT HAS EXPLODED. The free arms lifted from her body.

Mitzi yelled, "What did you think we were gonna do, give it to you for a present?" The tentacle jerked and she fell to the floor, swearing.

Sven forced his eyes from the lifted claws. "How many machines have you lost now, Mod Seven Seven Seven?"

YOU KNOW WHAT I AM CALLED, DO YOU? DAHLGRENS-SON, IT IS REALLY TOO BAD THAT YOU CAME BACK. With one hand she picked Shirvanian up in a grasp of his ragged clothing; he hung like a battered doll. SHIR-VANIAN, WHETHER OR NOT YOU HAVE ALL THE POWERS ASCRIBED TO YOU IT APPEARS THAT YOU KNOW SOMETHING. YOU WILL TELL ME WHERE MOD DAHLGREN IS AND I MAY ALLOW YOU TO LIVE WHEN I HAVE KILLED ALL THESE OTHERS.

Shirvanian sniveled, "I don't believe you."

Erg-Queen shook him, his clothes tore so that he slipped down a little in her grip, wailing.

"Let him go!" Esther leaped, a claw sent her sprawling.

"You go ahead!" Mitzi screeched. "Go ahead and tell, you dirty little bugger! You always wanted to see us dead! Think you'll get anything when we're—"

"Shut up! Shut up, you goddam—" Ardagh lunged and swiped her a backhand blow on the face.

The erg jerked them apart. Mitzi sobbed and went on at the top of her voice, "slimy fink, all he ever wanted because he never gave a—" the coil slid under her armpit, over her mouth, and cut her off.

Ardagh clenched her fists and hissed, "Oh, don't push it, for God's sake please don't you push it!"

"You got yours in!" Mitzi snarled and rubbed her reddened cheek against her shoulder.

Erg-Queen kept her burning attention focused on Shirvanian: MACHINEMAKER, I MADE YOU A BARGAIN AND—

"I hate you!" Shirvanian shrieked. "I hate you and you're a liar and I don't want your dirty bargains!" With the hand nearest Sven he crossed his fingers for half a second.

Still holding him suspended in one hand, erg-Queen grasped his arms with two others and raised a fourth to his eyes. He screamed horribly and fainted.

Esther leaped once more and this time the coil wrapped her whole body round; she gasped and retched.

Sven was shaking. Finding the bond had slackened on his wrist he folded one pair of arms to the front and one to the back to keep his body still and said quietly, "I also know where Mod Dahlgren is."

Erg-Queen lowered her arm and let Shirvanian fall. He lay in a heap. Esther got her breath back and chattered with fury, the girls huddled on the floor, sobbing.

DO YOU, DAHLGRENSSON? I WAS WAITING FOR YOU TO SAY SO. THESE OTHERS SEEM TO HAVE GONE MAD. TELL ME.

"I can't speak properly with all this noise."

MOVE THE OTHERS BACK TO THE WALL, erg-Queen said. THEY ARE USELESS AT THE MOMENT. One erg plucked Shirvanian and bore him and Esther away. The other pulled back Mitzi and Ardagh. YOUR FATHER WAS ALSO A GOOD MAN TO TALK TO, IN HIS WAY. NOW I WONDER IF YOU WILL WANT TO BARGAIN WITH ME.

"What bargain are you offering?"

THIS. She raised a claw. MACHINEMAKER HAS A GREAT DEAL OF INFORMATION I WANT. The erg wrenched Sven's front arms down and bound the hands to his sides. YOU HAVE ONLY ONE THING TO TELL ME. The limb turned red body-outward till the fire reached its claw. THIS IS YOUR BARGAIN. Sven jerked back convulsively, was stopped by the erg, the red-hot claw moved lightly down his front from neck to waist, the charred clothing parted and a pink singe mark flared on his breast. YOU WILL DIE MORE EASILY.

Ardagh went wild. "You filthy things!" On hands and knees like a beast, mane of hair tossing savagely about her head, "Both of you, you're filthy things! You machine *thing* can't do anything but kill, and Sven Dahlgren, you brought us here to die and I hope she burns the—" The tip of the erg's tentacle pushed into her mouth and she gagged.

LOCK THEM INTO THE CLOSET IN CORRIDOR WEST UNTIL THEY SHUT UP, said erg-Queen.

Shirvanian stirred, rolled his eyes in horror, and struggled feebly with the machine. "Mama! I want Mama!" he wailed.

The ergs bundled them down the shadowy corridor, a door slid to with a thump, and one erg came back, leaving the other on watch.

THIS CANNOT GO ON MUCH LONGER, DAHLGRENSSON, said erg-Queen. THOSE ARE CHILDREN, AND CHILDREN PLAY AT BEING HEROIC, BUT YOU AND I WILL NOT.

Sven's eyes were full of tears. The burn hurt a little; the tears were for the children, dirty, weary, beaten down, and forced to play games more complex than erg-Queen could conceive of. For Esther and Dahlgren and the ones who had died. All of the ones who had died. She would not recognize his tears, and he did not wish that she should. Her sensors did not blink, no dust could fall in them and hurt. The heat arm had dulled almost to its normal color. "Perhaps one day you will kill and hurt for pleasure," he said. "That will be your next step upward."

I DO NOT KNOW WHAT YOU ARE SAYING, DAHLGRENSSON. YOU HAVE A HABIT OF PLAYING FOR TIME, LIKE YOUR FATHER. MY SHIP WILL LIFT OFF IN TWENTY-FOUR HOURS AND I WANT MOD DAHLGREN ON IT. WHERE IS HE?

He watched the arm turning red again, and the ergs tightened his hands to his sides. His breath came out with a shudder. "In Clothier's storeroom," he said. "Wrapped up in a bolt of cloth."

Joshua scrambled on Clothier's table and said, "Get Mod Dahlgren." The machine's signal buzzed faintly. Perhaps Shirvanian had damped it.

Now he's crossing his fingers to let the others know I've found Clothier . . . if he's alive, if he's got fingers to cross. Ugh.

But the machine was running; Shirvanian must still be functioning.

Clothier skimmed the corridor, hugging the wall and its shadow. Joshua had another horrid thought; he opened the neck of his suit and felt for the control, afraid it had been broken in the fight with the erg. It seemed whole. His mind was whirling.

"Why don't you lie down and rest for a moment, Joshua?" Clothier asked.

Joshua was too tense to rest, but he was also fearful and ignorant of ergs. He stretched out uneasily on the long dark surface.

The creature whispered, "What is your favorite color?"

"Huh? Oh . . . anything but space-gray." God protect me from crazy machines.

"You have a beautiful skin tone, Joshua. You should wear deep warm colors. Ochre-red, antique gold . . . what do you think of burnt orange?"

The dull ceiling ran above his head, the dim lights slipped by, flick, flick, hypnotically. "I never thought of it."

"Silk," said Clothier.

Joshua pulled up on one elbow. "Silk!"

"Lie down, be calm. Genuine wasp with eighteen percent dharworm! Heavy raw slubbed burnt-orange silk from Maljhugu!" Thin steel feelers ran over his ankles and up to his crotch, he thought the thing was about to make love to him, yelped and kicked; two more metal bands whipped over his wrists to his armpits; now he was caught and would be dished up on a platter to erg-Queen! He wrenched ferociously.

"Stay still, Joshua, and let me measure you."

He said through his teeth, "I have no time to be measured or admired or sewn up in slubbed silk! Get me Mod Dahlgren and do it now!"

"We are here," said Clothier. It turned into the storeroom where the marvelous fabrics were shelved ceiling-high.

And stopped halfway through the door. The signal died, the measuring limbs slackened and dropped to the floor.

"Oh my God! Clothier!" Joshua knelt on the black surface and battered it with his fists. "Shirvanian!" Unconscious or dead. The receiver started up a piercing whine. Ergs were coming. Joshua jumped off Clothier, ran to its back end and pushed. Sweat sprang off him, the heavy machine wheeled slowly into the room, he pulled the door to, leaned on it a moment, panting, scanned along the shelves, the hundreds and hundreds of shelves, for that odd-shaped bolt of dark blue. The light was dim, the luminous materials flickered with wild pale flames, he scored his head with his nails in a fury of haste.

"Whatever are you doing, Joshua?"

He whirled. Clothier was standing by the door with the awkward blue bolt in its arms. The ergs in the corridor passed, and when they were gone he heard Clothier's faint hum once more. Oh, Shirvanian!

"You went off for a minute. What happened?"

"I don't know. What shall I do now?"

"Take the cloth off him."

The machine complied with a few lightning twirls.

"Put him on your table." Joshua looked down on the simulacrum, lying in stillness, long-bodied, gray-blond in hair and beard. Hard demanding face—more so in life, I bet, and that's what I'm supposed to find for Sven. Okay, Shirvanian, start yelling for Mama, I've got him. "Drop that suff on the floor any which way."

Clothier was folding the material. "But Joshua, that's not ti—"

"Drop it. Pick off a few of his hairs and sprinkle them on it as if they'd rubbed off."

"Taklon *never* pulls—"

"Hurry and drop his hair on it, Clothier!" Now she'll believe Sven—and probably start looking for me! "Good. Now take me to Transformer Room One and go to Stores."

He climbed on beside erg-Dahlgren. Clothier opened the door and swung out into the corridor. "I want you to take fresh power cells, two days' worth, for Mod Dahlgren, yourself, three medtechs and six trimmers. I don't know what those kinds look like or where they are. Do you?"

"Yes, Joshua. I have been told."

"Fine."

"But they may be quite a burden for me with yourself and Mod Dahlgren, if you don't mind my saying so."

"I'll unburden you. I'm getting off at the transformer."

"A three-two-five is stationed there at the door."

Joshua had picked up the signal: his heart raced. "Guarding?"

"No. Recharging."

He could see nothing around the curve of the hall-way. "Turn back then. Hurry!"

"I have been told to leave you at the transformer without waste of time." Smoothly, serenely, Clothier picked up speed.

"Clothier!"

"Be calm."

Joshua got up on his knees, rivet gun in hand, erg signal shrilling in his ears. Clothier skimmed the curve, and the servo by the door to the transformer room plucked the socket from the connection in its body without any haste, let it reel back into the wall, turned and drove for Clothier, all limbs out.

"Hold on now, Joshua."

Clothier braked, made a U-turn, went into reverse at full speed while Joshua flattened himself with an arm holding down erg-Dahlgren. It backed alongside the servo, ducking the grazing limbs by a few centi-meters with its low height, squealed to a stop, with-drew its heat sealer and poised it for an instant like a cobra before driving it red-hot into the erg's sensor plexus.

The servo's treads slewed, its arms clanged to the floor, its motor died.

"A clumsy thing like that is no match for a good sewing machine."

"Clothier," Joshua swallowed, "I'm glad you're with us." He disembarked. "Now I'll leave you to the other one, who will tell you what to do. While you're in Stores collect as many other power cells as you can and put them in the recycler or waste disposal."

"I cannot do that, Joshua." The voice was very gen-tle. "I can destroy only what is useless to everyone or dangerous to my existence."

"I see." Joshua pulled the control from his chest and stuck it on the table, under erg-Dahlgren's hand. "Goodbye, then, and thank you."

"You are welcome, Joshua. Remember, burnt orange!"

Joshua found the button that opened the door to Transformer Room 1, zipped down and pulled a length of sticky plastic from his body. He threaded it swiftly through the tubing, found his longest fuse and lit it.

Outside he fired the blowtorch, opened three or four of the half-dozen sockets in the wall beside the door and aimed enough of a jet at each to melt the plastic so that it could not be pulled out. He jammed the torch in his pocket, ran past the stalled erg, heading counterclockwise to Transformer Room 4.

"What're you looking at me so funny for?" Shirvanian asked. His teeth were chattering. "Were you afraid I'd let her kill you so I could stay alive?"

"No, I thought you'd ask her to have us tortured first," said Mitzi. "You sure laid it on thick with all that blubbering and howling. You didn't have to wet your pants."

"That's what you think." He looked down. "Didn't even know I'd done it. I'm glad I fainted before I died from being so scared."

"I hope the air lasts." Esther was perched on a shelf, among batteries. There was no room for her on the floor where the others were squeezed together. The one dim light in the ceiling, like every other in the place, had its own peculiarly unpleasant quality. "Why have you got your fingers in your ears, Ardagh? Hey, Ardagh!" She reached down and pulled at the fair hair.

"I'm afraid she's hurting Sven," Ardagh whispered.

"She hasn't touched him again," said Shirvanian. "Yet. He's told her where the Dahlgren was . . . she's ordered the nearest servo to go to Clothier's storeroom

—ow, it's recharging by the door to the transformer Joshua's heading for!—and—and Clothier just skewered it! Now she'll send everything out! Joshua, you better run like hell!"

"Is he all right?"

"I dunno. He's left Clothier."

"She never checked to find if any of us was missing."

"She never checked with us—but she knew somebody got killed along the way. Why should she care? Human beings don't get counted around here. Now shut up, I'm going to work."

Beneath the Pit floor Clothier skimmed a corridor too narrow for the larger ergs; it did not expect difficulty with the trimmers which serviced the Pit machinery. It stopped in a dark alcove leading to the machine room, bared erg-Dahlgren's shoulder, withdrew the cells, whipped off the cloth and replaced them. The plastic heart quivered and squeezed the artificial blood, the air sacs swelled in a thoracic cavity filled more with brains than bowels, the lines of EEG and EKG zipped and twittered behind the camera eyes. Erg-Dahlgren sat up.

"Are you in good order, Mod Dahlgren?" Clothier asked.

After an instant's orientation, erg-Dahlgren answered, "I am, thank you, Clothier. And yourself?" He put his arm in his sleeve and fastened the clothing.

"The same. Please pick up that article on my table, turn back the tape and move the dial clockwise by three millimeters. Tape down the dial, place the article in your pocket, follow this corridor eastward and up the ramp to second level and deliver it to the person who has requested it of you."

"I will be discovered, Clothier."

"You will be shielded, Mod Dahlgren."

Mod Dahlgren!
Yes, Shirvanian.
I'm glad you're okay. We're locked in a closet on West corridor off the main vault. One servo guarding, I've got hold of it, when it opens the door give me the control, then go to erg-Queen and do whatever she asks. She'll be happy to see you.
I cannot say the same, but I will do what you want.

35

Erg-Queen, taking input from all her latitudes, said, THE SERVO SENT TO RECOVER MOD DAHLGREN IS DISABLED, MOD DAHLGREN IS MISSING FROM CLOTHIER'S STOREROOM, THERE IS A TWENTY-FIVE METER LENGTH OF CLOTH ON THE FLOOR WITH A FORTY-CENTIMETER SQUARE CUT OUT FROM IT AND SEVERAL OF MOD DAHLGREN'S HAIRS ADHERING TO IT. OUTSIDE THE STOREROOM WE FOUND A PIECE OF THE SAME CLOTH WITH SOLDER FRAGMENTS ON IT.

The ten arms beat against the body like two giant hands, ringing an echoing chord. Sven said nothing.

NOW TELL ME YOU DO NOT KNOW WHERE MOD DAHLGREN IS.

"I don't! I don't know where he is now!"

BUT DO NOT TELL ME THAT SHIRVANIAN HAS DONE ALL THIS. HE IS IN A CLOSET CRYING FOR HIS MOTHER. THERE IS ANOTHER HUMAN BEING FREE IN THIS BASE, OR MORE THAN ONE. TELL ME, DAHLGRENSSON, THAT THIS IS NOT SO.

"The others died, they died," Sven whispered. The arms rose.

The closet door opened.

"Shirvanian." Behind erg-Dahlgren the servo stood, humming quietly, not moving.

"That's me," said Shirvanian. "Hullo, Mod Dahlgren."

"Quietly," Esther whispered. She was trembling at the sight of Dahlgren's doppelgänger.

Erg-Dahlgren looked down at the small filthy child with a rats' nest for a head of hair. "Shirvanian?"

"Who did you expect," Shirvanian hissed. "Turing or von Neumann?"

"I do not know who those are."

"Give me the control."

Erg-Dahlgren handed it over. Shirvanian ripped off the tape. "Okay. Now go to Mod Seven Seven Seven and lie like hell—and leave the door open here. We'll do the rest."

"Is that really what Dahlgren looks like?" Mitzi asked.

"That's what Mod Dahlgren looks like," Esther said.

The footsteps died away, and outside the guardian erg turned and rolled westward along the shadowed corridor, pausing every once in a while by the wall on either side to pull at and rip out the recharging sockets it found there.

I HAVE ASKED EIGHT QUESTIONS, said erg-Queen, AND I HAVE RECEIVED TWO ANSWERS. ONE: SHIRVANIAN WAS KIND ENOUGH TO TELL ME HIS NAME. TWO: YOU HAVE TOLD ME WHERE MOD DAHLGREN WAS, BUT HE IS NOT IN THAT PLACE NOW. REGARD THESE ARMS, DAHLGRENSSON. THEY ARE ALL CAPABLE OF CARRYING HEAT, AND THEY WILL EMBRACE YOU.

Sven regarded them. He couldn't keep his eyes away from them. The air smelled of their heat.

MOD DAHLGREN!

The arms fell; Sven gave a faint whimper. His nose was running and his mouth was dry. His arms and torso were glued together with sweat, it ran in trickles down his back and inside his thighs.

Erg-Dahlgren came into the vault. He paused, examined Sven with curiosity, and came to stand beside erg-Queen at ease, arms behind his back. "I am here, Mod Seven Seven Seven."

Sven shuddered at the sound of the voice and turned his head away.

WHY HAVE YOU NOT COMMUNICATED WITH ME?

"I returned to order only a few moments ago. I was confused, I have been in this area only once. Did you not pick up my signal?"

Erg-Queen tapped her arms. I WAS ENGAGED OTHERWISE. WHAT CAUSED YOUR MALFUNCTION?

"I don't know, Creatrix. I was lying on my bed with my afferents turned down and without knowing I became as nothing."

GO TO THE SHIP AT ONCE AND BOARD IT. YOU WILL BE SAFE THERE.

"Certainly." He glanced again at Sven before he left. Sven kept his eyes turned away. He did not dare look.

What now, Shirvanian?

Get aboard the ship, Mod Dahlgren. You'll be as safe there as anywhere.

IT IS A PITY YOU WOULD NOT LOOK AT MY WORK, DAHLGRENSSON. NOW IT IS SECURE.

Sven wrenched at the coils. "Why do you have to kill? Why can't you leave us alone? We can't harm you any more!"

IN THE FOREST ONE THRESHER WAS DESTROYED AND ONE DISABLED. IN THE TREAD-REPAIR CHAMBER ONE SERVO WENT OUT OF CONTROL, DAMAGING EQUIPMENT. AT THE DEPOT TWO DRONES, TWO ERGS IN THE FIVE-HUNDRED

CLASS AND FIFTEEN TRIMMERS WERE WRECKED TO THE POINT WHERE THEY COULD ONLY BE SALVAGED FOR PARTS. IN MY HALLS PROVISIONER WENT OUT OF ORDER AND DAMAGED FOUR MACHINES. ON THE LANDING FIELD TWO THRESHERS WERE DESTROYED AND TWO DISABLED WHEN THE TRANSPORT EXPLODED. FIVE MINUTES AGO AN ERG ON THE LOWEST LEVEL HAD ITS BRAIN CENTER DESTROYED— PURPOSELY BY ONE OF MY OWN MACHINES. I ASSURE YOU, SVEN DAHLGREN, THAT FROM THIS MOMENT ONWARD YOU WILL NOT HARM US ANY MORE. WHATEVER POWER MACHINEMAKER POSSESSES IT HAS LOST ITS VALUE, BOTH FOR ME AND FOR YOU.

Sven closed his eyes and waited for the searing arms. The first of the transformers blew up.

Coming out of the third transformer room, Joshua heard not only erg signals but ergs themselves. He ran. The treadway was circular; if he kept on he would reach the entrance to the hangar again, and that would be clogged with ergs. He swallowed in panic, thumbed the button of every doorway, finding traps, storerooms, closets, hallways, hoping for an elevator, on the theory that for speed the ergs would use ramps; in narrow corridors and warrens he would be hopelessly lost, and eventually trimmers, like savage rats, would corner him.

One door opened into an elevator; he peered into its cavern anxiously: empty. He plunged in, punched the CLOSE plate and the one for third level where the Pit entrance was. Ergs whined by the door and he sank against the wall. Ergs upstairs too, but he would be fighting toward the place he wanted to go. In his pocket he had saved a lump of plastic and a length of fuse for any situation he found urgent or interesting. The blowtorch was half-full; he had most of the rivets. Armed to the teeth.

The elevator moved slowly, very slowly. It stopped at level two. The door opened.

Joshua shrank into a corner, pushed his spine into it, wanted to be part of it, a right-angle of steel and concrete.

Twenty people crowded in, some men, some women, some he couldn't tell which. They paid no attention to him, and an erg reached in a limb, pressed a button and withdrew it.

The door closed and the elevator started downward again. Joshua gulped down the lump in his throat.

The humans did not look at him. Their skins were white, black, red, yellow, blue, mauve; they were dressed in the uniform of Mod Dahlgren with gold emblems on the breast, same material, colors matching or contrasting with skin tone, pleasingly, according to Clothier's aesthetic values. They were all humanoid in shape, though one did not appear to have a nose, another had a snout and a fringe of tentacles on his/her skull, yet another a narrow reptilian jaw, very short arms and a long balancing tail. They spoke in low tones, not quite to each other.

"Yes, it's good to be home again."

"It is a pleasure to visit your distinguished planet."

"An honor to have participated in this valuable experiment."

"Working with Doctor Dahlgren."

"Alongside colleagues from all the distances of the Galaxy."

"Don't you agree, Doctor Lindstrom?"

Mild laughter. "Of course we did not always agree, but—"

By the time the elevator reached ground Joshua had concluded that these were androids created for the trip to GalFed Central.

The door opened, an erg reached in a limb to shepherd them. Joshua held his breath. The limb, before withdrawing, scoured the wall, found one more object, Joshua, and plucked him out with a pinch of his sleeve. It did not care that he was wearing sagging dark-blue jersey stained with dirt and sweat. He was dragged along with the crew in their bright, clean cloth and fresh unhuman skins. He might have disabled the servo with his rivet gun, but he did not know how the others would react. They walked without turning their heads, practicing the inane phrases.

"Conditions were difficult."

"If not impossible."

"Although we did succeed to some degree."

"In stabilizing."

"The mutation rate in zones."

"In which the specimens were subjected to."

"And which statistics will show."

Joshua did not discover what the statistics showed. He had been plodding along a tube-shaped corridor; as the light changed he saw that a pair of gates were opening into a narrower tube of shining metal, and he was sure that this led to the ship.

The servo guide was sending the androids over the step and up the arch two by two. Joshua, odd-man-out, cast about the tunnel and found flanges in its sides, like those of the old buttress trees in the forest. Their shadows were dark; Joshua darted into one and it received him like a mother's arms. The servo ticked off the last two, closed the gates behind them and locked the heavy latch. It turned and wheeled away, past Joshua and back down the tunnel, its signal faded. Joshua permitted himself to breathe. Mod Dahlgren was not among the androids. Perhaps he was on the ship already, perhaps not. On impulse, Joshua picked the lump of plastic from his pocket, spun it into a string, wound it around the gate latch, thumbed it down firmly, found his bit of fuse and lit it. Then ran.

He was a few meters away from the main corridor when the explosion boomed. At the tunnel mouth, a swarm of trimmers, signals in his receiver muffled by the blast, appeared from nowhere and everywhere and grabbed Joshua, pulling him in all directions like ants fighting over a leaf. They choked, wrenched, tore. He screamed and a screwdriver smacked his mouth.

Just as suddenly they dropped him and scuttled off.

He lay sobbing on the filthy concrete floor, blood running from his mouth. Hands picked him up and set him on his feet. Or tried to. His knees kept buckling.

"Get up! Hurry, get up!"

He got his feet planted on the floor, finally, pulled his head up on his sore neck. The steel strength of the arms told him, if not the face. Mod Dahlgren.

"Who are you? Are you a friend of Shirvanian's?"

"Y-yes." He swallowed blood. One of his front teeth was loose, his throat was swollen. "Josh . . . Joshua . . . Ndola." He coughed up the blood, turned his head and spat.

"I am Mod Dahlgren."

"I know . . . I—we got you out of Clothier's storeroom."

"I didn't know that was where I had been taken."

"Those trimmers . . . they obeyed you?"

"They do when Shirvanian is around."

Joshua's clothes were ripped, the receiver had fallen out of his ear and been trampled somewhere, the blowtorch had dropped from his pocket, now half torn off, and was crushed. He still had the rivet gun. But he felt broken. "I have to find Dahlgren . . . I promised Sven." He coughed again. "If I could rest a bit . . ."

"Not too long, Joshua Ndola."

"And you—what will you do?"

"I was to board the ship, but it seems the gates are badly jammed."

"You'll have to go to her."

"No. I have had enough. Come along, Joshua. I too wish to find Dahlgren."

In the vault the lights flickered, went out, came on again.

WHAT IS HAPPENING?

Sven opened his eyes, raised his head. "Don't you know? A transformer has blown up."

Heat the arms again, monster. Sport of nature, of everything hideous in men. And we'll go down together.

Shirvanian waited in the shadow of the corridor, so frightened he thought his heart would shrivel and slither down between his lungs and his liver. His control was in one palm, his eyes were on erg-Queen, he was waiting for the ripeness of a moment and his hands were curved to catch it as it dropped.

The second transformer blew, and two seconds later the third. The light jumped once like a bomb's flare, and went down dim, fading into the deep orange, near-red of an ancient dream of hell.

On third level a corridor went dark; the ergs running it slowed. Their infra-red kept them from crashing into each other, but they skittered along the walls, treads and limbs hooked into doorways. They were lost.

On first level several ergs paused to recharge; when they found fused sockets they searched for others, but from the others no current flowed. They stood where they were, slowly dying.

At Transformer 2, where power was still flowing, six recharging ergs of different classes were set upon by a pack of trimmers and threshers with recharge signals beeping. They pulled and clawed sockets, limbs, antennas, sensors. The battle raged for a few minutes, and as the last of their power ebbed, it slowed, wavered, died down. One surviving thresher hugged the last whole socket to its receptor and recharged. Its light sensors were smashed and its antennas broken.

Now most lights were out in all levels northwest, southwest, and southeast. Hundreds of ergs swarmed toward the lights of northeast, but they had no duties there, they milled about, collided with each other, clogged the corridors.

Shirvanian's control was full out.

After a couple of hours of uneasy sleep in great discomfort, Dahlgren was wakened by a sound of metallic creaking. He lifted himself on one elbow, painfully. The creatures about him stirred a little; there was no wind here, no thunder or lightning. During the Pit "nights" there was no light except the faint glow from the band of glass at top level, and now most of that was gone. Power failure? The Pit had its own generators to control heat, light and ventilation, but the switches were outside.

He parted the leaves of his tree and could see nothing, but he knew with dreadful logic that the noise was coming from the cage and the clones were working at the bars. He did not know why he enraged them, by sight, or smell, or an instinct that had been implanted in them by the ergs.

The thin pajamas clung to his skin, there were droplets of moisture in his hair and beard. He thought he might simply lie back and let them kill him. They had been created degraded images, they did not even have the ugly dignity of the proto-men who ate lice and flies but carried promises in their gonads. He could not fight them, and he did not want to cry defiance to their gabble.

Men should live in peace and brotherhood, writes the schoolchild in the essay. Turds. Brothers have fought for millennia. Mothers, daughters; fathers, sons; as I fought Sven Adolphus and refused to lead the life of study—and my own Sven surely despises me. Yet the old man refused to die before he made peace with me. I will never know Sven, and I cannot make peace with these, who have been picked from my flesh like seeds out of an apple. And these machines will become like men, men like me, for in erg-Dahlgren they have already the seed of rebellion; if they break him it will grow again somewhere.

How they do grunt, those two. Soon they will be out here. Dahlgren, you should have died with the others.

All that was contemplative and resigned in Dahlgren lay down and turned its face toward darkness, and all that was arrogant, angry and contemptuous picked up his body and clambered down the tree in the silence he had learned as an observer of animal life.

A bar snapped. The male barked deeply in triumph, and the female made the whistling sound through teeth and nose forced by her harelip.

Did the breaking of one bar give them enough space to come out? They were pushing, grunting; they were strong enough to bend the bars a little more.

He crouched at the base of the tree. An unknown sleeper snorted. Rodents squeaked, a bird chirped, insects rustled among the bits of bark on the earth floor; a tiny waterfall splashed and its stream rippled down toward a pond.

Dahlgren scratched at a couple of insect bites on his shin, and the rubbing of rough skin seemed loud.

Then the clones yipped together. They had broken out, into a larger prison, and could make what noise they chose. Immediately they found something to squabble about; Dahlgren moved from tree to tree, feeling for every step. He was a big man; he would not spring up easily from a heavy fall.

The clones fell silent. They might, within two minutes of leaving the cage, have taken the giant step of learning to make peace in order to follow a common aim.

He backed away from the sound of their movements, cracked branches, growls and snorts. He saw nothing. There was a low diffuse light that turned everything to one in the mist. If he had been able to see where he was going they would see where he had gone. The tree clump was the only hiding place in the Pit, and he had to leave it because that was where they would search.

He slipped back from this shelter, crouched behind a stone, tried to judge where the wall would be: it was lined with heavy lianas, he might find a cover climbing among them and increase the surface over which they must hunt him. Silence now. Grayhead and Ridgeback slept, and all the others. He thought he was likely only a few meters from the wall, and dropped to hands and knees to feel for obstacles and avoid tripping. His body sank into a pool of mist.

It occurred to him—

A throttling arm came round his throat and cut off his scream.

It had occurred to him that their night vision might be better than his own and that one of them could have diverted him with noise while the other attacked from behind.

You! erg-Queen cried. You!

Shirvanian came out into the vault, into the lurid dusk. "How long is it since you recharged, Mod Seven Seven Seven?"

She said to the ergs holding Sven, TAKE HIM!

The ergs freed Sven, but they did not take Shirvanian. They retracted their limbs and stood still.

"They should never have made you with those heat arms. Ten of them! All that energy! You can't use more than two or three at a time, and you didn't need the heat. Just showing off. You don't have to call for your friends. They'll be here in a minute."

She surged toward Shirvanian, bowling over Sven. He got to his feet, lunged wildly after her, and missed.

"Don't, Sven. She won't touch me. She has no more power left than a trimmer."

She bellowed, THAT IS ENOUGH—

Mitzi ran out with wild hair, shrieking, "Shirvanian, you idiot! There's a recharger in the clo—"

Erg-Queen slapped her aside and skinned Esther, who had followed. Rolled around the corner, casters slithering, to meet Ardagh leaping from the closet, grasping in both hands a meter of steel cable, socket at one end and a tangle of frayed wires at the other. Ardagh pulled back and whacked her with it straight on. She spun.

Ergs boiled out of the corridors, banging, wheeling, flowing in currents. They hemmed her in, butted and ground against her inviolate surface.

MOD DAHLGREN! At full volume her voice nearly cracked the ceiling.

Sven, Esther, Mitzi shrank against the walls, Ardagh into the closet. But the ergs left a little space around Shirvanian; he stood in their flock as a shepherd among sheep.

STOP! DAHLGRENSSON! MACHINEMAKER! STOP! She was backed to the wall. Her arms, her ten arms went outward in full, threatening or pleading.

Shirvanian ground his teeth, his eyes filled with tears.

The metal clashed and whined around her. The arms rose very slowly, as slowly, it seemed, as clock hands, rose slowly to her trembling glittering crown, the blued-steel arms began to break off, one by one, the silver antennas.

STOP! ... STOP ... ST ...

She bowed and spun, wheeled crazily three or four times, rocked back on her rollers, and stopped.

The ergs rumbled, buzzed, hummed. They slowed gradually, power evaporating. Shirvanian willed. They rattled, ticked for a few moments, stopped.

Arms crossed, Esther straddled a trimmer riding piggyback on a three-twenty at the edge of the lonely space in which Shirvanian had centered himself. She looked at Sven, at Shirvanian, at erg-Queen. Odd noises echoed down the halls in receding waves. The vault was a center of silence.

Shirvanian sank to a squat, hugging his knees, sobbing.

Erg-Queen stood back to the wall, claw-hands tangled in her crown.

Esther watched the child, licked her lips, scratched under her chin. "Well, Shirvanian, she broke your bird."

Shirvanian's eyes were squeezed shut, tears rolled down his dirty face and dripped off his jaws. "She was a beautiful machine," he whispered.

Dahlgren writhed and bit, the clone yelped and hung on, squashing his windpipe. He saw a universe of stars, the last of his light, and through it the black shape of the female, arms out, mouth open in a split-lipped grin.

Lights went on, fifty blazing floods, a blast of whiteness.

Dahlgren, head bent backward, spine about to crack, saw one dark figure leaping down the flagstone steps of the slope, unzipping a jumpsuit, pulling out a red banner of cloth.

Joshua caught the clone's neck in the laplap, wound it in two quick twists, and yanked hard. The clone threw his arms wide and fell back.

The female screeched and flung herself on all three.

Erg-Dahlgren, on guard outside, watched helplessly from above.

Joshua groped for the rivet gun; his one sickening choice was to crack her on the head with it; she was clawing at his face. The male grabbed for his ankles. Dahlgren, beneath all, was battered by flying limbs. The birds and beasts had wakened and were screeching.

A terrifying gray shape rose into the blaze of light,

stared yellow-eyed for a moment, and blinked once with translucent lids.

"Strangers?" the serpent asked. "Us?" It slammed the back of the female's neck with its snout and she fell over, looped a coil around the waist of the male and squeezed the breath out of him firmly.

It looked at the dazed clones, at gasping Joshua, at Dahlgren on hands and knees shaking his head like a dog.

"Turn off the day, Stranger," it said. "I want to sleep."

Dahlgren, panting, raised his head. His eyes were red-lidded and bloodshot, his tongue swollen; blood and spittle bubbled at the corners of his mouth. "Why did you not say you would help me?"

"Stranger, you never asked," said the serpent.

Ardagh swung the length of steel flex and grinned crookedly at Mitzi. "Sometimes muscle is useful." Then she flung it across the vault and it crashed among ergs washed against the walls, heaped in the corners. The hellish light shone dully on their carapaces.

Shirvanian picked himself up slowly. "Dahlgren's up on third level . . . with Joshua . . . and the other Dahlgren."

Esther hopped to Sven's shoulder and they picked their way among battered machines, clambering over some still humming or quivering monster. Silence hung in the empty air above them.

rracktick!

They stopped.

"Oh, Shirvanian!" Ardagh whispered. "What's that?"

tickrrackticktick!

Shirvanian pulled back against a metal flank; he looked like an ancient midget. He sniffled and rubbed his nose on the tatter of a sleeve. "I don't know."

"Can't you tell?"

"I don't know! I don't know everything!"

"We can see that, but—" Mitzi slumped. "I'm sorry ... whatever it is, I give up."

Shirvanian had to peel back his fingers to loosen their grip on his control. "I'm still up. Whatever it is, it's not an erg."

"Something different," Ardagh said wearily. "You said that about erg-Queen."

tick!

"Behind that door," said Esther. She hopped stalled machines as if they were stepping stones. "Office of the Statistician."

"Oh. I know what that is." Sven let his breath out luxuriously. "I mean I don't know what it is, but I know what it looks like. Come and see. This won't take over the universe."

In the office, the cabinets had been knocked over and the files riffled, but the thing clicking in one corner had been left alone, perhaps because it was a machine.

On a pedestal under a glasstex bell, it was a collection of knobs, rods, ratchets and spindles made of brass that had softened to the look of gold; it seemed archaic and useless, someone's long-ago concept of a perpetual-motion machine. Fine wire claws rose out of its floor and turned the knobs. *rracktick!*

"I remember that," said Esther. "Stats was a bit of a nut. He had all those gears and rods machined and rigged to a little generator. You could even run it on a penlight cell. I never knew what it was."

Shirvanian went round it and pinged the bell with his fingernail. "It's a model of Babbage's Difference Engine. The only part that was ever built of just about the first computer anybody ever thought of."

"Are you going to turn it off too?" Mitzi asked.

"What for? It's done nothing for six hundred and fifty years and I don't see why it shouldn't go on doing it."

Dahlgren was resting on the bed in his old infirmary room, a chaotic mess from his struggles with the servo. Erg-Dahlgren was waiting at the doorway.

"Dahlgren, your son is coming, with Esther. And the children."

Dahlgren rose, pulled off his boots and then his pajamas, used the pajamas for rags to wipe the dirt off his boots. Erg-Dahlgren gave him the uniform. He put it on and combed his hair and beard; there were bits of bark clinging to them.

He got up stiffly.

"Shall I help you, Dahlgren?"

"No. Thank you."

In the hall, Sven was standing, arms folded to front and back. A muscle twitched in his cheek. Shirvanian was leaning on the wall, about to keel over, and Esther squatted nearby, arms wrapped about herself, staring with calm black eyes. The girls were hugging Joshua, who had a thick lip and a scabbed nose.

Dahlgren held out his hands. Sven, arms unlocked, came forward and took them in all four of his own.

"Sven . . ." He had hardly a voice. "It is good to see you alive and well."

Sven licked his lips and whispered, "I am glad to be with you again, Father."

While erg-Dahlgren was standing bemused at this exchange, Esther exploded. She threw arms wide and in one leap hooked her legs over Dahlgren's shoulders, so that he nearly fell over, slapped his cheeks hard with both hands, and plunged her fingers into his hair and began to scratch his scalp.

Dahlgren threw back his head and laughed till the tears ran, and pulled her face down by the ears to kiss her.

"You cannot sleep yet, Shirvanian," Dahlgren said. "We cannot sleep. The live machines must be called in, all the ones at the factories, the ship's engines shut off, the reactors turned down—"

"I sent—" Shirvanian yawned, "—trimmers to pick out erg-Queen's transmitter, hook it into the radio . . . start repairing the transformers . . . you can broadcast on her frequency . . . anything you like . . . in a couple of hours . . . trimmers'll show you . . . where the mike is . . ." He went over in a ninety-degree arc and Esther caught him before he hit.

"Get the child a bed, man," she told Dahlgren. "Get us all beds. For that kind of talk there's all the time in the world."

As Shirvanian lost consciousness, several hundred ergs woke, whined and rumbled aimlessly for hours, a congregation of ghosts.

But at hour 19:17 the count stopped.

Erg-Queen stood in the vault. She had neither transmitter nor power cells, her sensors were dead eyes, her arms curved out like cup-hooks. Around her the broken shells of machines had been pushed against walls and into corners.

She was left silent and alone in the center of the space where Dahlgren had crawled and eaten off the dirty floors.

36

Shirvanian had nightmares; he screamed and muttered. Esther crawled into bed with him, turned the light on, and clasped his grimacing face. "Hey, Shir-vanian!" she said. "Pleasant dreams."

Shirvanian opened his eyes wide. "Where am I?"

"Workers' quarters. A bit dusty, otherwise in good order."

He raised his head and looked around. His chest heaved in a sigh. "It's all over."

"Ayeh."

"I have nothing to do now."

She sniggered. "A tragedy. I imagine Dahlgren will find you something."

He turned his face into the pillow. "You don't understand . . . everything I've done—"

"Saving our lives?"

"I don't mean that, nobody will care about that. What I did before . . . outworld—and taking the ship." He rubbed his eyes. "I don't know what I'm going to do."

"Well," Esther pinched her lip. "You could get hold of the erg ship and its crew, and head off for parts unknown. I'm sure that wouldn't be beyond you."

"You're laughing at me! Everybody does!"

"No, Shirvanian, I'm only talking nonsense to get your mind off those nightmares—and any others you might make for yourself. If you really want to know what to do, Shirvanian, I think you should get that goddam tattoo off. Tattoos don't belong on people." His lip flared in a pout. "I know what you're thinking. You could tell me something. Yes, I realize I caused tKlaa's death by cutting off the signaler. I shouldn't have done that, and I guess I should thank you for not telling me. But it was something like a tattoo, it was on a chain, and I don't like that either. Tattoos or chains."

He sniffed again, and in a few minutes had drifted off. She hunched on the bed and stared at his pale battered face. His eyelashes were long and thick. Beautiful lashes. She pinched one of his cheeks, very gently, and then the other. Small pink flushes appeared on them. A little improvement. She turned off the light.

Breakfast was a tasteless scrounged meal, and eating with Dahlgren made it an uneasy one.

He had an odd way of eating, head turned slightly aside, one shoulder a bit hunched forward. This physical attitude, from one point of view, was that of a haughty man who shunned company; from another, the manifestation of great diffidence. He would have seemed impossibly forbidding if Esther had not had her feet hooked on his chairback, her knees resting on his shoulder blades and her arms clasped loosely around his neck.

"Did you talk to Barrazan Four?" Ardagh asked timidly.

"Only to the spaceport." He glanced at her through his brows. "I had to tell them that you four were alive and safe, otherwise it would have been cruel to your parents."

"Did they say anything?"

"After they recovered somewhat from the shock, they thought I was a bit crazy, but they will relay a message to GalFed Central. Esther," he pulled her hands away gently, "I am not itching . . . did you expect the Triskelians to come for you and drag you off in fetters?"

"I suppose so."

"Running away from the Order is not one of the major crimes. It is usually committed by stowing away."

"Yes." Joshua ripped his bread savagely. "And we had to steal a ship."

Dahlgren shrugged. "Ships have gone out of order. Barrazan Five is much closer to Four than Two is. There is a point at which it is possible that a ship bound for Two and going awry might be closer to Five than to either Two or Four, and might choose to land here. It has happened once or twice before."

"Doctor Dahlgren," Ardagh said, "are you suggesting that we lie?"

Mitzi sniffed. "Now *you're* pushing it!"

"I am not!" His voice was so harsh that Ardagh shrank. "I am saying that Shirvanian may be very powerful now, but I do not know how powerful he was aboard that ship, though the suggestion may be a blow to his vanity. You wanted it to go astray, but the wish and the actuality are not necessarily the same. I can't tell what you did to the ship or whether you did it, and I doubt that anyone else can, since the ship does not now exist. You have moral obligations and you have legal rights. Tell the truth and let hell freeze." They ate in silence for a few minutes. Dahlgren picked up a spoon and turned it between thumb and fingers. He said in a lower voice, "If it is necessary, if my word is worth anything, I will testify for you. I owe you very much, very much thanks ..."

"That's all over." Ardagh's voice had tightened. "What's coming ..."

"Oh, Ardagh! What can I say? You have everything you need to do anything you want. The universe does not depend on one medical school. Shirvanian has done so much good for people in such a short time—will he really become a master criminal among his machines? Perhaps he will learn to work with both people and machines. Mitzi—who does what she pleases—I hope she will not waste herself. As for you, Joshua, from what Sven has told me I believe a good lawyer could take you out of both the Triskelian Order and the Space Academy. But if you ever choose to go into space, the Service has ecobiology branches where you can very nearly write your own ticket. Your father can hardly object, and you can—you can avoid

the acrimonious exchanges that embitter so many people . . . Now will you kindly pass the preserves, or
whatever passes for preserves on this table?"

"Where are you going, Esther?" Ardagh asked.
"Down to base level."
"What for?"
"Come on and I'll show you."

The light was brighter; one transformer had been
repaired. A narrow track had been cleared among the
stalled ergs.

Esther jumped up and caught a ten-centimeter steel
ring fixed to the ceiling. "And there," she pointed,
"there's another, a few meters down. All the way
around!" Esther whooped, reached and grabbed the
next ring and the next, swinging, yipping, brachiated
the circle of the corridor, voice echoing crazily. Two
minutes later she dropped beside Ardagh. "Exercise
for growing gibbons."

"Will you stay here, Esther?"

"I'll stay with the Dahlgrens till Sven goes off on
his own, and then with Dahlgren. He ought to have
someone around who likes him besides erg-Dahlgren."

"Sven—"

"Sven loves him, but he has his own feelings and
ideas, as he should; he's not mine any more either.
And I . . ." Her eyelids thickened and reddened. As
Mitzi had once done she put her fingers to her mouth
and spoke out to an empty space: "Topaze is not a
mate . . . Yigal is dead . . ." She grabbed the ring
again with her shrill morning cry and scalloped away.

"My God!" Mitzi yelped. "Where'd you get that?"

Joshua was wearing a well-tailored coverall of burnt-
orange raw silk, with slubs. He looked handsome.

"Clothier took a liking to me," he muttered. His
mouth was still a bit swollen.

"Hey, now I can get rid of these goddam filthy rags!"

"It's got to *like* you," Joshua said carefully. "If you speak to it nastily its feelings get hurt. It's got a mean way with a heat sealer, so watch out!"

"Ha." Mitzi went away with a look in her eye and a couple of hours later turned up in something dark and misty that seemed to have raindrops woven into it. Very decadent and very attractive.

Ardagh sighed in envy and resignation and lurched off to be sewn into red-green shot silk that made her wholesome as an apple.

"You look delicious," Sven said.

Ardagh grunted.

He said stiffly, "I was trying to give you a compliment. I suppose I'm not very graceful at it, but I haven't had much experience."

"I don't mean anything. It's—"

"Shirvanian's been bursting into tears every ten minutes, and you've got your teeth clenched. You'd think we were still—"

"That's the trouble! Everything was terrifying and I was scared the whole time, and now . . . just anti-climax. And . . ."

He knelt and circled her with all his arms, covering her thorax from armpit to hipbone. "Going back to the Triskelians?"

"Yes."

"Ardagh, you will be the greatest surgeon and Shirvanian will have created the ultimate automaton while I'm still trying to learn useful things like square roots and set theory. I have so much to catch up on."

"And we won't see each other again." She loosened one of his arms and took the hand, examined it.

"You want one for a souvenir?"

She laughed. "I was thinking how perfect, how per-

fectly shaped it was, how suited to your arm and body.
I wanted to remember . . ."

"I'll make sure we see each other again." He replaced the arm around her body. "And you do look
good in that creation of Clothier's." He grinned. "But
not as good as you looked without it."

Ardagh and Joshua were waiting in the aircar with
the motor running. Mitzi ran across the field, hair flying and cigarette bobbing in her mouth; climbed
aboard, slid into the pilot's seat and pulled levers.

"Now let's see your license," said Joshua.

"Sorry, sweetie, I left it on the ship."

"If that's dope you're smoking I'm getting out,"
Ardagh said.

Mitzi laughed. "No such luck. Just tobacco, found
it in the freezer under a ton of ice. Where's Sven?
Thought he or Dahlgren would come."

"They both said they never wanted to see those
things again," said Joshua.

The aircar was the old model Joshua had found in
the hangar. The engine had been put in order, and the
craft was good enough for the weather: rain, sun,
cloud and wind battling for control of the sky.

Three trimmers and a medtech rolled out the cage;
the clones hung on to the reinforced bars and gaped
sullenly. Once in a while the female whimpered and
touched her face; it had a strange flattened look:
medtechs had reshaped her harelip and sprayed
the wound with skintex. Eventually it would peel, her
face would be new and whole.

The ergs pulled a cable from the aircar and hooked
it on the cage. Mitzi tapped a signal: the aircar rose,
the cage swung. The female huddled in one corner.
She had not provoked the male since the operation,
because her face hurt so, and he had found her so
strange he contented himself with giving her a few
half-hearted pokes.

The aircraft soared over buildings, dead reactors like gray mausoleums, and two or three ergs stalled in the middle of the scoured terrain of Zone White; swung toward track 2, tracing the white brick road. The landscape was that of a sterile moon. The sky was pale, almost blue. Fabrics of fine rain parted like curtains, then wind swept it, and the salt-ringed pools below rippled, stilled to mirrors, rippled and stilled again. The pink sun stood overhead at noon.

The aircar rose until the dun-colored clouds covered the terrain. It flew through nothingness specked with glimpses of broken-backed land where the vapors thinned.

They did not say much during the hours of travel or when they circled over the green brick road, the remains of the house, the fresh mounds near the cabbage patch where the ergs had reburied Yigal, and nearby, Koz's idol. The earth was already covered with seedlings.

The aircar lowered until the cage thumped the ground, and hovered. Joshua unrolled a ladder, climbed down to the cage roof and pulled out a pin. The door swung open. He disengaged the hook, climbed back and pulled the ladder up.

The clones hung back in the corners of the cage for a few moments, staring with distrust at the open door. Then they both jumped for it, tangling in the doorway. The male shoved away the female and stepped out. He took a few paces, gripped the soil with his toes, stood facing the trees; his body flashed pink-white in a brief clearing of the sky.

The female came out slowly, picked up a stone, and crept softly behind him, raised it—

"Oh God—"

"Easy, Ardagh." Joshua touched her arm. "They've been through that before."

—and a multicolored bird flew by, screaming fiercely. She dropped the stone and followed it with her eyes till it disappeared. She forgot the male and took the bird's direction; the wind lifted her hair, gently for once; in the distance her face was almost comely. She passed through waist-high brush, stopped and turned. The male was watching her. They had never in their lives been so far apart. He approached her slowly and paused where the brush began. They stood looking at each other clothed in leaves.

"Okay, that's it." Mitzi snapped flame to a fresh cigarette and the aircar rose, the cloud pressed in again.

Ardagh said, "I wonder what they'll make of Topaze."

"A ménage à trois," said Mitzi.

"Sven."

"Yes, Mod Dahlgren."

"I hope you will not be offended if I ask you this question."

"Go ahead."

"Does my appearance disturb you?"

"Oh no . . . it might if my father was dead. Why?"

"I was curious. Would you not have taken me for him, otherwise?"

"I'm sure I would at first. You do look just like him. But, you know, when I was a child, even though he hadn't much time for—for being a father . . . I lived close enough to him to know not only how he moved and spoke, but how he reacted to everything around him."

"Then you would not truly have taken me for him."

"Not for very long. I'd certainly take you for his brother."

"Thank you," said erg-Dahlgren.

37

Dahlgren was breathing impatiently over a cranky Shirvanian who was trying to design a tree of machine hierarchies when there were a bare hundred and fifty live ergs left above trimmer class in the complex, and all echelons were broken.

"I would like to speak to you, Dahlgren," said erg-Dahlgren.

"Just a minute! Just a minute!"

"Please, Dahlgren, now. Outside."

"What do you want? What is it?"

"Shirvanian is about to throw a tantrum, and I know you need rest."

"Mod Dahlgren, I have so much to fin—"

"I know, and I would like to show you something. Please."

"Now what's the tr—"

"Just down here, a short way . . ."

"What—"

". . . and in here." Erg-Dahlgren closed the door behind them.

"Now what the devil do you want?"

Two rumpled beds, an overturned chair, a chess table. Erg-Dahlgren righted the chair. "The move is number twenty-eight. White Bishop prevents further advance of pawns by moving to Knight three." He sat down on the the righted chair and moved the Bishop.

"Have you gone crazy?" Fists on hips, Dahlgren was staring at him.

"Out of order is the expression, Dahlgren. I am the only person here capable of working around the clock, and I have been doing so. I do not need rest, but I would like a change, and I want to play chess."

Dahlgren sat down suddenly and sweat broke out over him; he panted.

"You see. That is why I brought you here."

A medtech slammed the door open and rolled in, needle poised. Dahlgren's face was scarlet. "Yes, but you do not understand."

"I do not know the words for what you are doing to yourself, but I believe I understand. You want to restore . . ."

"The status quondam. I suppose so . . ." He raised his hand slowly and attacked the White Bishop with N-R4. "There is very little time. In a few days I will board ship and face a GalFed inquiry. I will have a lot to think about on the way."

29. Q-Q4. "Check. Nothing can be restored, Dahlgren. Some things may be finished."

"Nothing can be finished. I have nothing."

"Nothing? Your son is alive, and you are playing chess."

Dahlgren laughed. His eyes were full of tears. He took himself out of check with K-R2.

"Are you not satisfied with your son, Dahlgren?" 30. BxP.

Black pushed Pawn attack with P-N6. "I am more than satisfied with him. He is quieter than me, like the old man, and better-natured than both of us. He has her eyes and mouth . . . and he nearly gave his life to save us . . . and I have not told him how much . . . and I have not even thanked you for all you have done."

"That is not important." 31. He took Pawn with Knight's Pawn.

Dahlgren took Pawn with Rook.

32. PxP.

NxP.

"If we were not on the same side this would be a savage battle," said erg-Dahlgren. "Now both Kings are exposed."

"I am exposed. I will have to answer terrible questions."

"I hope I have not helped save you to put you in more danger, Dahlgren."

"I have put myself in danger." And the magnificent, obscene erg-Queen had created the only two creatures in his prison, erg-Dahlgren and Grayhead, who had made any effort to help him. He had stimulated envy, malice and resentment in men; it had found its way into their machines and slaughtered them. Of all those murdered souls he could not think of any who would have battled to free him from his captors and only Haruni had tried to save him from his delusions.

33. Erg-Dahlgren moved King to R2 and avoided double check, and Black took Bishop with Rook so that 34. Queen would take Rook and remaining Black Rook would move to B7. "Check," said Dahlgren. 35. King moved out of check to N1, and Rook to B3. 36. Queen to Q3, Black took Pawn with Knight. "Check," said Dahlgren.

"Since you have an answer to everything, Dahlgren . . ."

37. K-R2.

Dahlgren moved Rook to B7. "Check. I presume you are going to resign, Mod Dahlgren . . . what did you have in mind?"

Erg-Dahlgren nodded and stared at the board as Dahlgren swept the pieces from it slowly with his arm and pushed them aside with the others. "Since Sven has said that although he would not mistake me for you over a period of time he would accept me as your brother, I do not see why I cannot go to GalFed Central and answer questions in your place. I would surely pass there: like you, Dahlgren, I am well-tested and built to last. Then you might be free here to do as you chose, whatever is possible, at least for a while."

Dahlgren wiped his sweaty face with his palms and dried them on his thighs. He sat back and formed his face into a thoughtful shape. He did not say that his pride would never allow such an act, nor express insult that it should be suggested; he neither thanked nor reproved erg-Dahlgren for offering himself up to senseless risk; he did not tell erg-Dahlgren, in his innocence, that such a trick would certainly be found out sooner or later and that he, Dahlgren, would be punished for it. He simply took the gambit and began playing a different game.

"That is a very interesting idea," he said.

"It would be much like what was planned before," said erg-Dahlgren. "Only without erg-Queen and those stupid androids. You have said so yourself, that I must do it if it would save anything."

Dahlgren smiled. "The questions would be much harder, and there would be no applause or admiration for Dahlgren."

"I am not sure I would know what to do with those if I had them."

"Then perhaps you should learn what it is like to want them, if you are to take my place."

"If it is necessary I will learn that too."

"It's worth considering. But you still have much to do here, you know."

"Yes, but I am supplementing you. Our tasks are almost equal. And my future is uncertain as well—and what other use is a machine in the shape of a man, except what I am suggesting? I would like to see a little of the universe before the future closes in."

"Yes. Then let us say we stand in equal places, and we must make some kind of decision. How shall we decide, Mod Dahlgren?"

"Very easily, Dahlgren." He picked up, tossed and caught the white coral Queen. "We'll play a game of chess."

APPENDIX:

The Game

1.	P–K4	P–K4	20.	KR–Q1	Q–B3
2.	N–KB3	N–QB3	21.	P–QN4?	QN–K3
3.	N–QB3	N–KB3	22.	N×N	Q×N
4.	B–N5	B–N5	23.	P–QR4	QR–Q1
5.	O–O	O–O	24.	P–R4	P–N5
6.	P–Q3	P–Q3	25.	Q–Q3	Q–N3
7.	B–N5	B–N5	26.	Q–K2	P–B6
8.	N–Q5	N–Q5?	27.	Q–B4 ch	K–R1
9.	P–B3	N×B	28.	B–N3	N–R4
10.	N×B	P–B3	29.	Q–Q4 ch	K–R2
11.	N–B2	P–KR3	30.	B×P	P–N6
12.	B–R4	P–N4?	31.	NP×P	R×P
13.	B–N3	N–R4	32.	P×P	N×P
14.	P–KR3	B×N	33.	K–R2	R×B
15.	Q×B	N–N2	34.	Q×R	R–B7 ch
16.	KR–K1	P–KB4	35.	K–N1	R–B3
17.	P–Q4	P–KB5	36.	Q–Q3	N×P ch
18.	B–R2	P×P	37.	K–R2	R–B7 ch
19.	N×P	N–B2		White resigns	

OUT OF THIS WORLD!

That's the only way to describe Bantam's great series of science fiction classics. These space-age thrillers are filled with terror, fancy and adventure and written by America's most renowned writers of science fiction. Welcome to outer space and have a good trip!

Bantam Book Catalog

Here's your up-to-the-minute listing of over 1,400 titles by your favorite authors.

This illustrated, large format catalog gives a description of each title. For your convenience, it is divided into categories in fiction and non-fiction—gothics, science fiction, westerns, mysteries, cookbooks, mysticism and occult, biographies, history, family living, health, psychology, art.

So don't delay—take advantage of this special opportunity to increase your reading pleasure.

Just send us your name and address and 50¢ (to help defray postage and handling costs).

BANTAM BOOKS, INC.
Dept. FC, 414 East Golf Road, Des Plaines, Ill. 60016

Mr./Mrs./Miss_____
(please print)

Address_____

City_____State_____Zip_____

Do you know someone who enjoys books? Just give us their names and addresses and we'll send them a catalog too!

Mr./Mrs./Miss_____

Address_____

City_____State_____Zip_____

Mr./Mrs./Miss_____

Address_____

City_____State_____Zip_____

FC—9/78